I0670356

DEDICATION

Mom

Because of you, I never stop trying. Because of you, I believe I can do it all. In the best of times and the worst of times, you have always been there for me. Your love and support is never ending. You taught me how to be a mom that my son can be proud of. The little memories are what will last a lifetime. I'm blessed that God gave me you for a mother.

I love you always

SILENT INNOCENCE

A FITZ SERIES

THERESA SEDERHOLT

Silent Innocence: A Fitz Series

ISBN: 978-0-9976692-6-8

This book contains strong language, graphic sexual situations, and violence. It is not intended for anyone under the age of 18.

Publisher: Theresa Sederholt © 2017
Cover designer: Robin Harper Wicked By Design.
Editor: Jacquelyn Ayres.
Formatter: Stacey Blake, Champagne Book Design

Friendship is a gift. It's the gift of family. It's the gift of love and gratitude. I fight to preserve that gift every day.

—Jin Chen

Chapter One

Tommy

"Hey, bug eyes, you sure we got the right house? It doesn't look like anyone is home."

I look down at the ragged piece of newspaper I jotted the address on and then back up to the house number. I wave the paper in front of him, proving to him I'm not some schmuck. "Yes, Stanley, it's a match and stop calling me bug eyes. I told you I can see real good now that I had them fixed. Best thing that ever happened to me was getting pinched. Two years into my ten year stretch and the state paid for everything, including my eyes."

"Sorry, dude, but we've been friends since junior high school. It's going to take me sometime to get use to the new you. *Especially* those fucking cigars you've been smoking; at least open a window."

I open my window and toss it out. "Happy?"

I made sure to check everything out the day before. This one lives in a two-story house; the owner lives upstairs and she lives downstairs. According to one of the neighbors, the owner lives in Florida for most of the year, so I won't have to worry about prying eyes. We've been in this car way too long. I hope this one is worth it. I would never question Vadik, but I don't like being this exposed for so long. At least it's finally dark now. Stanley is fidgeting with the tranquilizer when I notice her round the corner . . . with a fucking kid, no less. I nudge Stanley. "Hey, there she is. What the fuck, why does she have a kid with her?"

"Maybe we should call Vadik."

I open the glove box and pull out my piece. "There's no time for that. I need this payday, and I'm sure as shit not taking a kid along with us."

"Maybe we could get extra for the kid?"

I shove the gun in my waistband and then cover it with my jacket. I grab the tranquilizer from him, put it in my pocket and pull out my tools to break in. I don't tell him too much. After all, the more you know, the more you have to deny. I'm not taking a kid, they are only trouble. "Pull the car into the side ally and kill the lights. I'll take care of everything else."

I hop out of the car, not giving him a chance to fight me on this. Once I'm in the hallway, I wait outside her door. I want to give her time to settle in. Plus, it gives Stanley time to get into position. When I step inside, I'm immediately standing in a small living room. I work myself into the corner and listen. I can hear a shower running and I slowly inch my way towards the noise. I tuck myself into the corner, so I can't be seen. I can see the bathroom door from my hiding spot. The door opens and my mark steps out. I realize it's the kid in the shower—*perfect.* I won't have to mess with the kid. She heads into the kitchen and begins taking stuff out of the fridge. I quietly step into the kitchen. That is . . . until the floorboard creaks. She turns around, sees me, and drops everything onto the floor.

"Please, my daughter is in the shower. I'll give you whatever you want—money, jewelry—whatever, but please, don't hurt her."

For a split second I think I just might get out of here quick and easy. That is until the bitch grabs a knife off of the counter and comes at me, waving it around like a crazy person. She charges at me like she's in a swashbuckling movie! *What the fuck?* She swings it around and I block it with my forearm as I reach behind me and pull out my gun. She connects the blade to my arm, cuts through my jacket and puts a nice gash in my arm. Blood is running down my hand and dripping onto the floor. In the corner of my eye, I catch sight of the kid, dripping wet, naked in the doorway. I turn the gun and take aim at the kid. My eyes never leave hers. The bitch stops instantly when she sees the kid.

"Now this is how we're going to play this. Drop the knife or I shoot the kid."

She quickly drops the knife and the kid starts running towards her. "GET BACK NOW!" I yell.

"She can't hear you, she's deaf."

All the fucking women in Brooklyn and I've got to nab one with a deaf kid. The kid is now latched onto her leg. "How do you talk to her? Do you do that hand stuff?"

"Yes, we sign. Please, what do you want?"

"Tell her to go into the bathroom and you'll be in soon. Do it now and I won't hurt her."

She does that sign stuff and the kid is crying and shaking her head no. I take a step closer and whatever she says to the kid finally convinces her to go back into the bathroom.

"What's your name?"

"Effy, my name is Effy. Please tell me what you want. I can help you get it."

"Now, Effy, like I said earlier, this is how we're going to play this. You and I are heading out of here." I press the gun into her back. We only take a few steps when the kid runs out of the bathroom and throws herself at her mother. The little brat is trying to kick me in my shins! I pull the tranquilizer out of my pocket and stick it in the kid. She drops to the floor in a heap. Effy's screaming and hitting me. One good punch in the side of the head and she's out, too. I pull the towel off of the kid and wrap it around my arm. I lift Effy off the floor and put her over my shoulder as I head out the door.

When I get outside, Stanley pops the trunk. He zip ties her hands and ankles and we head out.

"What the fuck went on in there? You're fucking bleeding like a dead pig."

"Let's just drop her off at the location and get the fuck out of town for awhile. I probably need stitches, the bitch cut me."

"No shit. What happened with the kid?"

"Of all the girls in Sheepshead Bay that could fill this order, I've got to get one with a deaf kid!"

"Deaf, really?"

"No, I just make this shit up for the hell of it."

"You know what they say about those people."

I know I'm going to regret this but I'll bite. "No, Stanley, what do they say about *those* people?"

"They are smarter than the average person, cause they need all their other senses to pick up the slack. Don't you know anything about superheroes? You know like Hawkeye and Echo, they are deaf superheroes that have special powers because they can't hear."

If this wasn't such a fucked-up situation I would probably be laughing. "Just drive."

"I'm telling you, I wouldn't have left the kid there."

"I used the tranquilizer on her, so she's probably dead since it was for an adult."

"You used the whole thing?"

"I don't know. It all happened so fast. I just wanted to get the hell out of there. How much longer before we get to the drop off?"

"We're almost there."

The drop off house is not that far away and when we pull up, Inga, who usually does the intake of the new girls, is already standing in the driveway, along with one of the guards.

"What the hell took you so long? Where is she?"

"She's in the trunk." I hold up my bloody arm. "Can you fix this?"

She doesn't answer and walks over to the back of the car while Stanley pops the trunk.

"Ke një vajzë të gabuar!"

"English, Inga, what's the problem?"

"I said you got the wrong girl! Look at how old she is; this can't be right."

She pulls out her phone, dials as she walks out of earshot and then starts yelling in Albanian.

"Shit, Tommy, you said we had the right address. This is fucked up."

"Yeah, well don't say anything about the kid or we're dead."

She hangs up and waves to the guard. She takes a picture of Effy and orders the guard to take her inside.

"Vadik needs to see you both right away. He said to meet him at the usual place."

I hold up my arm. "What about this?"

"I think that's the least of your worries." She turns and walks away.

"Stanley, we have two choices: skip out now and hope we can get far enough away from all of this or, meet with Vadik and try and talk our way out of this mess."

"I don't know about you, but I'm not walking into the lions' den. I'm getting as far away from this as possible. And maybe, just maybe, I can stay alive."

I know I fucked up and he's right—that's really our only option. "Okay, let's go, but I still need to get my arm stitched up."

We quickly head the hell out of Brooklyn before things get anymore heated.

Chapter Two

Fitz

Yesterday was MJ's last day at work. She went in today to empty out her desk. I offered to go with her but she said I was just trying to get out of putting the crib together. So, I promised while she was at work today, I would finally get this thing together. I only promised that because I figured I could get Andy to come over and do it. Instead, he went off with Mom to put the finishing touches on the baby shower they are throwing us. Like I don't have enough crap to put together. Why does this thing come with a frigging fifteen-page book on how to put it together?

Instead of taking my overtime pay, I banked it. I never needed the money but I figured someday I would want time off. I have enough to stay out four months. If I did that, though, then I'd have to requalify on everything. Besides, by the end of the three months, MJ will be kicking me out the door. Suddenly, Captain Hart's familiar ring tone vibrates through my phone. "Hey, Captain, you know

I'm still on vacation, right?"

"Yeah, yeah, I know, but please come to the station today. I need to run a case by you. I swear—*just* for your opinion."

I look down at the pile on the floor, which will someday resemble a crib, along with the fifteen pages of instructions. I know I shouldn't be smiling right now but damn, I just might pass this off to Andy yet. Life is good.

"I'm on my way," I announce before ending the call and heading downstairs to grab my keys on the way out the door. It's a beautiful sunny day, perfect for riding Wanda. When I start her up, the rumble reminds me how wonderful my life really is. Well, except for the fact that if MJ had her way, she would have slapped a For Sale sign on poor Wanda. My grip on her gets a little tighter—*never.*

I make it to the station in no time flat. Inside, there's a commotion going on but I'm able to slip past them. Hart is in his office with the door closed, but I can still hear him yelling. I know when to steer clear and this is one of those times. I'll just wait until he cools off. I find an empty chair next to a little girl. Her focus is straight ahead with an empty, blank stare. She's got the most beautiful green-blue eyes I've ever seen.

"Hi, I'm Fitz. What's your name?" Nothing, not even a blink. How could someone not blink for so long? She is sitting so still with her hands tucked under her legs. What kid doesn't fidget? I notice Brad sitting at his desk, so I head over.

""Hey, Brad, what's the story with the kid?'

"Hello to you too, Fitz. Aren't you on vacation, trying to get ready for the baby?"

"I'm ready. Well, everything but the crib. Hart needed to talk to me about a case. What's the story with the kid?"

"She was found wandering around the streets. Someone called us and now we're waiting for CPS to pick her up. We have no information. Hell, she won't even tell us her name."

"Do you mind if I give it a try?"

"Knock yourself out."

Something about the kid is pulling me in. Maybe it's because she reminds me of MJ. I take a book off Brad's desk, walk behind the girl's chair, and slam it to the ground. Everyone jumps at the noise and all heads turn towards me. Everyone except the girl. I take my chair, pull it in front of her, and sit down. When MJ was in grade school, she had a friend who was deaf. She made sure Andy and I learned how to sign. MJ's younger than us but that never mattered. Andy always did whatever she said because that's Andy. And me, well, I've had it bad for her my whole life. I decide to start off simple.

"My name is, Fitz." At first her eyes follow my hands and then when I stop signing her eyes finally focus on mine. A lone tear slides down her cheek as her bottom lip quivers.

"My name is, Stella. My mommy needs help. Can you help her?" I'm barely following along.

"Where is she?"

"A man with a gun took her."

My jaw gets tight at the thought of what this kid might have witnessed. "Took her from where?"

She starts signing really fast now and I'm trying to keep up. "Please, slow down. I know you're scared, but I haven't signed in years. Start at the beginning and tell me what happened."

"Mommy and I were walking home from the store. When we got inside, Mommy made me go in the shower while she cooked dinner. She usually comes in right before I'm done to help me wash my hair. When she never came in, I went out to get her. There was a man with a gun standing in the kitchen. His arm was bleeding. He was trying to pull Mommy out of the house. I ran to her and tried to pull her towards me. She told me to go back into the bathroom and stay there. I did, but then I got scared and ran out again. She said be brave and wait for her, but then I felt something pinch me, like a boo-boo shot and I fell asleep. When I woke up, she was gone."

"Do you know who the man is? Have you ever seen him before?"

"No, never."

"Tell me what you did when you woke up."

"I shut off the shower and got dressed. I know mommy said to wait for her, but she never came back. I went out to look for her. I got lost and a policeman took me here. Mommy told me never to go with strangers, but policemen are safe."

"Do you know your address?"

She takes a deep breath and closes her eyes. When she opens them her tears begin to fall.

"Only part of it. I'm sorry. Mommy and I have been working on it."

My heart is breaking for this little girl. "Stella, how old are you?"

"I'm six. Can you help my Mommy–*please*?"

"Tell me the part of your address that you remember and let me try to figure out the rest."

I quickly write down what little bit she can remember.

"I'm going to have you hang out at Brad's desk while I see what I can find out for you."

Before I can get up she leaps into my arms, wraps her arms around my neck, and holds on so tight. At first, I'm taken aback, but then I remember being young and scared to death. I hold her tight and pray I can give this little angel a happy ending. I carry her over to Brad and introduce them before I head toward Hart's office. I look up, and he's waiting for me in the doorway. His arms are crossed and there is a distinct smirk on his face. He glances at Stella and then back to me. I'm guessing he witnessed my interaction with her.

"Hey, Fitz, sorry I had to call you in. I wanted you to look at a case that seems to have stalled. I never expected you to come in and jump right into the middle of a mystery. We didn't even know she was deaf. I didn't know you signed."

"MJ; need I say anything more?"

"No. She's the best thing that ever happened to you. So, what did you find out?"

"Her mother was kidnapped and she was a witness to it. I got a partial address, and she never saw the guy before. It sounds like the guy drugged her." I pass him the paper with the address.

"You got all of that in five minutes? Amazing." He shakes his head as if in disbelief. "I promise I'll get someone to find out where she lives right away, in the meantime, I need you to look at this." He passes me six folders that are not very big, which is not a good sign.

"Give me the express version before I look these over."

"From what we could piece together, five girls have gone missing and the sixth one was just found murdered. There is no sign of the other five girls."

"What do you need from me?"

"That's just it, Fitz, I'm not really sure. Maybe just a new set of eyes. You seem to have a knack at seeing things that none of us can."

"I'll take all of these upstairs and go through them, but I can't promise anything."

I get up to leave when all of a sudden there is a lot of ruckus going on outside of Hart's office. Stella comes barreling through the door and grabs onto my leg. I pull her off me and squat down in front of her.

"Hey, what's wrong?"

"That lady is trying to take me."

"You need to go with them while Captain Hart tries to find your mommy."

"He scares me. I don't want him to help me; I want you."

"Fitz, CPS is here for her. What's she saying?"

"She doesn't want to go with them. You scare her. And she wants me to help her."

"Tell her I'm a good guy, and I will help find her mommy."

"I tried, she's not buying it. Where's that address I gave you?"

He passes me the paper. I scoop her up and put her on top of the desk while I type the partial address on Goggle Earth. When I turn the screen towards her, her eyes grow wide and she points to the screen.

"That's your home?"

"Yes."

"I need you to stay here with Captain Hart. I promise he is big but not scary. I will go check your house."

I hand the files back to Hart. "I'll look at these later. I'm going to run over to the house and see if I can figure out what happened. In the meantime, she stays with you. Make up some sort of excuse for CPS."

"Fitz, you're on vacation, and I am still the captain around here. Why am I keeping her with me?"

"My gut is telling me to keep her here. Don't scare her." Before he can fight me on this, I'm already out the door.

Chapter Three

It's especially beautiful riding my bike along the waters edge. You can't get this feeling driving a car. MJ thinks I need a car after the baby gets here. I think she will do anything to keep me off of Wanda. I grip the handles a little bit tighter. *Don't worry, girl, I've got your back.* When I pull up to the house in Sheepshead Bay, the mail lady is just coming down the front steps. I catch her before she heads off.

"Good morning, I was wondering if you can tell me anything about the people that live here?" I quickly pull out my badge and show her. Mail ladies can be tougher than some cops I know.

"You're the second person to ask about the people that live here."

"Really? Who else was asking?"

"Mrs. Gaylord, next door," she shuffles her finger in that direction, "she said an insurance man came by yesterday. He said he was following up on a claim. Is everything okay?"

"I'm not sure yet. What can you tell me?"

"Effy and Stella McPhee live on the first floor. Stella is deaf. Over the summer, she taught me how to sign. She's one tough little girl. Effy is a good mom; they are always together. Don't know nothing about the father. She never talked about him. I ain't never seen anyone other then the two of them around here."

"Who lives upstairs?"

"Bob and Emily Jensen. They're retired and live in Boca Raton, Florida. Their mail is forwarded to them. They hardly ever come up here anymore, probably cause Bob is in a wheelchair now. Effy watches everything for them. This is a real quiet neighborhood. Everyone looks out for each other. Are they okay?"

I get out one of my cards and pass it to her. "I'm sure they are, but if you think of anything else, or see anything that doesn't look right, can you please call me?"

"Of course. I'll keep my eyes open for you." She leaves and I head up the steps.

It's a traditional two-story, two-family home. I knock—nothing. When I try the knob, the door opens into a hallway. On the left is the door for the first floor apartment. In front of me is a flight of steps leading up to Jensen's apartment. I gather up the mail from the floor and quickly flip through it. Mainly junk mail and some magazines. I try the knob on the door to Effy's place and it's not locked. When I step inside, the first thing I see are pictures on top of an entertainment unit of Stella and a beautiful lady that, I'm guessing, must be her mother, Effy. I pull a pair of gloves out of my pocket and put them on. Most guys carry a condom in their wallet; I carry crime scene gloves. This is the reality of my life. When I get into the kitchen, there is a big mess on the floor: food, blood, and a syringe with the needle still attached. It looks like there is still some sort of liquid still in it. I'm sure the lab will be able to process it and tell me what it was that knocked Stella out. I back out of the room the same way I came in and then check the rest of the apartment before I call the captain.

"Hey, you need to get CSU out here. Everything fits Stella's story. I spoke to the mail lady and she said it's just Stella and her mom,

Effy McPhee."

"Wait, Fitz, did I hear you right? Effy McPhee is the kids mother?!" he shouts. I pull the phone away from my ear.

"Yeah, why?" I ask once he quiets down.

"Fuck! This just took a turn for the worse. If it's who I think it is, Effy McPhee is the daughter of Senator Sidney McPhee from Virginia. He's on the short list for Vice President. If that's the case, then the feds will be crawling up our ass on this one."

"Are you sure about this?"

"Yeah, I read an article last week that talked about the men and women on the short list. He stood out because of his work on a bill for children with disabilities. He talked about how is granddaughter was his inspiration. I think there was a picture, too. Hold on, let me pull it up online."

While I wait for him to look that up, I head into the master bedroom and take a closer look around. There is no sign that she has anyone living here long or short term.

"I found it. Yep, this just got really fucked up."

"I'll wait here until you get a team out. How is Stella doing?"

"She was trying to teach me to sign. I thought I was doing good but she keeps laughing at me, so who knows? At least it seems to be taking her mind off things somewhat. When the team gets there, fill them in and then come back here."

He hangs up, and I continue to look around Effy's room. I finally find a couple of photo albums. All of them are of Stella. She has no group photos of family members. The only picture I find of the senator is face down in the back of the book. Why? I dig around a little bit more and find another photo album tucked under a stack of sweaters. Almost like she didn't want anyone to see it. Inside there are pictures of Effy while she is pregnant. There is a young man with her and she looks really happy. I put it back where I found it and head to the strong box that's sitting on a shelf in the closet. The key is sitting in it so apparently she's not worried about theft. I open it and start digging through it. Not really sure what I'm looking for. I find Effy's passport and birth certificate. Then, I find Stella's passport and birth certificate. The father's name is listed as Jason Blackburn. I find an article about the death of Jason Blackburn at the courthouse. There are six sealed envelopes addressed to Stella. Maybe the senator can shed some light on all of this. I put everything back and before I head out front to wait for CSU, I stop in Stella's room and take her Teddy bear off the windowsill. Maybe having it will be comforting for her. When I stop outside the house, the sun is bright. I look down and notice drops of blood and a partially smoked cigar. It's crushed, but it looks like a fat type of cigar, maybe a Robusto. I follow the trail until it comes to a stop in the alley. I'll let the team know when they get here. Knowing I have a few minutes before they arrive, I head next door to talk to Mrs. Gaylord.

I ring the bell, but no response. I see the curtains move a little so I know someone is home. "Mrs. Gaylord, I'm detective Rodriguez. I need to ask you a couple of questions." I hold my shield up so when she peeks out of the curtains again, she will see I'm legit. I wait a little bit more and then I hear the lock before the door creaks opens a crack.

"I don't know nothing, now go away."

"You don't even know what I'm going to ask you. Did you talk to the insurance man that stopped by here?"

"I didn't open the door. He finally went away."

"Ma'am, this is important. Did you spy on him out the window? Can you tell me what he looked like?"

"I wasn't spying. I'm a widow detective; I don't open my door for anyone. He was just an average, white guy. He had a strange hair cut. You know kids today do the craziest things with their hair. All kinds of crazy cuts and what not. He was kind of skinny. Maybe his mother should feed him better."

"How did you know he was an insurance guy?"

"When he was knocking on the door, he said he was an insurance adjuster. That's all I know."

"Did he say what company he was with?"

"No, I told you, I didn't open the door. Is everything okay with Effy and Stella?"

"I'm not sure yet." I pass her my card. "If you think of anything else, will you please call me?"

"Of course, but I don't know what else I can tell you." She takes the card, backs up, and abruptly shuts the door. I head down the steps just as Brad pulls up with the CSU right behind him.

"Hey, Fitz, Captain said you would fill me in."

"It looks like everything happened in the kitchen. The owners live upstairs but they are in Florida. From the little bit I looked around the apartment, there doesn't appear to be a boyfriend or husband. It pretty much played out the way Stella explained it. There is a lot of blood in the kitchen and then there's a smashed cigar in the street and a blood trail into the alley. Make sure CSU collects it all. Maybe we will get lucky and his DNA will be in the system. I have to get back to the station. Let me know if you find anything else."

I'm about to head out when my phone rings the familiar tune "With Eyes Wide Open" by Creed; it's MJ. "Hey, babe, everything okay?"

"I was tired, so I left early. Where are you?"

"The captain called and asked me to come by, he needed me to look at a case. One thing lead to another and I kind of got sucked into helping a deaf kid out."

"Fitz, I've heard a lot of excuses in my day but that one takes the cake. You better get used to not seeing the inside of that station for awhile."

I know MJ is nervous about the baby; I honestly don't know why. She is great with kids. "I promise I'm not going to be long.

When I get home, I will rub your feet for you."

"I accept all bribes involving foot massages. When are you going to trick Andy into putting the crib together for you?"

I make sure to cross my fingers before telling my wife a little white lie. I also know I'll be confessing to Father O'Connor this week. "Babe, I would never do that." I'm sure she's sitting on the couch, feet up, and rolling her eyes at that one.

"Sure, Fitz, and I fell out of the turnip truck yesterday, right in the middle of the Belt Parkway. I'm going to waddle over to the couch and take a nap. Call me when you're on your way. Love you."

"I promise I won't be long, love ya."

Now that I've confirmed who the kid is and that her mother was kidnapped, Hart will have to get used to the feds crawling up his ass on this one. I'll look at the other cases for him and be back home before MJ wakes from her nap.

Chapter Four

I can barely get through the front door of the precinct. There is a mob of reporters in front, blocking my way. I've always avoided reporters like the plague. I quickly put my head down, skirt past them, and head into Hart's office. He's on the phone and Stella is asleep on a chair. When he sees me, he hangs up.

"Hey, couldn't you at least put her on the couch upstairs?"

"I tried but she refused to leave the chair, eat, or even drink anything until you got back here."

"Why is there a crowd out front?"

"It has to do with that other case I wanted you to look at. Right now, my focus is on Effy McPhee. I was able to get in touch with Senator McPhee. He's on his way."

"Did he say anything about Effy?"

"No, why?"

"Just a hunch; no big deal."

"Talk to me, Fitz; your hunches are usually dead on."

"I think Effy might not have been in touch with her father. I have no proof other than the one and only picture of the guy was face down in the back of a photo album. Like I said, it's just a hunch." I sit on the edge of the desk, put her teddy bear down in front of her, and then move the hair out of Stella's face. Her eyes flutter open. She takes her bear and hugs it. She has a huge smile on her face as she sits up and looks around the room, her smile quickly fades.

"Where's my mommy? Did you find her? I want my mommy?" Her eyes fill with tears and her lip is quivering. She's signing so fast; I wish I was better at this.

"I found your house. I'm trying to find your mommy. I even brought you your teddy bear. Is he your favorite bear?"

"His name is Sam and when I come home from school, he's always by the window waiting for me. Sam is my best friend. I tell him everything."

"Can you remember anything more about the man that was in your house?"

"He had more hair than you. He was taller than mommy. I don't know; I was scared!" She's fighting back the tears.

"Okay, okay, don't get upset. I have some ideas on how I can find your mommy. In the meantime, do you want something to drink?"

"Yes, please."

"Okay, I'll be right back. Captain, walk with me to the vending machine."

I take a paperclip off Hart's desk and bend it on my way to the vending machine. I'm thankful we don't have the electronic machines. I stick the clip in the slot for chips and turn the dial till the chips fall to the bottom. When I turn to talk to Hart, his mouth is hanging open.

"Don't look at me like that, I give the vending guy twenty bucks a month. The thing is as old as the hills and only takes change. Who carries change anymore?"

"I never knew that could be done with a clip, amazing."

"Even now, after all these years, I'm glad I can still amaze you. Now, when is the senator going to get here?"

"He should be here soon. Apparently he was already in New

York doing some fund raising. What did you learn at the house?"

"Like I was telling you earlier, it doesn't seem like Effy has a relationship with her father. Stella never mentioned a grandfather and Stella's birth certificate listed the father, but he's deceased. There was an article about a shooting at the courthouse where he was killed. Maybe the senator can shed some more light on him." I run through everything with Hart from the large amount of blood on the floor to the description the neighbor gave me of the so-called insurance guy.

He's smiling and shaking his head. He puts his hand on my shoulder and squeezes. "You couldn't have been there for more than ten minutes and you probably know more in that short amount of time than the crew I sent over. I want you to sit in on the interview with the senator."

"You know I'm on vacation, plus, I still have to convince Andy that he should put that damn crib together."

He's waving his hand like he's shooing away a fly. "Yeah, I know—vacation, but I still need you to look at that file. It's not that hard to put together a crib."

"Fucking fifteen-page manual!" I practically yell. *He doesn't get it.* "Listen, I was thinking, since this case is going to be turned over to the Feds, what about having Stella work with Travis on a description of the guy? He's not only the best sketch artist the Feds have, he's also a tech wizard and that might come in handy. I think he could help. Plus, we could get Mrs. Gaylord to work with him, too."

"I was thinking the same thing. He might be a little unconventional but he really helped out on the Chambers case. It can't hurt. Let's start with Stella."

He heads out front to meet the senator while I head back to his office to give Stella chips and soda. Probably not what her mother would give her, but my choices are limited. At least the chips are a vegetable. I take a seat next to her and open the bag.

"Thank you. Did you find my mommy?"

"I promise as soon as we hear something, I will let you know. In the meantime, I'm going to see if my friend Travis will be able to work with you to draw a picture of the guy you saw." Her eyes grow wide as she puts her soda and chips down. She doesn't say anything. I'm starting to understand that when she is scared, she slides her hands under her legs. It's her way of staying silent.

"Don't worry; I'll be there with you. He's a really cool guy."

"Promise?"

"I promise." I just made a promise to see this through. No matter what happens, I will not let Stella down.

When I look up, Hart and the senator are standing in the doorway. When Stella sees him, she gets up and tries to move behind my chair. Is she afraid of this man or is he a stranger to her? Her fingers are digging into my arm. I get up, turn, and then crouch down so I'm blocking the senator's view.

"Stella, do you know that man?"

"Yes, my mommy said he's my grandfather."

"Are you afraid of him?"

"Yes, he always makes Mommy cry."

Her eyes grow wide and her tears begin to fall again. Damn it, what the fuck has this man done to make this kid so scared? I stand up, pulling Stella behind me.

"Fitz, this is Senator McPhee."

I cut him off in midstream. "I know who he is, sir. What I would like to know is what he has done to make Stella so afraid of him?"

Hart cringes and McPhee's jaw gets tight, as his cheeks turn red. Guess I just pushed a hot button—too fucking bad.

"My granddaughter is not afraid of me. I'm sure it's seeing her mother abducted that has her scared. Thank you for everything you've done, but the FBI will be taking over now." He waves his hand, dismissing me. It only makes me want to punch the fucker in the face. He steps towards Stella, but she grabs my leg with a death grip.

"Apparently, Senator, your granddaughter has a different opinion." Before he can answer, four men come in and it doesn't take a rocket scientist to figure out it's the Feds.

"How about I take Stella to the diner across the street to get her some real food to eat. She already told us everything she saw. Captain Hart can fill you in." I have to play nice with everyone if I want them to bring Travis in. "In the meantime, maybe you can get your tech Travis Gage here from Quantico to work with her on a sketch." I don't wait for an answer. I take Stella's hand and lead her outside via the back door. Too many prying eyes out front.

When we step outside, I scoop her up and race across the street. We get inside and my usual booth is available. Truth be told, this place has been my home away from home for many years. I get Stella situated and while she's coloring, I pull out my phone to let MJ know what's going on.

Me: Hey beautiful, what are you doing?

MJ: Looking at my feet and wondering why you're not here massaging them.

Me: Do you feel up to meeting me at the usual diner?

MJ: Are you okay?

Me: Yeah, but I need your help with the little girl I told you about.

MJ: I'm on my way.

"So my wife is on her way here. While we are waiting, let's pick out some stuff to eat. Pancakes, eggs—anything you want."

"Peanut butter and Fluff, please, and apple juice. You have a wife?"

"Yes, don't look so surprised."

She giggles and it's adorable. Manny comes over and I order my usual along with Stella's order.

"Why did that man take my mommy away?"

"That's what I want to find out."

Before too long, MJ walks in and I get up to hug her. "Hey, babe, I want you to meet a friend of mine. Stella, this is my wife, MJ."

"Hello, Stella. Have you been keeping Fitz busy?" MJ automatically signs.

"He's trying to find my mommy."

My phone starts to ring and it's Hart. "I'm going to step outside and take this call. You can start on my food when it gets here." I get up. Manny is walking by with the food, and I swipe a piece of bacon. "Hey, Captain, what's up?"

"I just spoke to the feds, and Travis was available. He's en route now and should be here within the hour. It helps that we have the senator's private plane at our disposal. Before you say anything, I know you're on vacation. But, Fitz, this kid has opened up to you. Please tell me you'll stay on and help. If I need to, I'll call MJ and smooth things over with her."

"MJ is here. I was just going to fill her in when you called. Has the senator received a ransom call or note?"

"No, nothing. I don't get it."

"Did you ask him about his relationship with his daughter?"

"Yeah, according to him, everything with Effy was fine. I also asked him about Stella and he said he doesn't see her that much and maybe she was just upset by everything that happened."

"Are you buying it? I'm not. Stella was genuinely scared of him. That type of fear comes from something she's seen." I look through the window and I see Stella laughing. I knew she would feel comfortable with MJ.

"Honestly, I don't know what to think."

"Did you get a chance to ask him about Stella's father?"

"No, he shut me down after I asked why she was afraid of him. After that, I figured he's not going to tell me anything."

"Okay, MJ is here now. I'm going to talk to her and see if she can get any thing more from Stella about the senator."

"Don't forget—I still need you to look at that other case for me."

"One thing at a time, Captain. We'll be back soon."

I head back to my table and find the two of them laughing so hard they are both crying. "What's so funny and where is my food!?"

"Stella was telling me about school. I was hungry. Don't worry, Manny is bringing you more."

"MJ, look, I know I'm on vacation but . . ." She leans over and kisses me in mid sentence.

"I would expect nothing less from you."

I am the luckiest guy in the world. I lean in and pretend I'm kissing her cheek but whisper in her ear. "Try and get her to talk about her grandfather and her father."

Manny drops off another plate of food and a huge chocolate egg cream for MJ. While she talks to Stella about the senator, I'm eating my food and pretending not to pay attention. Apparently, she has only seen him three times that she can remember. One time, she had to have her picture taken with him. The other two times, he came to her house. He didn't talk to her, only her mom. Both times, he was yelling and left her mother in tears right before he hit her. After that, she never saw him again. My stomach is in knots at the thought of the old man hitting Effy. I'm letting MJ do all the talking. She seems to be opening up more with her.

"Stella, do you know why he was yelling at your mom, or why he hit her?"

"No. His face was so red. I tried reading lips, but they were talking so fast. The only thing I saw was when he called her stupid. My mommy said that's a bad word and I'm not supposed to use it." Her lip is quivering again and she bites down on it, trying not to cry. It hits me: maybe she was able to read the kidnappers lips. I stop MJ and I start to sign.

"Stella, when the man was trying to take your mom, were you able to read his lips?"

"No, I was crying and holding onto my mommy's leg. She sent me back into the bathroom. I went but then I got scared and ran out again. That's when he stuck a needle in me. When I woke up, I was alone."

"Okay, let's head back to the station. My friend Travis should be here by now. MJ will stay with you while you try to give him a description."

We head across the street. I hope between Travis and MJ, they can get a description together that might actually help us find Effy alive.

Chapter Five

Effy

"*Stella—Oh dear God, Stella.*" When I open my eyes, I have no idea where I am. The only thing I do know is I'm in some sort of cage. I remember Stella running towards me and I remember trying to fight him, but then he injected her with something. I screamed and tried to fight him off, after that—*nothing.* Why would anyone want me? Is this because of who my father is? Where is Stella? What did that creep inject her with? Is she still alive? I curl into a ball on the cot, lean over the side and hurl. "*Stella, Mommy loves you,*" I whisper so softly for fear someone might hear.

I've got to figure out how to get out of here. I need to get to my baby. I get up and try to take stock of everything. It's dark, my head is pounding, and it takes my eyes a bit to focus. When they finally do, I realize the room is filled with cages. Each cage has a cot and it looks like there is one girl in each cage. I'm not even sure how many cages there are. I try to reach my hand into the cage next to me, but it's too far. I get up to walk towards the door but there is a chain around my ankle and it's bolted to the floor.

"Hello, can anyone hear me?" I shout out.

"Shh, if she hears you, she'll come down and hurt us all."

"Who?"

"All I know is her name is Inga. She brings us food and a bucket to wash up. There is also a bucket under your cot, you need to use that for a toilet."

Oh my God, this can't be happening. "Why are we here?"

"I have no idea, all I know is I've been in here for a couple of weeks."

"Weeks! What do they want with us?"

"I don't know. One girl kept yelling and banging on the bars. Inga came down with two guys. They put on the lights, pulled her out of the cage, and beat her to death in front of us. After that, we got the message. If we don't yell and fight them, then maybe we can get out of here alive."

I try to make out the other girls in the cages but it's too dark. "How old are you?"

"I'm thirteen. We're all around the same age except for the girl they killed, she was older."

Oh my God, they're so young. "How many girls are here?"

"Including you, six. Now you need to be quiet or they will come back."

I can barely make out her climbing back into her cot. We are being kept like animals. What the hell are they going to do with us? I've got to figure out a way out of here. I have to get to my baby. I've got a huge lump on my head and when I touch it, the pounding starts and a wave of nausea comes over me. I lie back down and curl into a fetal position, trying to will away the urge to puke. I need to try and make sense of all of this while I figure out how I'm going to get out of here.

Fitz

When we get inside, MJ takes Stella upstairs away from all the prying eyes. I step into Hart's office and quietly close the door behind me. The feds are looking over some maps with Hart, and McPhee is on the phone, his voice is low. He can't possibly be that stupid to think whispering will stop everyone from trying to hear what he's saying. I take the files that the captain wanted me to look at and have a seat. When I begin looking through them, I realize they are all missing persons except for one. The last one, Jin Chen, was murdered. Her name sounds familiar but I can't place it. The medical examiner's report said her death was caused by blunt force injuries of the extremities. Layman's terms: she was beaten to death. She was beaten so bad that the medical examiner had to use dental records to identify her.

I take the pictures of all the missing girls and I keep flipping from one to the next. They don't resemble each other at all. Every girl is a different nationality. The only thing they have in common is they're all young kids. How does the dead girl fit into all of these missing girls? Why does Hart think they're connected? Why does this girl's name sound so familiar to me? Just as I'm about to ask him, McPhee ends his call and glares at me.

"I need all non-essential employees to leave the room." Does he think his glare on me will make me cower or back down? Fucker doesn't have a clue. Before anyone can say another word, I get up and put the files back on Hart's desk. I turn to the asshole and inch my way into his personal space. "I'm not a non-essential employee. I'm a detective and I'm here at the request of Stella McPhee . . . you know . . . your granddaughter."

"What do you have to do with my granddaughter? She's six for God's sake; what does she know?"

"Apparently, more than you do. Right now, my wife is working with her to put together a sketch of the man that abducted Effy. It's because of Stella we have any information at all."

He steps back and turns his attention towards Hart and the feds. "Gentlemen, what I'm about to tell you must not leave this room. In five days, President Caine will be announcing that he has selected me to be his Vice President in the wake of the sudden death of Vice President Webber. We need to find my daughter before that announcement."

My fists are balled by my side. I feel like flames are about to shoot out the top of my head. What kind of fucking asshole is this guy? He doesn't care that his daughter has been kidnapped. Oh no—he only cares because it might interfere with his fucking political plans.

"Have you gotten a ransom call, yet?" I spit out between clenched teeth.

"Look, Fitz, Hart told me you have a track record of solving cases that no one else seems to be able to solve. Personally, I don't think we need you. It's up to the FBI; if they think you have something to bring to the table, then you can stay."

I take a deep, calming breath before the urge to knock all his teeth out takes over. "Look, McPhee, I'm on vacation. The only reason I'm here is because I made a promise to your granddaughter. I could not care less about you and your political aspirations. So, back to my original question: have you gotten a ransom call, yet?"

"No." He's practically growling out his answer.

"Captain, the press was here when I got here this morning. It was before we even knew who Effy was, why?"

"It has to do with that other case I asked you to look at. Do you think it could be related to Effy's disappearance?" Before I can answer, all four feds and McPhee begin drilling Hart about the case. "Look, everyone, I called Fitz in to look at it because we're at a standstill. I don't know if it's related; all I know is that a half a dozen young girls have gone missing. Fitz, did you look at it?"

"I was just starting to dig into it when the good senator showed up. I can take a closer look now." The senator rolls his eyes, making me aware that my snarky remark doesn't go unnoticed. I reach for the folders, but one of the FBI guys grabs them. This is why I don't like to work with partners or anyone else, for that matter. They are all huddled over the files. I get up and head towards the door.

"Where are you going?" The look of angst on Hart's face tells me he doesn't want to be left to deal with these guys.

"Look, Captain, I don't think I'm needed here. I'm going upstairs to see how Stella is making out with that sketch." I don't give him a chance to protest; I quickly head out the door. I grab some cans of soda and head upstairs.

When I enter the room, I find MJ, Stella, and Travis laughing. Travis notices me first and throws his hands in the air. "Thank God you're here. Stella is trying to teach me to sign. I think I just called Captain Hart a dog in a dress!"

"You've got to watch her; she signs really fast. It's good to see you. Sorry it's under these circumstances." I put the sodas down and pull up a chair.

"Don't worry, after the baby comes, Olivia and I will come up for a real visit, not a working one," he says before bringing his focus back to his handy work. "With MJ's help, we were able to put together a sketch. I was just getting ready to print it out for you."

He hands me his tablet so I can see what this guy looks like. He's an average looking white guy with no identifying scars. He does have a tat on one finger—a skull with cross bones. He has long hair but only on one side of his head. Maybe in time she might remember more but, right now, I think she's on overload. When I pass him back his tablet, I don't need to say anything. He's smart enough to know this is not going to be very helpful. However, I would never let Stella see my disappointment. I sit across from her and MJ pulls Stella closer to her. I have a bigger problem: her grandfather might want to take her, and I can't let that happen. I'm going to have to play nice with this asshole. It's not going to be easy.

"Sweetie, you did a good job with that sketch. Can you hang out here with MJ for a little bit longer?"

"I just want my mommy."

"I know, sweetie, I'm trying really hard. I need to get this sketch out. I promise I'll be back really soon."

Travis pulls his chair close to Stella's. "How about you teach me some more signs?" She smiles and begins showing him some stuff.

"MJ, walk me to the door, please?"

I pick up the tablet and head towards the door. "Listen, she is deathly afraid of her grandfather. Even though he convinced CPS that he is some sort of loving grandfather, I can't send her off with him. I'm going to try and convince the senator to let her come home with us. We can sign and she is comfortable with us. At least I know she'll be safe."

"Babe, I would expect nothing less. I'm not letting her go off with a man that she is afraid of. Do what you have to do to make it happen." She kisses me and then smacks my ass to send me on my way. I know how lucky I am and I thank God everyday for my beautiful wife and wonderful family.

When I get downstairs, I head right into Hart's office and pass the tablet to one of the feds. "This is the guy that Stella said abducted her mother. It's pretty generic but at least it is something. Has anyone tried to contact the senator yet?"

They are all huddled around the desk looking at files. Hart finally looks up, "No, we think somehow the abduction of these other woman might be tied to it."

I step closer to where everything is spread out. I'm staring at all the photos and notes but mainly their faces. "What links them?" All heads turn toward me.

"That's what we're trying to figure out. Do you have any ideas? Did you get anything more out of my granddaughter?"

"No, not yet. Listen, Senator, it's getting late and Stella has been here all day. I've been thinking; she's the only one who's seen the guy who abducted Effy. I think we should keep her hidden; taking her back to your place would be too obvious and risky. She feels comfortable with my wife and me; how about I take her back to my house?"

He's staring at me like I have three heads. I realize he has no idea that Stella could be a target. All he cares about is finding his daughter before the big announcement about him being named VP. He looks at the feds for answers but they seem to be waiting for him to take the lead. I nudge Hart to help me out here.

"Sir, if it's any consolation, I can vouch for Fitz. Stella would be totally safe and comfortable with MJ."

McPhee waves his hand at me like he's shooing a bug away. "Whatever, just keep her away from the press."

Fucking ass. I head upstairs to talk to MJ and find Stella asleep in her lap. "Hey, babe, I need you to take Stella home with you. Keep her out of sight. I'll call Andy to come hang out with you till I get home."

"Why does my brother have to hang out there?"

"Safety in numbers. Besides he can start working on the crib." I give her a huge smile, and she just rolls her eyes.

"I knew you were going to pass it onto him and I know why. It's just another reason why I love you. I need you to carry her to my car."

I scoop up Stella and she hardly moves. Poor kid is mentally and physically exhausted. We head out back and I get her strapped into MJ's car. "Be careful and text me when you get home. I'll call Andy and tell him you're on your way."

I watch her leave and I'm happy that both of them will be away from all this craziness. I try Andy and it goes right to voice mail. He's either on the phone or he didn't charge it. I try Mom's house; they have a landline.

"Hello," Dad answers on the first ring.

"Hey, Dad, where's Andy?"

"Hello to you, too. He's in the kitchen with your mom. Did you get the crib together?"

"I don't want to talk about that. I need to talk to Andy; his phone went to voice mail."

"That's because it's sitting next to me, dead as usual. Hold on, I'll get him." I hear him yelling for Andy. Hell, the entire neighborhood hears him.

"Hey, what's up?"

"MJ should be home any minute. She has a little girl with her. I need you to get them inside and make sure you stay with them till I get home."

"I thought you were home?"

"If I was, I wouldn't be calling you. I got called into work, I'll explain everything later. Oh and while your there, I need you to put the crib together." I hold the phone away from my ear and wait for it.

"Fuck, Fitz! I knew it, I should have made a pool and this way I could have made some money."

"Yeah, love you too. Thanks." I hang up before he has a chance to rib me anymore.

Now with everyone nicely tucked away, I head back inside the precinct to take a closer look at these missing girls. If there is a link, I'll find it. I'm not about to leave it up to anyone else to figure it out.

Chapter Six

Effy

I hear a door open and a dim light comes on, helping me to see a little bit more. It looks like I'm in a regular basement. As my eyes begin to adjust more to the lights, I realize it wasn't a dream—I really am in a room with cages filled with girls. All of them very young. *Dear God, what the hell is this?* A woman and a very huge man come down the steps. They go to each cage, unlocking them and passing out food. When she gets to me, she tells me to step back. She's got a heavy accent, Russian, maybe. I can't be sure. The guy steps in and hands me a plate. My hands tremble, causing me to almost drop it.

"Please, why am I here?"

"Shut up and eat. Don't give me any problems and you just might make it out of here alive." He walks out and she locks the door. As they head towards the stairs, she tells the girls their time here is almost over. When she reaches the top of the steps, the lights go out. I've heard about human smuggling rings, but I thought that happens in other countries not here in America. *It can't happen here.* I need to escape. I need to get to my baby.

Why would they want me? I'm too old to be sold like these younger girls. Maybe they don't know who I am. If they knew, I'm sure they would hit my father up for a big ransom. What the hell are they going to do with me? Maybe I should tell them to call my father. Maybe they wouldn't take me away with the others. I drop to my knees and pray. Right now, that's all I have. I pray that my baby is safe. "*Hang on, Stella.*"

Fitz

While Hart and the FBI are trying to figure out their next move, I start skimming through the pictures and reports for the missing girls. It hits me quickly that not only were they all young, ranging from eleven to thirteen. They were all taken from the general area that this precinct services. The girl that was beaten to death was twenty-one, but she looked younger than that. I push aside the missing girls and concentrate on the dead girl. That's where the answers are locked away. Her name was Jin Chen. Jin was a senior at John Jay College. She was studying Computer Science and Information Security. The crime scene report states that her body was dumped near the Plumb Beach area. That area is known for late night hook-ups, whether in cars or on the beach. The people that frequent the area don't care. Was she there for a hook-up or was she really dumped there? I pull out the ME's report to try and gain some more insight. I see Gail was the ME on this case. I've worked with her for years; she's not just a colleague but a great friend. At first glance, the report seems pretty clear: dead girl on the beach. When I read further, two things jump out at me: a dead Cellar spider was found imbedded into her skull and a tiny storage chip from a USB drive was found in her colon. I know that should freak me out but it's the bug that freaks me the fuck out. Bugs, why does it have to be bugs? Just the thought of those fuckers creeps me out. The fact that it was in her skull sends a shiver up my spine.

"Fitz, what is it?"

I look up and realize I was totally in a zone. "Sorry, Captain, I need to talk to Gail."

"Did you find something?"

"I need to clarify something with her."

He turns back to the conversation with the senator while I take the report to the printer and make a copy for myself. When I get back to Harts office, everyone is still huddled around the desk. I put the report back, step outside, and shoot a quick text to Gail.

Me: Hey, can you meet me for coffee?

Gail: Hello to you too, stranger. What's up?

Me: I have questions on the Jin Chen case. Are you available now?

Gail: Aren't you on vacation?

Me: I thought so but you know life happens.

Gail: Do you want me to come to you?

Me: I've got Wanda today. I can pick you up.

Gail: I'm getting ready to leave now. I'll skip Wanda thank you very much. I haven't eaten all day I'll meet you at Deli 52. I'll be there in 30.

Me: Make it 45, I want to swing by the house to check on MJ.

Gail: Send her my love. See you soon.

I'm about to go back into Hart's office but I realize no one other than Hart even notices that I'm gone. I wave goodbye and hightail it out of there. I want to check in at home before meeting Gail. When I head out back, I find a woman standing by my bike. "Can I help you?"

She trails her fingers along Wanda's seat, and the hair on the back of my neck just stood on edge. "Nice bike."

"Who are you and what do you want?"

"Why is Senator McPhee in the police station?"

"And you are?"

"Hudson. I'm a reporter."

"No comment." As I climb on Wanda she steps in front of my bike. She places both hands on the handlebars.

"Please give me something to work with."

"You're a new face; what rag are you with?"

"I'm an independent reporter, trying to make an honest living."

Some people can lie and some can't lie to save their life. She is the latter. "What are you in high school or something? Look, Hudson, I've heard it all, so cut the bullshit. What's your full name?"

"It's just Hudson. You know, like Cher? And for your information, I'm a senior in college. I want to know why McPhee is here?"

"Are you even old enough to know who Cher is?"

She rolls her eyes. "Yeah, you know, "Turn Back Time," "Half Breed," and all that shit. Now why is McPhee here?"

"Well, Hudson, like I said—no comment. Let go of Wanda—*now!*" I look down at her hands and then up towards her as I start up Wanda. The noise drowns out anything else she has to say. She steps aside and I pull away. When I look back, I see her throw her hands up and walk away. Just what I need now, the fucking press on my ass.

Vadik

Everything was going great. I've been filling orders at a nice clip. That is until Tommy picked up the wrong girl. Inga texted me a picture; I have no clue what would posses him to think this was the girl I asked for. He knows they have to be young. The younger they are, the more money I can get for them. I have no idea who this girl is, but maybe I can get something for her. I mean, she's pretty, but she's got to be in her late twenties—too old for my needs. Didn't he learn anything after that Asian bitch? This was supposed to be the last one for a while. Now I have to figure out what to do with her. Maybe I can throw her in as a bonus. Everyone likes to get something for nothing. They want to feel like they got a good deal and my buyer is no different.

I told Inga I needed to see Tommy right away. He never showed up. He knows he's in trouble and probably skipped. I've got to find out who this broad is and if there's anyone looking for her. I've got a contact at one of the precincts; I'll see if he's heard anything. Hopefully, she's a nobody and won't be missed. I'll try and get what I can for her and if not, I'll dump her like the last one.

Fitz

I'm lucky that Andy and Stephen live directly across the street from us, with an added bonus of Mom and Dad right around the corner. We've been in the same neighborhood for as long as I can remember and I can't imagine living anywhere else. I pull up just as Stephen is climbing the steps to go inside.

"Hey, Stephen, I need to talk to you. Besides, Andy's at my house."

"So, what else is new? You think he's mothering MJ now? Imagine how bad he's going to be after she has the baby." I laugh, knowing that he's right.

"I need some advice on a case I'm working on and, before you say anything, I know I'm on vacation."

"I'm not saying anything, I knew it wouldn't last. What's going on?"

I reach in my pocket pull out a dollar and press it into his hand. He looks down at it and back up to me.

"Guess I'm giving you the family discount again. Have a seat."

We sit on the stoop and I tell him everything about Stella and Effy, including what a douchebag the senator is.

"So what do you need from me?"

"I don't want Stella to end up in the system. And I sure as shit don't want to let the senator get his hands on her. What can we do?"

"Jesus, Fitz, nothing is ever easy with you. Do you think Effy is dead?"

"Well, there has been no ransom demand. Every minute that goes by without a sound lessens the chance that she'll be found alive."

"Are there any other family members that might lay claim to the child?"

"I don't know, but I can't leave anything to chance."

"Are you thinking you want to take custody of her?"

"If it's possible, I would. You know I was around the same age as Stella when I lost my mom to violence. She was a witness to it, just as I was. I wouldn't want her to grow up with the same fears that I had."

"Is the grandfather that bad?"

"I don't know him at all. What I do know is that she is afraid of him—deathly afraid. On top of that, he is going to be named the new VP. Her life will not only be turned upside down, she'll be put under a microscope."

"You know if he is made VP, and she ends up with him, he might be able to use her disability to get secret service protection assigned to her. That might not be such a bad deal."

"Doesn't the protection come automatically with the job?"

"That's what people think but the truth is protection does not extend to the vice president's immediate family."

"Even if he could get her the protection, it would be a very lonely life for her."

"Do you know if Effy had a will?"

"I didn't see one when I did a quick look through her strong box, but that doesn't mean she didn't."

"Okay, let me discreetly look into this. For now, let's go see what's going on at your house."

We get up and head inside. "Hopefully, Andy got the crib together."

He bursts out laughing. "I should have taken the bet with my father in-law. He knew you were going to get Andy to do it."

"Am I that predictable?"

"Fitz, you are very black and white. It's either right or wrong, there is no gray line in your world and that's why you're great at what you do."

"I'm going to take that as a compliment."

When we get inside, the house smells like chocolate chip cookies. "Hey, Andy, your better half is here. Where's MJ and Stella?" I call out. Stephen and Andy have been married for years, yet, every time they see each other, it's like the first time.

"They are both taking a nap. I put the crib together; you owe me big time. Did you intentionally buy the hardest crib in the world to put together?" He asks as he enters the living room to greet us.

"Of course; just to piss you off. How is Stella doing?" I head into the kitchen with Andy on my heels.

"She's a great kid, Fitz. I hope you can find her mother alive. I wouldn't want what happened to her to be the last memory of her. Do you have any leads on her?"

My last memory of my mother was of her brutal murder by my father. I try to live my life in the present, and I'm so grateful for all that I have. Andy's family took me in as one of their own, but every now and again, that nightmare comes back front and center. Sometimes, no matter how much you try, the pain hits you like a sucker punch to the gut. "I have no leads. Did Stella say anything more about what happened?" I know I'm grasping at straws, but I wish she could give me some sort of clue.

"No, nothing new. What about her father? Do you know anything about him?"

"Not yet. I just started looking into the case. Stella didn't mention him and I didn't want to flat out ask her, at least, not yet." I glance at the clock. If I leave now, I won't be to late for my meeting. "I have to meet Gail but I wanted to check on everyone. Can you guys stay here till I get back?"

"Of course. Go before it gets any later. I'll order a pizza for everyone. Give Gail a hug." Andy pushes me out the door but not before I grab a couple of cookies.

Chapter Seven

When I get to the deli, Gail is already there waiting.

"Hey, sorry I'm late."

"No problem. How's MJ?"

"She's tired and mothering all of us more than usual. According to all the books I read, I think she's close." The waitress comes over and we quickly order.

"So you have questions on the Jin Chen case. Is this in an official capacity? Cause if you're still on vacation, I really can't go into details with you."

"It's official; Hart called me in to look at the case. Six girls have been taken, all around the same time. Jin was one of those girls and she showed up dead."

"Why would Hart call you in for that?"

" He was stuck and thought a new set of eyes might help. It was not supposed to be anything official. So when I got to the station, there was a little girl sitting on a bench. Apparently, she was found wandering around the streets not too far from the station. No one realized the girl is deaf and had no one to communicate with. Thanks to MJ, I know how to sign. Fast forward: the girl's mother was abducted and the kid witnessed it all. The mother is the daughter of

Senator McPhee. This kid, Stella, is afraid of the grandfather and he agreed to let her stay with MJ and me. This whole thing is one big cluster fuck, but now you're up to speed on everything."

The waitress drops off a basket of bread and our drinks. Gail is just staring at it. "Hey, you okay?"

"No. If Stella's mother is in the hands of the people who killed Jin, the chance of finding her alive just became very slim."

I lean in a little closer. "Why? I mean, I know all the text book reasons why, but what is your gut telling you?" I pull the autopsy report out of my pocket and pass it to her. She holds her hand up and pushes it away.

"Please don't. I don't need to see that report again. You know how sometimes a case will just stay with you and not in a good way? Well, the Jin case is like that for me. She was beaten by two people. She had bruises on her body that resemble a woman's high heel shoe. Her skull was crushed by a man's boot. It was large, I measured it at a size fourteen. The tread of the boot print might be some sort of military boot. The logo from the bottom of the boot was imprinted on her left side just below her ribcage. I sent it to trace but they said it was a popular military brand and they weren't holding out much hope. She was petite and looked so young. If I didn't know her real age, I would have placed her at about fourteen."

I can feel my blood pressure going up at the thought of what this girl went through. "What made you think she was dumped and not killed at Plumb Beach? Maybe it was a hookup gone wrong."

"At first, I thought that was the case but when I found the spider imbedded in her skull, I knew she was dumped there. Plus, she was dead at least three days when her body was found. She was dumped right at the edge of the parking lot. Anyone who pulled in there would have seen her body right away. But, again, it was the spider; they are not found at the beach." I feel a shiver run up my spine. I fucking hate bugs.

"Are these spiders indigenous to a certain area?"

"They are a very common spider. I double-checked in the *Platonic: World Spider Catalog.* They are often mistaken for daddy longlegs."

"So, she could have been killed anywhere. Why was there a memory chip in her colon?"

"I only tell you my findings, you're the one who solves the mystery. The only thing I can tell you is that she should have passed it but she suffered from chronic colonic diverticulitis. It's not common in the Asian culture but I'm sure her western diet, coupled with stress, played a part in her developing this disease at such a young age. You're looking at me like a deer in headlights." Probably because I'm trying to figure out what she's saying. She shakes her head slightly like she's figured out my confusion. "Diverticulitis is an inflammation or, when it's really flared up, an infection in one or possibly more small pouches in the digestive tract. I found the tiny chip in one of those pouches."

"Wow, were you able to get anything off of it?"

"I have no idea. I gave it to Stacey in the crime lab to process."

The waitress drops off our food. Gail picks at her pastrami sandwich while I devour mine. No doubt our conversation is killing her appetite. "We can hold off on the rest of this until you finish eating." I push her plate closer to her. Maybe taking a break will bring back her appetite.

"Are you all ready for the baby?" She quickly changes the subject.

"Yeah. Andy got the crib together today, so the room is officially done."

"How is he feeling?"

"He's doing good. You know with Parkinson's, he'll have good days and bad, but he has more good ones. He has a lot of family support, so that helps. Truth be told, I could have put that crib together but having him do it and think that I couldn't really helped him."

"I figured that was the case. You always put everyone else's needs first. You're a good man and a royal pain in the ass."

"Thanks, I think." I try to swipe her pickle from her dish but she smacks me!

"Never mess with a girl's pickle. Now tell me, do you think all these cases are related?"

Gail is a lot like me: a dog with a bone. "I'm not sure, yet. Hart thinks so, but I haven't had a minute alone with him to find out why. I think Effy, that's McPhee's daughter, is somehow in this same mix. I'm just not sure how."

"How old are the other missing girls?"

"Young, why?"

"Maybe that's the common denominator. Jin looked a lot younger than she really was. Is there anything else that would link them together?"

"They all live in the area that the precinct serves, but I haven't really gotten a chance to dig into everything yet. I wanted to look closely at Jin's case first."

"Do you think her case could be related to the Long Island serial killer cases?"

"No, all the girls in that case were prostitutes. Everything I've read about Jin doesn't suggest she was a prostitute."

"Do you want me to do a search for similar cases in the past like Jin's?"

"Yeah, that would be very helpful. I just have that twist in my gut that's telling me the answers are staring me in the face. I feel like I'm missing something, but I'm not sure what."

She pushes away her plate and is tearing the paper from her straw into a million tiny pieces. I pull the paper from her hands. "Gail, what's bothering you?"

"Jin's beating was beyond brutal. It was sadistic. She wasn't raped, but she suffered . . . bad. She had marks around her left ankle, like she was restrained somehow. She died a very slow death."

"Did she fight back?"

"No, that's the thing that bothers me. She had no defensive wounds at all. She wasn't drugged—nothing. Why didn't she fight back, Fitz?" Her question, almost a plea.

"I don't know, yet, but I think you've had enough of this. I'm going back to the station to look at those cases. If I need anything, I will let you know."

I pay the bill, walk her to her car, and make sure she gets off okay before heading out. What is it about this case that's bugging me? Why didn't Jin fight back? When I pull up to the station, the crowd is out of control. I head around back where at least I won't get mobbed. Thankfully, no sign of Hudson. Maybe she got the message. When I get inside, I find Hart is alone in his office.

"Hey, Captain, where did everyone go?"

"Where the hell have you been?"

"I had to check on MJ and Stella. After that, I met with Gail for dinner. Are there any new developments?"

"No, do you have anything?" He's looking to me as if I can solve this overnight.

"I just started looking into all of this. Where are the files?"

"The Feds took them upstairs. Look, I think there is enough people on this case now. You can go back to your vacation. Let me walk you out." His door is open and he is talking loud, well . . . louder than usual. Before I can question him, he presses a thumb drive into my palm as he shakes my hand. He follows me out back, looking around the entire time.

"Fitz, copies of the files are on that drive. Everything that was in the original ones. Whatever you do, please don't let that drive out of your sight. You never got any of this from me. As far as anyone is concerned, you couldn't offer any help with them."

Something has him spooked; this is not like him at all. "You know that I will keep everything safe, including Stella. Now, do you want to tell me what's really going on?"

"We have a leak. I'm not sure who. It just seems that things are getting out and I'm not sure how."

"Is the word out on Effy?"

"Yeah, a reporter asked me about it. I don't think it's a kidnapping for ransom. No one has made any contact. The Feds swear they haven't leaked anything. You're the only one I trust."

"What reporter?"

"It doesn't matter."

"Yeah, it does. What fucking reporter?"

"Some chick with one name, Hanson or something."

"Hudson?!"

"Yeah, that's it: Hudson, you know her?"

"I found her hanging around back here when I left earlier. How the hell did she find out?"

"I told you, I think there is a leak. Anyway the senator is preparing to go live about the kidnapping."

"Fuck no! What about Stella?"

"The only thing that is out there is Effy McPhee is missing. The senator said he will only speak about Effy."

"Well, he's a fucking idiot. It's only a matter of some simple investigating before the press finds out about Stella. Don't forget, just because she can't hear that doesn't change the fact that she is an eyewitness. The senator is going to put her in more danger than she already is. Did you try talking to him?"

"They brushed me off like I'm some rookie."

"Let me ask you, what makes you think these cases are connected?"

"The age of the girls, plus they were all taken from the area that this precinct services."

"I noticed that, too. It's really odd, but it would make sense if there is a mole."

"I know. Look, go home. I will feel better knowing that you're there with MJ and Stella."

He's really rattled by all of this. "I will, but I'm going to have Travis pop in to sweep your office." He cocks his head and before he can protest I squeeze his arm. "I trust him with my life and you know you can, too."

He barely whispers an okay before he's headed back inside.

Chapter Eight

Hudson

I'M NOT GOING TO BE pushed aside, not by Detective Rodriguez, and not by Captain Hart. My best friend is dead and I want answers. Maybe if Rodriguez knew everything I have so far, maybe then he might be more willing to talk to me. I thought Jin was crazy when she said that she thought somehow the death of Vice President Webber could be tied to the missing girls. It was supposed to be our final project for our Political Science class. It was just a theory, but then when Jin went missing. I started to question everything we found out. When she turned up dead—*murdered*, I realized it might not be such a crazy theory. I have to find Detective Rodriguez and get him to listen to me. Maybe he doesn't remember Jin, or her parents, but maybe if I remind him, he'll want to listen. He's my last chance . . .

Fitz

It was late when I got home. Stella was asleep in the guest room. MJ was fast asleep, too. She's up and down all night long. I quietly crawled into bed, trying not to wake her. I've never been a heavy sleeper and now that MJ can go into labor anytime, I only cat-nap. I feel her struggling to move around the bed, apparently trying not to wake me. When I roll over, I find her sitting on the bed with the light from her phone, reading the autopsy report. I reach over and take it out of her hands, but she is trembling. "Hey, I didn't mean for you to see that. Are you okay?"

"Fitz, why didn't you tell me Mr. Chen's daughter was murdered?"

I turn on the light on the side table and that's when I notice she's been crying. "You know her?"

"Yes, you do, too. I know the last few years have been crazy for us, but her parents own the dry cleaners around the corner from my old apartment in Brooklyn."

It finally hits me—that's what's been bugging me. "Shit, MJ, how could I be so dense?"

"When you're on a case, you go into a zone."

I pull her into my arms. "That's no excuse. I need to go see Mr. & Mrs. Chen tomorrow."

"I would like to pay my respects; can I go with you?"

"I would rather you stay close to Stella. I promise as soon as this is over, I will take you to see them." I pull her close to me and mindlessly run my fingers up and down her belly. She eventually falls back to sleep, leaving me to run this case over and over again in my head.

I feel the morning sunshine on my face. I reach for MJ, hoping to snuggle for a little bit before starting my day, but the bed is empty. I hear the shower running and decide to join her. When I turn around to get up, I find Stella standing by the bed. She's looking at me like one of the kids from *The Shining*. I nearly lose my shit!

"Jesus, Stella, you nearly gave me a heart attack." Her eyes grow wide, her hands are trembling.

"Is my mommy never coming back?" Her signing is very slow, like someone who is apprehensive about asking a question that they really don't want an answer to.

"I'm doing everything I possibly can to bring her home—*promise*." I open my arms and she climbs into my lap. I rock her as she silently cries for her mom. A mom that seems to be the only person that is there for this kid. Not that bastard of a grandfather who should be the one to comfort her. This just serves to remind me that family by blood isn't always family.

MJ has long since finished her shower, walks in, and puts a cup of coffee on the nightstand for me. She sits on the bed and strokes Stella's back. Stella looks at her and smiles. These two have grown pretty close in such a short time.

"Fitz, I know we can't go back to her home to get her clothes, so Andy, Mom, and me are taking her shopping."

I know I can't keep everyone under lock and key, but at least Andy and Mom will be with them. "Okay, just stay together and text me when you get back home," I say almost as a plea. She agrees, gives me a kiss, and they leave as I head into the shower.

My first stop today is to pay a visit to Mr. Chen. I can't believe I didn't put it together that Jin was his daughter. Right now, he is the only lead I have. When I pull up to the store, it is closed, but I see Mr. Chen working inside. I knock a couple of times and when he sees me, he opens the door.

"Hello, Mr. Chen, how are you? I'm so sorry for your loss. Where is Mrs. Chen? I would like to pay my respects."

"She's upstairs. She does not want to leave the house. She does not believe that Jin is dead. I'm closing up the store; my heart is just not in it."

They loved this store and all the neighbors. Brooklyn neighborhoods are like a close-knit family. If Andy and I did something wrong, by the time we got home, Mom already knew. "I'm sorry to hear that. Can we talk for a bit? I would like to know exactly what happened."

"Why don't we go in the office and you can ask me whatever you would like."

I know this place like the back of my hand. I installed the security system when Mr. Chen was having problems. That system ended up saving lives, MJ's included. We have a seat in the back, and now comes the hard part. I need him to open up about everything he knows about his daughter. I vaguely remember Jin working around the shop after school.

"Sir, please tell me what you know about Jin's life outside of her family. I know she was a senior at John Jay College. What else can you tell me?" I sit back and let him talk. He might not have any information relevant to the case, but sometimes in life, the best thing we can do for someone is to listen.

"Fitz, Jin was a good girl. She was working hard in school. She was the first person in our family to go to college. She wanted to make us proud. This was her last year and she wanted to get a place with her best friend. I understood how she felt. I knew I couldn't keep her home with us forever. My wife blames me; if I would have told her no, she would not have been taken from us." His voice cracks at the end. He closes his eyes and begins to cry. I get up and get him some water.

"If you're up to it, I have some questions." As I sit back down, I place my hand on his shoulder and give it a slight squeeze.

"I would do anything to find out why someone did this to Jin. Please, ask me whatever you would like."

"Where did Jin live?"

"She found an apartment not too far from here. I can write it down for you." He jots it down and passes it to me.

"What did the police tell you when she went missing?"

"Fitz, I want you to know I did ask for you first. They told me that my daughter's apartment was not in your precinct. I was told I had to wait twenty-four hours and file a missing persons report. They tried to tell me she probably just went off and would turn up. I know my daughter; she would never do that."

I know I can't save the world but it still feels like a sucker punch in the gut that I was not there for him. "What can you tell me about Jin's roommate?"

"She is a very nice girl. They have some of the same classes. They were working on a final project together that took up a lot of their time, so my wife would make up care packages and take it over to their place. I can assure you, Fitz, I checked Hudson out before my daughter asked permission to room with her."

Hudson?! Did I hear him right? What the fuck—Hudson? I can literally hear the blood pounding in my ears. "Mr. Chen, what did you find out about Hudson?"

"She comes from a nice family. They live in Westchester. Jin said her father was an investment banker. Her mom was a stay-at-home mom. They seemed like ordinary people, Fitz. Do you think she might be in danger, too?"

"I don't know what to think, but I do know the first thing I need to do is talk to Hudson." *This is unbelievable.* We get up and he walks me to the door. "I will let you know what I find out. Please let Mrs. Chen know I was here and I promise to come back with MJ."

I hightail it out of there and head towards Jin's apartment. When I glance at my side mirror, I notice I've picked up a tail. Apparently, I've ruffled someone's feathers. When I slow down, I notice it's Hudson. What the hell is she up to? I pull into the bus stop since parking in Brooklyn is non-existent and she pulls in behind me. Before I can even get off of my bike, she is running towards me.

"Why the hell are you following me?"

"I need to talk to you. It's important and you blew me off."

"You said you were a reporter. You never said you were Jin's roommate."

"My minor is Journalism. I thought maybe if you thought I was a reporter you would take me seriously," she states frantically. "Look, Jin and I were working on a project. I thought she was just being paranoid, but now I think that project might have gotten her killed. Can we please go someplace quiet to talk?"

"Go home; I'll meet you there." She doesn't argue with me. She races back to her car and takes off. I follow closely behind her.

Vadik

After putting some feelers out about this girl, I got back the worst possible news. She's a senator's daughter. On top of that, she has a kid . . . a deaf kid who witnessed the whole fucking thing. My client is not going to be happy. Even though demand for these girls has been high, my discretion is why I get paid so much for them. The younger, the better.

I own a pizza parlor, which gives me the perfect cover. The kids hang out here, and I get to know them. They feel safe and their parents feel safe leaving them there while they do their shopping. It's a win-win situation for everyone. Well, everyone except the girls. I make sure they are never taken from here. I have video games and pinball machines—free for the kids to play. They get to know me. They start to trust me. After a while, they are telling me everything about their lives. Once I have all their information, I'm able to tell my crew where to snatch them from. This, however, could be a major complication.

I'm pacing around my office when I hear a commotion out front. I have cameras hidden, which are voice-activated. I trust no one, but today the commotion is coming from the mother of one of the girls. She wants to put up flyers of her missing daughter. If I let everyone put up flyers, it would draw attention to my place, and I can't have that. Not too long ago, some broad was in here asking about that Asian bitch. Now this? The problem is that this current group of girls was not spaced out enough. My contact at the station said some red flags came up. Add to that, one of the girls is the senator's daughter . . . my lucrative business just came to a screeching halt. Tommy and Stanley are off the grid, but I need them found—*now!* I know I got the address right; the only thing I could figure is Tommy got it wrong. They fucked this up. Now, they need to get that kid. In the meantime, I need to have Inga get the girls that we do have ready to ship out. Everyone, that is, except the senator's daughter. I need to figure out what I want to do with her. I grab my phone and shoot Inga a text.

Me: Get everyone ready to go, except the new girl. We need to be ready to leave on a moments notice. Have you heard from Tommy and Stanley?

Inga: The girls are ready when you are. I haven't heard from either of them. I told you Tommy needed medical attention. I asked around and he hasn't reached out to any of our people.

Me: If you hear anything, let me know.

Pulling out the senator's daughter only leaves me with five girls to transport. My client is not going to be happy, especially when I tell him it's going to take longer to fill his standing order. He resells these girls for his cause. What that is, I don't ask. I have my own cause—retirement. Half my money goes to an investor that discreetly handles it for me. The other half goes into an off-shore account in the Virgin Islands. I literally get off with every transfer I make. It's a thrill I never get tired of. Now that Stanley and Tommy fucked everything up, I'll be lucky to get out of this alive. First things first, I need to let Aafii know that the shipment will be short.

Me: Shipment is ready to go. It will be one short.

Aafii: Why the rush and why one short?

Me: Things are a little heated around here with all the

missing girls. My source said they are trying to link the dead Asian girl to the missing ones.

Aafii: You should not have dumped her out in the open. How the hell did she even find out about you?

Me: I'm not sure, but my source at the station said they found a chip from a USB drive in her gut. He's going to try and get it so I can see what's on it.

Aafii: So why are you one short?

Me: My guy grabbed the wrong girl.

Aafii: Are you fucking kidding me? Who did he take?

Me: Effy McPhee, senator McPhee's daughter. My source said he's going to be named the next Vice President.

Aafii: Tell me about the girl.

Me: She's got to be in her late twenty's. She has a kid that's deaf.

I was going to leave out the part about the kid, but a quick Google search is all it will take to find out about her. I do, however, omit the part about her being a witness to Tommy's fuck up.

Aafii: Bring me the girl. I'll let you know what I decide about the kid.

Me: If you say so. I'll meet you tonight at Teterboro. After that, I think we should lay low for a few months. While the dust settles and I can move my operation.

Aafii: We will talk about that later. I'll see you tonight.

I'm going to try texting Tommy. Maybe I'll get lucky and he'll answer.

Me: You grabbed the wrong girl, but I was able to salvage the fuck up. I need to know about the kid. What did she see?

Tommy: I swear I had the right address. 1352 Bragg Street.

Me: 1352 Brown Street. It doesn't matter, the buyer will take her too. Back to the kid; what did she see?

Tommy: What does it matter, I hit her with enough of a tranquilizer to knock out a horse. She's probably dead.

Me: Stay out of town for a while. I'll let you know when you can come back.

Tommy: Whatever.

I need to find out the status on the kid. Aafii wants her alive, but if she is, she can identify Tommy. Somehow, I think this is going to be one big cluster fuck and I'm smack in the middle of it.

Me: Inga, small change of plans. We leave tonight. Bring the new girl.

Inga: I thought she was a mistake?

Me: Not anymore.

Now I need to find out why this kid is so important. Why keep a witness alive? Maybe the answer lies with the senator. A quick search on the internet and the answer is staring me in the face. The Vice President died suddenly and the senator is in the running for the job. What better leverage than to have a VP's daughter and possibly granddaughter as a pawn. The big question is: where is the granddaughter now? Maybe my contact at the station knows. If not, it's to his benefit to find out.

Chapter Nine

Fitz

The drive to Hudson's place does not take long. If she really believes that Jin was murdered because of whatever they are working on, then the apartment is not a safe place for her. God only knows what these kids got themselves into. When I pull up, Hudson is already out of her car waiting on me. I take a minute to run everything through my head one more time.

"Detective Rodriguez, why are you just sitting there? You're not going to crap out on me, are you?"

She trying to sound tough; she is anything but. "If what you're telling me is true, then your apartment is not safe."

"You're joking, right? I was just here an hour ago; it's safe."

She doesn't wait for my protest, she's already heading up the front steps. It's a renovated brownstone with multiple apartments. Judging by the mailboxes, two are on the first floor and one on the second. Her apartment is on the first floor, in the back of the building. When we reach her place, the door is wide open. Before I head inside, I pull her behind me. “Stay out here and be quiet.”

A quick look around and I head back out to the hallway. “The place has been tossed. I want you to go inside and see if anything is missing.” I pass her a set of gloves. “Put those on, don’t touch and don’t talk.”

When we step inside, I hear her gasp. If she didn’t come looking for me she would have been here when this happened. They even went so far as to dump out the cereal boxes. Definitely professionals. When we get back outside, she begins to cry. “If you plan on doing this for a living, you might want to ditch the tears.”

She puts a hand on her hip and pokes a finger in my chest. I think I just pissed her off. “I don’t want to do this for a living. It was a final project for our Political Science class!”

So she just confirmed she’s not a reporter. No big surprise there. She’s not reporter material, and she never will be. “Do you know what was taken from your apartment? Did they get your computer? Do you think they found whatever you were working on?” I know I’m hitting her with rapid-fire questions and I don’t want to scare the kid, but this is bad. Her and Jin are in someone’s crosshairs and now Jin is dead.

“I brought all of Jin’s personal stuff to her parents house last night. My computer, along with Jin’s notebooks, is in my backpack, which is always with me. Everything else is on three thumb drives. Jin had one. I have one. The other one she hid at her parents’ shop.”

I grab her hand and pull her outside. “Get on my bike—*Now!*”

“What’s wrong with you? Why are you yelling at me? I’m the victim here!”

“Not only are you in danger, but you just put the Chen’s in danger. We need to leave now and I’m sure they have some sort of tracker on your car, which is why they probably came after you left. Get on—*now!!*”

I start up my bike and she get's on. I'm driving like a maniac. I try calling the dry cleaners and no answer. They live above the cleaners so they could not have gone far. I call Hart's cell phone and tell him to get someone over there stat. When I pull up, the entire building is engulfed in flames. "Stay put."

I grab one of the fire fighters and she tells me Mr. & Mrs. Chen were not in the building at the time of the fire. They are standing next to an ambulance unhurt but clearly shaken up.

"Mr. Chen, what happened?"

"After you left, I went upstairs to tell my wife that you came by. I finally convinced her to leave the house . . . just for a walk around the neighborhood. When we came back around the corner, we saw two men running from the store. I tried to run after them but they were too fast for an old man like me. Then, I saw the fire. Fitz, everything we had left of our daughter was inside our home. Now it's all gone." He pulls his wife into his arms and they both break down into tears. How did this spiral out of control so fast? I look over to check on Hudson and she is not there! Shit! I need to find her, but I can't leave Mr. And Mrs. Chen. I'm about to call Hart when I see him pull up.

"Hey, I need to find someone. I'll explain it to you later but right now I need you to put Mr. & Mrs. Chen in a safe house. No one can know you have them!"

He knows me well enough that he doesn't question it. Now I need to figure out where the hell Hudson went. I head back towards her place because realistically I don't know anything about her. I pull up just as she is getting out of a cab. At least she's alive. A pain in my ass, but alive. I step in front of her, blocking her from getting anywhere without me.

"What would posses you to come back here? Please, make me understand."

"I wanted to get my car. I thought I would go home. At least I know I will be safe there."

"You can't go home!"

She steps closer with her hand on her hip and her finger in my chest yet again. This girl is trying my patience. "You. Can't. Stop. Me!"

"The fire was arson. Whatever was in Jin's stuff was important enough for someone to burn down a building. Do you really think you want to put your parents in that kind of danger?" Her face pales as reality hits.

"My parents are dead. I wouldn't be putting anyone in danger. Besides, I have no where else to go." Instead of poking me, she wraps her arms tightly around herself. "Why is this happening?"

"Why does Mr. Chen think your parents are still alive?"

"I don't broadcast my personal life. That's why it's called personal."

Now come the tears. Why me? "Come on, I have someplace you can stay."

She climbs on my bike without a fight. We head off to the one place I know I can leave her that she will be safe. My parent's house.

We pull up and she's not moving. She finally pulls her helmet off and gets off my bike. "Where are we?"

"My parent's house, Patrick and Annie Justice."

"Aren't you afraid I'm going to put them in danger? You wouldn't let me go home, but it's okay to put your parents in danger? What kind of lunatic are you?"

"The good kind of lunatic. Look, my dad is a retired NYPD detective. My mom will put the fear of God in anyone. Trust me, you'll be safe here." We head inside and before we can get upstairs, my mom is already half way down the steps.

"Fitzgerald, is everything okay? Did you eat? Whose your friend?"

She didn't use my middle name, so I'm not in that much trouble, yet. "Ma, calm down and give me a minute, geez. Where's Dad?"

"In front of the TV, where he always is. I swear that thing is warping the world." She's waving her hands as she heads back upstairs. We follow closely behind her.

"Mom, this is Hudson. She is helping me on a case. Hudson, this is my mom. Is dinner ready?" Food always distracts her from fifty questions.

"Almost. I'll set another place."

I pull Hudson aside. "I need to talk to my dad. Don't worry, she won't bite." I can't help but laugh at the look on her face. Dad's sitting in front of the TV with the remote in hand, channel surfing. Typical guy.

"Hey, Dad, I need your help." He lowers the volume so he can give me his undivided attention.

"Does this have to do with Stella? I met her today; cute kid. MJ told me about Jin. I hope they catch the bastard and do to him what he did to her."

"I'm not sure if it has anything to do with Stella. Let me fill you in on what I know."

I quickly give him the lowdown on what little I know. When I tell him what happened to Mr. & Mrs. Chen, he leans in closer to me. "Do you think this girl is somehow responsible for the fire?"

"Honestly, no. I think these two girls stumbled onto something. I need her to trust me enough so she will tell me in detail what that something is."

"How can I help?"

"First, I need you to keep her safe. I don't know who else I can trust. Hart took the Chen's to a safe house, so he's not available. Other than her name, I know nothing about her."

"She can stay in MJ's old room. In the meantime, let me try talking to her."

I have nothing to lose. We head into the kitchen and find

Hudson wrapped in my mother's arms, crying. "Hey, what's going on in here?"

"Fitzgerald, why didn't you tell me everything this poor child has been through?"

"Well, Mom, I don't know everything she's been through. That's why I'm here. Hudson, you need to tell me everything or I can't help you."

My mom steps back and wipes away Hudson's tears. "You can trust my son with your life. Tell him everything . . . let him help you find a way out of this mess." She squeezes my arm as she walks out and reminds me to go easy on her.

"Hudson, this is my dad. Now, why don't you sit down and start from the beginning. Leave nothing out, no matter how insignificant you think it might be." I sit down and pull a chair for her in front of me. She sits down and takes a deep breath as she wipes away her tears.

"It all started with our Political Science class. Our professor paired Jin and I together for the final project. The project is based on the rise of human trafficking in the United States. We split the project into two parts. For the first part of the project, Jin created an algorithm that was supposed to only show how HT was on the rise. However, it also showed that in the past year, less boys then girls were abducted. On top of that, the age of the victims dropped. We noticed that numerous girls had gone missing from Brooklyn, but no boys. So, Jin started to search why no boys were taken and she tried to figure out where these girls were being sold. We thought our research would take us to the Nogales/Arizona border since it is so easy to cross. At first, we thought we would find Coyotes doing the smuggling, but that didn't pan out. Instead of shipping them to Mexico, we found that now most of the girls are being sold to the Middle East. We were shocked that the girls were ending up there. Then we tried focusing our attention on the MS-13 gang.

Especially since they've been known to be involved in HT. Add to that, their presence was becoming larger in Long Island. It seemed a logical conclusion to think they might be behind everything, but we couldn't find anything to tie them to the latest string of missing girls. Not to say that there is no gang connection, but it just wasn't there.

Jin also found that, recently, all the girls were being taken from an area that your precinct serves. That was the first red flag. It wasn't until we got to the second part of the project, which was to follow the money, that we realized why." She stops to take a drink of water but her hands are shaking so bad that she gives up. "During this time, I was doing an internship for an international bank. So, it seemed only logical that I would do the research on the money trail. I was supposed to monitor any odd wire transfers. Jin gave me some different area's to focus on. The Middle East gave me a plethora of information. I started seeing a pattern. There were three wires every time a girl went missing. The wires were all from the same account. Then I traced each wire. They went to a holding company called Crypto Holdings Inc., in New York City before they were distributed to their final destination. The first one was the largest and went to a bank in Queens. The next two wires were sent to the same bank in Brooklyn but to two separate accounts. Then, I stumbled upon a rather large wire from the same account that went to a brokerage house in DC. That account only received one wire. It was easy to see where the money was going, but privacy laws made it hard to trace the owners of the accounts that received the money. Once I had all the information I could find, I gave it to Jin. If anyone could find the owners, I knew she could.

"While I continued to try and find out more on who originated these wires, Jin put all her focus into trying to figure out who the people were who received the money. First, she looked at the wires that went to Brooklyn. She said those were easy to figure out. She found out that someone in your precinct owns one of the accounts. The other one went to the owner of a pizza parlor not far from your precinct. She couldn't find anything on the owner of the one that went to Queens, but she was not giving up on it. She did some more digging and found that the DC wire went to an agent who was assigned to protect the sitting Vice President. We talked about it and I finally convinced her that it was probably some sort of technical error. But, when the VP up and died suddenly, Jin freaked out. She had a crazy theory that he was murdered and that the agent had a hand in it. I thought she was subscribing to a wild conspiracy theory. I told her that I didn't buy into that whole tinfoil hat brigade thing, and to just to drop it and focus on the other wires. We still needed to know who the owner of the pizza parlor was and who owns the account in Queens. We needed to know why the owner was getting the wire. She assured me she would put aside her theory on the VP and just concentrate on the other wires."

She rubs her hands up and down her jeans no doubt trying to steady her nerves. "Jin was working day and night trying to figure it out. I had a bad feeling about everything and told her if all this information is true, then we are in a world of danger. I finally convinced her that we were in over our heads and we needed to do something with all the information we accumulated. This was beyond our Political Science project. She finally agreed, made copies of everything we had accumulated and put it on those three separate USB drives."

"Why did she hide it at her parent's house? Why not go to the FBI or Homeland? Not everyone is dirty."

She closes her eyes and rubs her temples. I'm quiet, giving her the time she seems to need.

Dad takes her hand and gives it a squeeze. "Take your time, Hudson."

"When I went home with Jin, she showed me the elaborate

security system her father had at a simple dry cleaners. Over dinner, I asked Mr. Chen why he had that type of system. He said he really didn't know much about it. He said a dear friend got it for him and installed it. Jin told me that friend was you. She said she was going to bring you everything. She said her father trusted you and she knew she could, too. You need to understand—at that point—we really didn't know who to trust. Never in our wildest dreams did we think we would stumble onto whatever the hell this is."

"I've been on vacation, but the captain would have told me if she came to see me."

"She was on her way to see you when she was abducted; your captain never knew."

I get up and pull three beers from the fridge, twist the tops and pass her and Dad one before taking a seat. I feel like I've been kicked in the gut. "Please, continue." My voice barely above a whisper.

"I went to the police department to find out if any progress had been made on Jin's case. I thought I would try and find you . . . see if I could really trust you. When I got there, the press was out front. I worked my way into the crowd to see if I could pick up any information. They were all talking about the senator's daughter being kidnapped and about him becoming the next VP. I freaked out. I went around back to leave and that's when I found you. But then you blew me off. That's everything I know up till now."

"I blew you off because you were claiming to be a reporter. Why?"

"I thought you wouldn't take me seriously if I told you I was a college student with a wild theory about Jin's death. Besides, it seemed the press were getting some answers that I couldn't."

She has a point but I would never admit it. "Who's the leak?"

She's picking at the label on her bottle. Dad pulls her hand away from the bottle and holds it tightly in his. "I know you're scared, but you have to trust someone. I promise you, you're safe here. If anyone can stop this madness, it's my son. Hudson, who's the leak?"

She seems to hesitate. I'm not sure if it's because she's scared or just overwhelmed. "Fitz, you need to understand—at first—all I knew was that it was a cop. I didn't know you, I only knew of you from Jin."

"You know me now. I can't help unless you trust me. Who's the leak?"

"Brandon Jensen."

I nearly choke on her words. "Are you sure Brad is the leak?" To say I'm in shock is putting it mildly.

"The money trail doesn't lie."

"Do you know who he is working with?"

"No, Jin was kidnapped before she could figure that out. She always said if you follow the money and then cut it off, these people would come out of the woodwork like roaches. She said it was only a matter of time and that the money trail would expose everyone. I tried to figure it out from the USB drive she gave me but it's encrypted. I also have her notebooks but they are in Chinese."

I get up, drain the rest of my beer, and toss it in the recycle bin. "So, what's your real name?"

"Hudson, I legally changed it a year ago."

"Why?"

"Personal reasons that have nothing to do with any of this," she says. She expects me to trust her but she won't give me an answer to a simple question. I look at Dad and he rolls his eyes.

"Where is your USB drive?" I ask. She is hesitating. "Look, if you don't give it to me, I can't help you."

"Before I give it to you, you have to promise me you will do everything in your power to find out who killed Jin. Her family knows you and they might trust you, but I know nothing about you. I need some reassurances that you won't just sweep this under the rug to protect one of your own." She gets up and puts her empty beer bottle into the recycle bin.

"Hudson, it's what I do best. In a jumbled mess, I can see what no one else can: the finish line. My job is to protect the innocent, not a crooked cop."

"Okay, I have to trust someone, it might as well be you." She reaches into her pocket, pulls out the drive, and presses it into my hand.

"I need you to stay here. I promise you'll be safe."

We head into the living room where Mom is waiting for us. "Hudson, is going to stay here for awhile. I will check in later." I kiss Mom and nod to Dad. I head out but not before stopping to pick up Hudson's empty bottle of beer.

Me: Travis, where are you?

Travis: I just finished Hart's office. It's clean.

Me: Get to my house ASAP I have a lot of stuff for you.

Travis: On my way.

Chapter Ten

I leave Wanda at my parent's house and cut through the alley towards home. Could Hudson be right about all of this or is she giving in to some sort of conspiracy theory? I'm sitting on my stoop, waiting for Travis, trying to make sense of it all. Andy comes out of his house with a dish of something. He comes across the street and sits next to me.

"Hey, why are you sitting out here?" I try to peek under the foil and he smacks my hand.

"I'm waiting for Travis. What's in the dish?"

"I didn't know if you were going to make it home for dinner, so I thought I would bring something over. Besides, I'm determined to win a game of trouble. I swear Stella must have rigged the game. Why do you have an empty bottle of beer in a Ziploc bag?"

"I need to run the prints off of it. What's for dinner?"

"Baked Ziti; Stella said it's her favorite. Why is Travis coming here?"

"We need someplace to work outside of the station."

"Fitz, what's going on? You were supposed to be on vacation for, at least, the next three months, but that was a bust. Now you're going into that zone you go into when you are all in on a case."

"I know you're worried and honestly, if I thought I could walk away from this, I would. Unfortunately, if it is what I think it is, that's no longer an option."

"Now you're scaring me."

That's the last thing I ever want to do. Stress affects his health. "I'll tell you when it's time to worry. Right now, I want to know what is going on with you and Stephen. Don't even try to deny it. Last night when he came home, he seemed like a broken man." He's looking down, avoiding eye contact, which confirms my suspicions.

"We've hit a rough patch."

"Hey, Andy, it's me. You can talk to me about anything, you know that. Every marriage will have some rocky roads. What's wrong?"

"Going through this pregnancy with MJ made me realize how much I really want a child. Stephen doesn't. That's more than a rocky road, Fitz, that's a fucking boulder in the road of life."

"Are you assuming that or did you talk about it?" He cocks his head and gives me the 'you're such an ass look'. "I'm not an idiot. Why doesn't he want children?"

"Because of my disease—plain and simple."

"What the fuck, Andy, are you guessing or did he come right out and say that?"

He looks me square in the eye, for the first time since this conversation started, what I see breaks my heart. "He said it, Fitz. After that, I walked away. Nothing he could say to me would change the hurt from his words."

"Jesus, now what are you going to do?"

"I don't know. What would you have done if MJ said she didn't want children? What if she used your job as an excuse?"

"That's a totally different situation. A job is just a job but an illness is not something you choose."

"That's my point. I didn't choose it, Parkinson's chose me. I'm making the best of my situation. Well, at least I think I am. All I know is, I'm not getting any younger. I have a lot to share and I don't want to only be known as Uncle Andy. I want to be someone's dad."

"Here comes Travis; we'll finish this conversation later. I'll be in in a bit." I lightly smack the side of his knee. He nods before getting up and taking the food inside. Travis pulls up on a Harley. I laugh; most people rent a car, only Travis would rent a Harley. He cuts the engine, comes up and sits on the step next to me.

"Wasn't that Andy? I hope he didn't leave on my account."

"He went inside to heat up dinner. Besides, I need to talk to you privately."

"Does it have something to do with that beer bottle in the bag?"

"Yeah, but that's just the tip of the iceberg."

"By the way, while I was checking Hart's office, I also checked his computer. It was clean. Do you know something I don't?"

I pass him the thumb drive. "Everything I'm about to tell you is on that drive. I haven't seen it, so, to what length, I don't know. Do you subscribe to conspiracy theories?"

"Working at the bureau, I've learned to desensitize myself to them. If I didn't, I could very quickly fall down that rabbit hole."

I take in a deep breath and tell him everything Hudson told me, including who the leak is. He never once stops me or questions me. He just takes it all in. He's like a human computer, processing every word. When I'm finally done, he reaches over and picks up the bottle.

"So this chick Hudson only has one name and she won't tell you why she changed it? I'll run her prints and see if she's in the system. I'll also swipe the rim and run her DNA through CODIS. Now, do you really believe her story about the VP being murdered? If that's the case, is McPhee in on it? Or maybe Effy was kidnapped so he would go along with whatever plan they have. This all sounds a little off the wall. Then again, I have seen some stranger things."

"You met McPhee, does he seem like a warm and caring father or grandfather?"

His silence speaks volumes.

"What about what she said about Brad? Do you really believe it? How well do you know him?"

"I've worked with him for five years. We've never partnered, but that's on me. Hudson kept saying '*follow the money*' who knows, maybe he couldn't resist the easy payday."

"Fitz, if all of this is true, then we have a bigger problem. Jin's medical report states that she had a storage chip in her intestines. Where is it now?"

"Shit, Gail gave it to Stacey at the crime lab to process it. I think Brad saw the medical report. If that's the case, then Stacey could be in danger. Let's go inside. I'll call Hart and let him know what little I can confirm. You can get started on validating what's on that drive."

We head inside and the smell is wonderful. Stella sees Travis and her face lights up. She has really taken to him. While he plays around with her, I pull MJ aside. "How are you feeling?"

"I'm tired from the shopping spree with Stella today, but I'll be fine. We had a lot of fun and it kept her distracted for a while, so it was worth it. I have a doctor's appointment tomorrow. I put a reminder on your phone."

"I need to make a call and then you can tell me all about your day over dinner."

"What are you not telling me?"

"I need to sort it all out in my head first. I have a girl stashed at Mom and Dad's house. She's in your old bedroom." Her eyes grow wide and her cheeks flush.

"Wait, I didn't mean it like that. I need her protected. She was Jin's roommate. There is a leak at the precinct, and I know I can trust Dad. I'm not randomly stashing girls in your old bedroom."

"Wow, you rolled that out without even taking a breath. Don't worry, do what you have to do. Tonight, I get my foot massage. Make your call; dinner is getting cold."

I kiss those luscious lips and then bend down and kiss my baby. "I love you both."

She heads inside, and now I have to get in touch with Hart.

"Hey, Captain, are you still at the safe house?"

"Yeah, I was waiting to hear from you. What's going on?"

"Your office and computer are clean. I might know who the leak is. Travis is working on it now. As soon as I can confirm it, I'll let you know."

"Don't pull that shit with me, Fitz. Who's the leak?"

"Brad." I wait, cause the captain gives everyone one-hundred percent trust. Break that and your life is over. 3.2.1 . . .

"Are you fucking kidding me?! Brad? Why?" I'm holding the phone away from my ear.

"Right now, I'm thinking money. Listen, no one can know that you have the Chen's at the safe house."

"Don't worry, I haven't said a word. When will you know for sure if it is really him?"

"Travis is working on it now. Gail gave the chip from Jin's intestines to Stacey in the crime lab. I'm worried. What if the same people that burnt down the dry cleaners go after the chip?"

"Security in that lab is really tight. It should be okay. How did you get all this information?"

"I have to go. As soon as I know more I will let you know."

"Fitz, don't hang up . . ."

I love that disconnect button. Besides, right now, I need to spend some time with my beautiful wife. When I get inside, I find a table filled with food, friends, family, and lots of laughter. When all is said and done, these are the memories I treasure.

Dinner was great but I could not take my mind off of my conversation with Andy. Stella is asleep and Travis is working on the thumb drive. Now it's time to pay up on a long overdue foot massage.

I'm working my thumb up and down her arch and by her moans, I think I'm doing good. I want to talk to her about Andy's situation but I can't break a confidence.

"Fitzy, What's the matter?"

"What makes you think anything is wrong?"

"You can't keep a secret and when you have to, it drives you insane. So, why not just tell me and avoid all the stress you're putting yourself through. Besides, you know eventually, I will find out."

I hate when she's right, which is most of the time. "I can't, which sucks. I really want to. I mean, you're my everything. It's just that I can't break a confidence. See? It sucks."

"Can you do my calves next, please?"

I'm massaging her calves, which are so tight, and now I feel bad I've neglected her.

"If I had to guess, I would think it has to do with Andy," she surmises. My hands stop and I'm trying not to give anything away, but MJ can read me like a book. "Fitz, I know what happened. I'm glad he finally talked to you about it. I know he was worried that you'd go off on Stephen."

"What are your thoughts on the whole thing?"

"Well, I understand why Stephen said what he did. I don't think he meant it to be mean or hurtful. Unfortunately, his words stung. You know, once it's out, there's no changing it."

"My first instinct is always to protect Andy. That's just what I do, what I've always done. I understand what happens when he is stressed out. But, shouldn't he be the judge of what he can or can't handle?"

"Yes and no. When he was first diagnosed, I wanted to do

everything for him. At one point, we came to blows and I had to back off. I realized that I was not helping him. He needed to learn his limits. Sometimes his head and his heart tells him he can do something, but his body has other ideas. It's learning to find a balance."

"I'm sorry I wasn't there for him when he was first diagnosed." I'll always feel bad about that.

"You were working that case with the feds in Virginia at the time. You needed to keep your head in the game to stay safe. We weren't purposely holding anything back from you."

I switch to her other leg and she lets out a little moan that is a direct link to my cock. "What should we do about Andy and Stephen? I think I should talk to Stephen," I suggest.

"And say what? He is entitled to his feelings. We might not agree with them but they are real." She points to an area that requires my attention.

"Maybe they need to consult Andy's doctor about it."

"Oh, Fitz, all the consulting in the world will not change what's in their hearts. The bottom line is: Andy looks to the future and Stephen only sees fear."

"Do you really think Stephen is afraid?" I begin kissing the inside of her thighs. Up one side and down the other.

"Yes, I really do. I think he figures if Andy doesn't get stressed, then they can keep his disease in check. It's not realistic, and it's denying Andy the experience of a lifetime. He has the support of his family twenty-four seven. I know how much Andy has to give a child. Denying him that makes me very sad."

"I still think I'm going to talk to Stephen. I don't want to assume anything. He can tell me to mind my business, but what kind of friend would I be if I didn't try? Now, I think I need to have my way with you, if you're up to it?" My fingers are gently stroking her *coochie,* as she likes to call it.

"My heart says yes, but my body feels like it's ready to explode. I've been getting cramping in my back all day . . . *sorry.*"

I climb up next to her and pull her into my arms. "There is nothing to be sorry about." She snuggles into me and I stroke her back. Soon, she drifts off to sleep.

Chapter Eleven

Effy

THERE IS A LOT OF noise and then the lights come on. My eyes finally adjust. Oh no . . . they are taking us out of these cages. They link each girl together, except for me. This can't be good.

"What's going on? Where are you taking me?"

I hear it before I feel it—a smack across my face. A smack so hard, it feels like my teeth will fall out. No doubt her handprint is on my cheek.

"You will do as you are told. If you give me any trouble, you won't live to regret it." Her words cut right through me. All I want is my daughter and I will do anything to see her again, to know that she is safe. I fall into line and climb out of the cellar. It's nighttime. How long have I been here? It's the end of fall; the days are getting shorter. Is that why it's dark or has sitting in the dark twenty-four seven made me lose all concept of time? We are ushered into a windowless van. One of the girls is crying again. If she doesn't pull it together, it won't be good. My hands are cuffed behind me but I scooch over towards her and let her lean on me for a bit. "Shhh, we will find a way to survive this, but if you keep crying, they will get mad."

Inga turns around and glares at me. "Shut up and back away from her, or else."

"She's only a child, a very scared one at that. Show some compassion for Christ's sake." She turns in her seat and this time she smacks me on the side of my head. The pounding headache instantly comes back.

"Do as you are told and shut up or the next fist will be to the girl's face."

I do as I'm told. I don't want to make any trouble for her. I'm trying to look out the front window to gage where I might be. We are coming up to a toll. Oh no, we are heading over the Goethals Bridge! I keep watching to see where we are going. If they take us to Newark airport, maybe I can make a scene to attract some attention. They don't take us to Newark; they stay on I95, and we end up at Teterboro Airport. My chest tightens. *I'm never going to see my baby again.* I close my eyes and silently pray for God to save Stella.

When we get to the last hanger, there is a private jet waiting. A car pulls up to the hanger, and when it finally comes to a stop, Inga gets out. The girls are all huddled together while I quietly watch what's going on outside. Stella and I have spent the last six months in a class to learn to read lips, but they are too far away for me to see. The doors to the plane open and the steps come down. A woman descends. She and Inga talk for a few minutes and then Inga waves to our driver. He gets out, opens the back door, and pulls us all out. At this point, every girl is crying. Inga comes over and leads them to the plane. Everyone, that is, except for me. Another car pulls up and man gets out. He walks toward me. He seems so familiar, but I can't place him. My world only revolves around my daughter and her needs. So, how could I possibly know any of these people? The lights from the other car are in our faces and I really can't see much. Finally, someone steps out of the car. I can tell it's a man but he doesn't look familiar to me. The man standing next to me goes to him and I step out of the light. I keep inching my way towards them. Their voices are low, but now I'm close enough and able to read their lips.

"This will be the last load for awhile. Once the heat from all this dies down, I can get you more girls."

The other man points towards me. "Did you find her daughter, yet?"

Oh my God, they are looking for Stella! That must mean she's still alive.

"My source said she is stashed at a policeman's house, that it'd be hard to get to her."

She's safe! Oh dear God, thank you.

"That's fine. Maintain surveillance on her. For now, I have the mother. If need be, I'll get the kid myself. The wire transfer has been completed. I will contact you if I need you. Take the cuffs off her and bring her here."

The familiar man comes back to me and puts one hand around my throat. "I'm going to take those cuffs off. You behave or I'll snap your fucking neck." His accent is heavy but it's the look in his eyes that scares me. He's so cold and dark, like a man with no soul. His voice is familiar and I'm wracking my brain as to where I've heard it before. He takes off my cuffs and I rub the red marks on my wrists. He grips my arm and pulls me towards the other man. It's only when he walks away that it finally hits me where I know him from—the pizza parlor!

"Why am I here?" I ask.

He takes a step closer, invading what little personal space I have. He has a heavy scent of cologne that is sickeningly sweet. "You're a pawn, nothing more. If you do what you're told, you might see your daughter again."

"What about the others?"

"Maybe you should be more worried about yourself. Get in the car." He opens the door and I climb in. I would sell my soul to the devil himself if it meant my daughter would be safe. If I do as I'm told, then maybe they will stay away from my baby. As we drive away, I look back and see the plane taxing down the runway. I close my eyes and silently say a prayer for all of them.

Fitz

MJ finally fell asleep. I check on Stella before heading downstairs. She is sound asleep, as well. I need to see what Travis has found out. He's by himself, lost in his computer stuff. "Hey, want a beer?"

"Jesus, Fitz, you almost gave me a heart attack. Yeah, I'll take one. Andy said to tell you he was tired and don't forget about MJ's doctor's appointment tomorrow."

"So, what have you figured out so far?"

"It's very sad that the world lost this girl. She was very talented. I'm following the money trail and I agree with her, Brad is the mole. I'm trying to find out why."

"I don't give a fuck if the world was coming to an end. Nothing could ever justify it. What about her claim about the VP?"

He looks up from his computer and takes a sip of his beer. "You know I don't easily buy into conspiracy theories, but I have to tell you, she might have been on to something. Maybe we need to dig further into McPhee, beyond regular vetting procedures. If something turns up, then we could address it at that time. I'm more interested in the pizza place."

"What did you find out about it?"

"It's the common denominator. According to Jin, every missing girl was seen at the place. I tried to find out who owns it, but it's buried in one holding company after another. I'll get to the bottom; it's just going to take me a little bit longer."

"Were you able to find out anything on Hudson?"

"Not yet, I need to get that bottle processed. After that, I will have more to go on. Where are you at with the kidnapping?"

I finally sit down at the table next to him. "No where and the only thing I have is what I gave you. There has been no ransom call. So why take her? That reminds me, Hart gave me a thumb drive with the case files on it. I'll get my lap top and we can compare them to what you've got." I head into my office, which is in the front of my house. The blinds are open and when I look out, I notice a car with someone sitting in it. The good thing about living in the neighborhood you grew up in is that everyone knows you and you know everyone. I head back into the kitchen where Travis is still glued to his computer.

"Hey, there's an odd car out front with someone sitting in it. I'm going to check it out. I'll be back."

"You want backup?"

"No, I rather you stay here." I grab my gun and head downstairs. When I open the door, the guy takes off. At least I'm able to get a partial plate number—2784. Apparently, I've ruffled some feathers, just wish I knew whose.

When I get back in the kitchen, MJ is sitting at the table having cookies and milk. "Hey, beautiful, you should have called me; I would have brought them upstairs to you."

"Fitz, I'm not an invalid. If you keep waiting on me hand and foot, I will be a beached whale. Now, why don't you fill me in on what's going on. Oh, and don't say nothing. It's not everyday my husband goes outside, barefoot in the dark, brandishing his gun."

I look down at my feet and realize I've been busted. "It's just work stuff; no need to worry." She's not going to buy it but it's worth a shot.

"You're almost as bad at lying as you are at keeping a secret." She dunks another cookie, pops it in her mouth, and gives me a smirk.

"I went into the office to get my laptop and I saw someone sitting in a car. I thought I would see if he was lost or something."

"Or something, with your gun drawn, *right?* Now why don't you start at the beginning." She leans back and puts her feet up, signaling she's not about to go anywhere without some answers.

"Okay, here is the express version. The girl I have stashed at Mom and Dad's gave me a USB drive with a lot of information. Travis is trying to decipher the information. I'm hoping something will lead us to Effy. There is a mole at the department, so I'm doing everything from here. Oh, and full disclosure, I'm probably going to call Lucas in the morning and ask him to come in on this. I know I can trust him."

"I thought he was retired?"

"He was driving his wife nuts, so he and Sal opened up their own private security agency. They also do some PI work when needed."

"I'm okay with having Lucas around. Now, what does this girl have and who is the mole?"

"She has a wild conspiracy theory that I'm hoping is just in her head. For the time being, we need to keep Stella close to home. And before you jump all over me, I'm not keeping you hostage. I just don't know what I'm dealing with yet. It looks like Brad is the mole."

She gets up and gives me a quick kiss and then squeezes Travis's shoulder. "Travis, I put some bedding on the couch for you. Don't stay up too late."

I watch her leave, lost in my thoughts of all things MJ. That is, until Travis nudges me out of my trance.

"Hey, that partial you gave me, it's registered to a Volkswagen that was reported stolen today."

"Are we ever going to catch a break?"

"It was reported stolen not too far from the pizza place. How about that for a break?"

"It's something. I think I'll check out that place in the morning, right after I stop at the crime lab. I want to make sure Stacey knows that everyone wants that chip. I'm going to call it a night. I've got a wife to attend to."

"Have fun."

Chapter Twelve

Andy

Another night of tossing and turning while Stephen sleeps like a baby. I wish I could figure out how to do that. At the end of the day, I'm not able to close off my mind and just sleep. The more I look at him sleeping, the more pissed off I feel myself getting. I get up and head downstairs, maybe a cup of chamomile tea will help.

After getting my tea, I head into the living room and curl up on the sofa. I've never been at a crossroads in my relationship with Stephen until now. Yeah, we argue and disagree but what couple hasn't? This, however, is huge and it really didn't hit me how huge until I met Stella. It's amazing how one little girl has made me want a future beyond my own immediate needs.

The quiet is deafening. I tell Alexa to shuffle my favorite playlist. Of all the songs to come on "Mercy" by Brett Young. My relationship is falling apart and I have to face the fact that there's no going back. You can't take back the words once you put them out there.

"Why are you sitting in the dark?" He flips on a light switch and I quickly wipe away a tear. The last thing I want is for him to add pity to the pile of everything he finds wrong with me.

"I couldn't sleep and I didn't want to disturb you."

He walks over and sits on the coffee table across from me. "I know I hurt your feelings. I didn't mean to but—" I hold up my hand, stopping him in mid-sentence.

"Stephen, there is no but, so please don't go there. You used the one thing against me that I have no control of: my disease. It's the one thing that I never expected from you. You broke my heart."

"Andy, you're the dreamer in this relationship, you always have been. I'm sorry, but I have to be realistic. You're young and we caught your Parkinson's early enough that we might be able to live a normal life together."

"Who defines what normal is? Maybe I am the dreamer, but I try to live each day to the fullest without falling into the '*why me*' pity party. Everyone has a gift, Stephen. Some people go through life and never realize what their gift is. Others know and share it with the world. I have a lot to offer a child, including how to respect and love others that are not what society deems as '*perfect*.' That's why you broke my heart. Your simple words gave control to my disease, while I fight everyday for that control. I love you. I always will, but this elephant in the room will never go away."

He leans in closer putting his hands on my shoulders. His face only inches from mine. "So, what are you saying, we're done? Is it that easy for you to walk away? After everything we've been through?"

"I would suggest counseling but you seemed pretty strong in your declaration that my disease is at the heart of this. Unfortunately, all the wishing and hoping won't make it go away."

He lets go of my shoulders and is now running his hand

through his hair. My eyes gaze down his bare chest and back up to his beautiful face, a face etched in pain. I want to take him in my arms and tell him we will get through this but this, right here, is far too big for me to compromise.

"I don't understand. I've done everything in my power to help you manage your Parkinson's. You're the one who is putting it between us. I've tried to make life easier, less stressful. And now, because I don't want to have a child, I'm the bad guy?"

"You just don't get it. You no longer treat me as an equal; I'm just someone you need to manage. Like you manage everything else in our lives. I feel like I'm walking on eggshells around you. In the end, you're making me feel like less than the man I know I am."

"Reality can be a bitter pill to swallow, Andy. You want to take upon the responsibility of a child. But, what happens when you are no longer able to care for that child? Or what if you—God forbid—die? Have you thought about that? It's not like a puppy that I can bring back to the pound. It's a lifetime commitment and it's not one I'm prepared to make."

"At any given time, any one of us can die, Stephen. Don't you think my sister thinks about that every time Fitz steps out the door? That hasn't stopped her from having a child."

"She's prepared to go it alone. I'm not." He gets up and walks away. Discussion is over and now I know, without a doubt, exactly where I stand. I turn the music up and Miranda Lambert is singing "Tin Man." The irony is not lost on me.

MJ

Fitz's was tossing and turning all night long. I know he is totally immersing himself in this case, I just wish it wasn't now. Right here, right now, I need him to immerse himself in this baby and me. Selfish, yeah, but I'm not perfect, no one is. The day we got married, I promised him I would start putting myself first. I was doing good, but then Stella showed up. In such a short time, I'm slipping back into my usual mode of taking on everyone's problems. Trying to bare their burdens for them.

I cuddle into him and place my hand over his heart. Even while he sleeps he wraps his arms tightly around me. If only we could shut off the world. "If only we could stay like this forever," I whisper as I lean up and gently brush my lips over his.

"MJ, what's wrong?" His voice is raspy and his grip gets a little tighter.

"I'm just feeling a little overwhelmed right now."

"With the baby? Are you feeling okay? Should I call the doctor?"

God love him. He instantly goes from sleep to panic dad mode. "The baby is fine, it's me. I'm having a pity party. I wanted this part of my pregnancy to just be us. Instead, you're knee deep in a case. You're stashing someone at Mom and Dad's house. Travis is camped out in the living room and now we are getting a guard. On top of all of that, Andy's marriage is crumbling. Don't get me wrong, I'm not mad that you're helping Stella. I just wish we could have a little bit of quiet time for us before the baby gets here. Like I said—pity party. It will pass." He's not saying anything. He keeps stroking my arm and his eyes are closed. Have I hit a nerve? "What is it, Fitz?"

"Before Andy spoke to me, I asked Stephen what options we had if Effy was dead. He was going to look into it. Now I'm wondering if

I should have asked someone else."

"Wouldn't her grandfather have custody?"

"It would depend on if Effy had a will and if she named someone to become Stella's guardian."

He shifts so now we are side by side. Our faces inches apart. I kiss him softly, breathing in his scent.

"Do you know who her father is?"

"There is a name on her birth certificate, but there was also an article about his death. I was hoping Stephen would come up with some sort of information on any other family members. MJ, I can't let her end up with her grandfather. I also can't let her fall between the cracks."

"Stop—you don't have to sell me. We've all become attached to her. I will help you fight to keep her safe."

"God, I love you. I know we were going to have this time for just us but, realistically, life will always get in the way. Neither one of us is very good at setting boundaries. You're a nurturer and I'm a fixer, and now things have become even more complicated."

"How so?" He's running his fingers up and down my belly. Every time the baby kicks, he smiles.

"It looks like there might be some validity to what Travis found on that USB drive. Jin stashed a copy of everything that her and Hudson were working on at her parent's dry cleaners. Hudson being the girl I've got stashed at Mom and Dad's house. Plus, both girls had a copy of the drive. On top of everything else, yesterday, the Chen's business and home was torched. Hart has them in a safe house."

"Oh my God, did Mr. And Mrs. Chen lose everything?"

"I'm not sure. I am going to stop by the fire marshal's office today and see what he can tell me."

"My heart is breaking for them. Thinking about all they have lost just put my pity party to shame. I mean, think about it—their only child, all their pictures and anything that had any memories attached to it—*gone*. How do you go on after all of that?" I feel a shiver run up my spine and he wraps me tightly in his arms.

"All we can do is offer them support . . ." His voice trails off and he has a far away look on his face.

"What are you not telling me?" He closes his eyes and takes a deep breath.

"I found out yesterday that Jin was on her way to see me when she was abducted. She needed help and when she finally decided to reach out, it was too late. I just wish she would have contacted me sooner. Maybe I could have protected her. Now I'll never know."

"As much as you want to, you can't be everyone's hero."

He runs his thumb over my lips before he kisses them. "I'll always be your hero, MJ." He presses his lips to mine, again. This time, he deepens his kiss. The need we have for each other is so powerful. My trembling fingers run softly down his cheek. "Make love to me, Fitz."

"Are you okay? I don't want to hurt you."

"You won't hurt me. With all the craziness going on around us, my need for you is what grounds me." With a huge smile on his face, he begins kissing me everywhere. The feel of his lips sends tingles all over my body. He's gentle, yet powerful. Knowing that my nipples are so tender right now, he brushes his lips over them before moving on. He nips my tiny superman tat, which is not so tiny right now. It looks like it's been stretched out with silly putty. He's my hero, now and forever. He wraps his arms around my legs, pulling me closer to him. His touch drives me crazy, but when he swipes his tongue up and down my coochie and then nips me, I loose all reason. "Fitzy, *pleeeease.*"

He gets up on his knees and rubs his cock up and down my coochie before he slowly enters me. I dig my heels into his rock hard ass trying to push him in deeper. "You're not going to break me. I need more."

"MJ, it doesn't have to always be fast and furious. Sometimes it's more fun driving in the slow lane." He's on his knees and slowly pulls back, lifting my feet, kissing them, and then placing them on his chest. At the same time, I see the door open and Stella walks in. Everything seems to be moving in slow motion. I push Fitz so hard that he flips off the end of the bed.

"MJ, what the fuck?"

I grab the blanket and toss it over Fitz. His mighty cock is still standing at attention. I grab my robe and throw it on, hopefully not traumatizing the poor child. He peeks out from under the blanket, his face as red as a beet.

"I can't believe I just got cock-blocked by a six-year-old."

I mumble under my breath "Better get used to it."

"Good morning, Stella, I thought you were asleep?"

"I miss my mommy." A speaking person would be able to express their fears through their words. For Stella, sometimes the only way she can speak is through her tears. She's fighting to hold them back but quickly loosing the battle.

"I know you do. I promise you, we are all trying to find her. Why don't we go downstairs and I'll make you some breakfast. Travis is asleep on the couch, you can wake him up. Maybe we can even get Andy to come and play a game with us."

"I thought you and Fitz were playing hide and go seek?"

I bite my tongue to hold back my laughter. "Not anymore, sweetie." I take her hand and head towards the door, leaving Fitz to sort himself out.

Chapter Thirteen

Hudson

I keep fighting the urge to run. This house is so quiet, but every time I get up and walk around, the floorboards creak. I give up and head into the kitchen for some coffee. When I step in, I find Mr. Justice reading the paper and having a cup of coffee. "Good morning, Mr. Justice. Are you always up this early or are you making sure I don't run away?"

"Mr. Justice was my dad; you can call me Pat. Now, as far as you running, my dear, I've been in this chair since I got shot. If you decide to run, I won't be the one chasing after you. Besides, I'm giving you the benefit of the doubt. You're an intelligent, young lady and I think you realize your options are limited. Right now, this is the safest place for you to be. The coffee is hot and I've finished picking my ponies for today's races, so if you want the paper, have at it."

I pour a cup and sit across from him. "Can I ask you a question?"

"You're half way there, go ahead."

"Why do you have a different last name then Fitz?"

“We adopted him when he was six. Now it’s my turn. Does your professor know any of the story you told us last night?”

“No, I told you everyone who knew anything.”

He takes another sip of his coffee and begins doodling on the newspaper. “Do you honestly believe this has anything to do with the VP’s death? I mean, you have to realize how crazy this all sounds.”

“Jin believed it. At this point, I don’t know what the hell to believe.”

“Last night you said your name change had nothing to do with this case. I’m curious, why did you pick only one name?”

“Like I said, it was personal. Sometimes less can be more.”

“And sometimes someone tries really hard to feed you a crock of shit, thinking you’re some kind of old fool.” His deep blue eyes are glaring at me, watching my every move.

“Pat, really, it was a family matter and I felt it was the best way to separate myself from the situation. Can we just leave it at that?”

“For now. What do you know about the pizza joint?”

Thank God, a change of subject. “Other than what I told you, nothing. I went by the place after Jin was abducted but it’s just your garden-variety pizza place. There were a couple of old style pin ball machines and some video games. There were a lot of kids hanging out. Just a regular pizza parlor.”

“How was the pizza?”

“What? It sucked. Why would that matter?” Now he has me really baffled.

“Hudson, when I was a kid, my mom used to take me for dinner every Friday night to a place called The Hole in The Wall. It was a run down little place that literately had a hole in the wall. There were maybe six tables in the whole place, yet, it was standing room only. They put their heart and soul into the food. When the kids took over the business, they decided to move to a bigger place.

After that, the food was never the same and eventually, they ran the business into the ground."

" Somehow, I think there is supposed to be some sort of lesson in that story."

"The pizza sucked, so maybe it was never meant to be a pizza parlor. It was probably always meant to be a front for something else. No heart and soul."

"What if the owner thought his pizza was the best in the neighborhood? Maybe he did put his heart and soul into it. Maybe he just has lousy taste in pizza."

Thought I had him but he's laughing. I'm really confused.

"Listen, kid, this is Brooklyn. The people here believe they invented pizza. There is a lot of competition, so it better be good or you'll be out of business in a heartbeat."

"You think we need to look further into the pizza place, then? Jin was working on that, I'm just not sure how far she got. Between school, my internship, and my other classes, I was on overload."

"Well, now you have my son to help you."

"What makes you think he wants to?"

His expression becomes hard to read. A cross between anger and pride. "I take it you don't know him very well."

"No, I only met him yesterday."

"My son has always been the one to right all the wrongs in the world. He's like a dog with a bone. He will solve it. It might not be the conclusion that everyone wants, but he always gets to the truth."

"I hope you're right. I'm going to try and get some rest." I leave him to his thoughts while I head back to my room.

Fitz

Cock-blocked by a six-year-old. I'm already on limited privileges. A sign of times to come. I head into a cold shower, intent on cooling my cock. I keep running everything over in my head. I hope Dad has gotten more information out of Hudson. The name change is bugging me, but I'm not sure why. I had a very restless sleep. Everything was going through my mind like a movie, a really bad movie. I need to prepare my argument on why MJ is going to have very tight security. She's fiercely protective of her freedom, but I hope she will realize there are no other options. "*MJ, I know you are capable of taking care of yourself. I just think with someone watching our house last night, we need more security and not just Lucas.*" I hear a giggle. I stick my head out from behind the shower curtain and find MJ leaning against the sink.

"Were you rehearsing your sales pitch?"

I step out of the shower and wrap a towel around my waist. "I wanted to make sure I didn't upset you while you're in this delicate condition." I trail my fingers over her belly, knowing how my touch affects her.

"You're partially responsible for my '*delicate condition.*' She gently nips my shoulder, sending a jolt to my cock.

"I haven't connected all the dots yet. I need to know you're safe," I remind her. She steps aside and watches me as I begin to shave. Her eyes dancing with delight. "You can't look at me like that, MJ."

"Like what?"

"Like you want me to devour you. After this morning, I thought my cock was on lockdown."

She steps closer and kisses my nipple, then she flicks it with her tongue right before she gives it a gentle tug. I hang on to the sink while she kisses her way down my side. When she gets to my tat, which, thanks to Mark Chambers, is now a Superman emblem with a lightening bolt running through it, she kisses it and whispers, "My hero." My towel falls to the ground. Before I know it, she's rolling her tongue around my cock. I try to concentrate on shaving but give up before I slice my throat. She's taking me deep, so fucking deep. "Babe, if you throat bump me one more time, it's game over." The throbbing of my cock is trying to keep up with the pounding of my heart. I pull back and lift her into my arms. I kiss her getting shaving cream all over her face, before I spin her around and enter her from behind. "Tell me if I'm too rough."

She's got a death grip on both sides of the sink. With every thrust she pushes her ass back towards me. "Harder, Fitz, please. You won't hurt me."

If I give her what she wants, this will end all too quickly. I slow down, lean over and nip her shoulder while I reach around and gently play with her nipples.

"Ohhhh, Fitz, please. Please, please—*please*."

"Please what, MJ? I want you to tell me what you want, what you need." I lean back, going low and slow, then I pick up the pace and push a little harder. When her breath quickens, I slow it down, again. Peaks and valleys, like a crazy wooden rollercoaster ride. How ironic that Sam Hunt is on the radio singing about doing 15 in a 30. My pace goes along with the beat of the music. That is until MJ digs her nails into my thighs, snapping me back to reality. With every thrust, I dip down a little bit lower, hitting her in all the right places. Now the throbbing of my cock has matched the pounding of my heart. Oh yeah, I close my eyes and let the freight train inside of me race ahead. I'm close, so very close. I want this to last, but then she reaches around and smacks my ass.

"Stop teasing me. Harder, Fitz, now!"

That does it; I can't hold back any longer. My throbbing cock races past my beating heart and I explode. I can literally hear a swish in my head. I close my eyes, lean back; it feels endless. My beautiful MJ quickly follows, crying out my name.

We both look up at the same time, catching a glimpse of ourselves in the mirror. Shaving cream is smeared on both our faces, and I can't help but laugh. I grab the washcloth and quickly clean us both up. "Guess I'm not really on lockdown."

She gifts me with a big, beautiful smile as her face flushes. "No, you're not. I know we can't lock the door, so we need to be careful with Stella around. We don't need to traumatize her any more than she already is."

After all these years, the sound of the door locking can still send me into a tailspin. I thank God everyday that she's so compassionate and understanding. I quickly lather up and pick up where I left off. "So, back to where we were before you had your way with me. Other than the doctor, do you have any reason to leave the house today?"

"What you're really saying is 'MJ, don't leave the house today.' Did you already make the call for more security?"

"Not yet. It's next on my list of things to get done this morning."

"Okay, I'll wait for you to come home to get me. We can go to the doctor's from here. In the meantime, I need to jump in the shower before you leave."

"Want me to wash your back?" I ask. She rolls her eyes and smacks me on the ass.

"Goodbye, Fitz."

Heading downstairs, I can hear Andy and Travis arguing in the kitchen. "What's going on in here?"

"Travis and I are arguing the merits of bacon."

"Andy, you liken it to a religious experience."

"I gotta go with Andy on this one, especially if it's extra crispy."

Travis raises his hands in surrender. "I give up. I'm taking that bottle you gave me yesterday, and I'm going to head to the lab. I'm also going to check in with Stacey. I want her to understand the depth of danger that surrounds anything to do with the chip that was found in Jin's autopsy. Where do you want to meet up?"

"Let's meet back here. I'm going to call Lucas in and anyone else he might have available," I relay.

"I spoke to Olivia last night and brought her up to speed. She left early this morning to come up and hang out here with MJ. She's been wanting to see her, so it was a good excuse."

MJ walks in and snags a piece of Andy's bacon. "No excuses needed; I can't wait to see her."

Travis leans over and gives her a kiss on the cheek. "Olivia, should be here soon, but for now, please feed that baby something healthy while I'm gone."

I grab a cup of coffee while MJ, Stella, and Andy are busy in the kitchen. I head into my office to call Lucas. He picks up on the first ring. "I need security at my house."

"What have you gotten yourself into now?"

I give him a quick lowdown on everything including the guy that was parked outside last night. I know I can trust him with the information the same way I can trust him with my family. Hell, he took a bullet for Andy. I know he's loyal.

"Shit, Fitz, Brad? Really? That's fucked up. Where is the USB drive now?"

"Travis has it. He made me a copy to stash for safekeeping. Hopefully, I won't need it."

"Well, you'll have Olivia inside with MJ. I'm going to put Kyle outside your place and Sal outside your parent's house."

"I thought Sal was strictly doing research?"

"He has been, but lately he's been getting restless so this will be good for him. If you think you need more, just let me know."

"Thanks, I'm going to my parent's place now. Maybe Dad got something more out of Hudson."

"You said Travis is doing a search on her, but let me dig around on my end. You never know."

"Okay, I'll wait here until Kyle gets into place."

I check in with Hart and all is quiet. I'm about to check my email when I see Olivia walking up the front steps. I quickly buzz her in.

"Hey, you, thanks for coming on such short notice."

"No thanks needed. Travis filled me in on everything."

We head into the kitchen and find everyone in a very heated game of Skip-Bo. "Hey, guys, look who's here."

Stella is looking at Olivia and then back to MJ. I forgot how much they look alike.

"Stella, this is . . ." Before I can finish, Olivia stops me.

"I can sign and read lips. In case you forgot, I also speak Russian, Farsi, Albanian, and Mandarin. I got this covered." She steps in front of me, squats down, so she's level with Stella, and begins signing. "Hi, Stella, I'm Olivia."

"You look like, MJ."

"I know. Everyone thinks we are sisters, but we are really friends. I'm going to hang out here today. Can I play cards with you?"

"Sure, but Andy cheats."

We all burst out laughing. I take MJ in my arms and give her a quick kiss. "I've got to run. Lucas's man should be out front. His name is Kyle. I'll be back in time to take you to the doctor."

I head out front and see Kyle is already settled in. I give him an update on everything before I cut through the alley to my parent's house. Sal is standing out front with my mom having coffee. I swear she will never learn.

"Mom, I need to talk to Sal. Is everything okay inside?"

"Everything is fine. Don't yell at him. We were just discussing my plans for today. I'll see you upstairs. Did you have breakfast?"

"Yes, Mom." I watch her leave all the time mumbling under her breath.

"Before you say anything, Lucas warned me about her. We were just setting the ground rules. She said she's going to the doctor with you and MJ today. What do you want me to do?"

"Stay here with my dad. I'll swing by and pick Mom up. Thanks, Sal, I know she can be a handful."

"No worries, my mom is Sicilian. Just picture your mom . . . on steroids. I got this covered."

I laugh and head upstairs. God, only knows what my mom is up to.

Chapter Fourteen

Mom is busy in the kitchen and Dad is glued to the TV. No sign of Hudson. "Hey, Dad, where's Hudson?"

"She's in her room. We had a nice talk this morning. I think your answers may be in the pizza parlor."

He's usually spot on when it comes to figuring things out. "Why?"

"They make shit pizza."

"That's it, shit pizza?"

He mutes the TV and looks me squarely in the eye. "It's got to be a front, son. Can't stay in business in this town selling shit pizza unless you've got something else going on."

Hudson walks into the room before I can finish asking him anything else. She looks exhausted, like she never slept.

"Fitz, I need to go home and get some stuff."

"Make a list of what you need and I can pick it up for you."

She walks up to me and with a hand on her hip and a finger pointed at my chest. This seems to be the norm for her when it comes to me. "You can't keep me a prisoner. I did nothing wrong. I'm the victim here."

"I'm trying to keep you alive, unless you want to join Jin on a slab at the morgue?!" Her face turns pale and she bites her bottom lip. Maybe to stop the tears or maybe to control her anger, probably a little bit of both. "I have a sketch I would like you to look at." I pull it up on my phone and pass it to her.

She stares quietly at it. Finally, she looks up at me and passes me my phone. "I've seen him, I just can't place where. Maybe it was at the pizza place."

"You never mentioned you went to the pizza place. Why?"

"With everything going on, I forgot. I went right after Jin went missing. I thought maybe I would see or hear something in there that would give me a clue about Jin. I know I was grasping at straws but I was desperate to find out where she was. Do you think the guy in the sketch has something to do with Jin's murder?"

"I don't know about that. What I do know is, he kidnapped Effy McPhee," I inform her. She sinks into the sofa and pinches the bridge of her nose. "Talk to me; what's going through your head right now?"

"I feel like I'm living in a giant jigsaw puzzle. The pieces are all scattered and I somehow hold the key to saving someone's life. Why me? Why is this happening? It was a simple school project. Most of it was supposed to be done on the computer. It was all hypothetical. Never in my wildest dreams did I think this was going to turn into the biggest cluster fuck on the face of the earth." She gasps and puts her hand over her mouth. "Sorry, Pat."

My dad wheels his chair closer to her and takes her hand. "It's okay. Take a moment to think, and then tell Fitz what you told me this morning about the pizza place."

I knew leaving her with my dad was a good idea. He is easy to talk to and never judges.

"The pizza sucked. I remember seeing a lot of kids just hanging out in there. Some were playing on an old-fashioned pinball machine." She takes a seat next to Dad.

"Close your eyes and picture yourself there. Talk me through everything, starting when you walked in the door," I say in a calming voice.

She closes her eyes and takes a deep breath and slowly exhales. "I walked in the door and there was a man behind the counter. He was as tall as he was wide. I waited for him to finish pulling a pie out of the oven. I ordered a slice and a soda. He rung me up and handed me my cup, then pointed towards the soda machine. While I was waiting for him to cut the pie, I filled up my cup. At the same time, a man walked in. They seemed to know each other. They had a quick conversation before the man walked past me to go in the back."

"What did the men talk about?"

"The man that walked in said 'Is he here?' The guy behind the counter said 'Yeah, he's in the back.' Then he said, 'Tom, you want a slice?' As he walked past me, he said 'Later.' He walked into the back, past the restrooms. I got my slice and sat down. I watched the kids for a bit. The man never came out of the back. When I got up to leave, I pulled out a picture of Jin and asked the man behind the counter if he ever saw her. He was quick to say no and cut off all conversation. After that, I left. How does any of that help you?"

"Did you see Tom's face?"

Her eyes grow wide. "When he opened the door, the bell chimed. I turn my head for a quick glance. Then, I went back to filling up my cup. When he told the man 'later' and walked past me, I didn't look up. After that, I saw his back as he walked away. Do you think it is the guy in the sketch?"

"You tell me, close your eyes and as he walks in, freeze the thought. Put yourself back in that moment and tell me anything and everything."

"I smell pizza and a strong smell of old cigar stink. He had on a black leather jacket. Oh my God, it's the guy in the sketch. Maybe Jin was right. Maybe the pizza place is where these kids are being taken from."

"Okay, slow down. How close is the sketch to the guy's face?"

"It was for a quick second, but he had some facial hair. He had an odd haircut. One side shaved and the other long. Ugh, why is this so hard?" She throws her hands up in the air, gets up, and begins pacing around the room.

"I've found that if you try to force it, it will never come. At least we know that the key is the pizza parlor. I would like Jin's notebooks. I have someone who might be able to read them. Maybe there is something in them that could help us."

She comes to a stop once again she's pointing her finger at me. "You expect me to just give you everything and then sit here like some damsel in distress while you run off on a one-man crusade? Guess again, Fitz. Hell will freeze over first before I let that happen. Jin was my best friend. Someone killed her and, for all I know, they are after me. And if that's the case, I'm not staying here. I will not put your parents in any more danger. Now, this is how this is going to play out. You and I will work together. Are you just going to stand there with that smirk on your face?"

My dad starts wheeling himself out of the living room. "Dad, where are you going?"

"Son, you know that movie with that little mini-me guy in it? Well, it looks like you've got yourself a mini-MJ. Good luck."

I could swear he was laughing at me. "Look, your place was tossed and we know they didn't get what they wanted, which means, they are looking for you. If I take you with me, then it's one more distraction for me to deal with. I promise, I will keep you up to date on anything I find out. I told you my dad can protect you, plus, I put a guard outside. You're going to have to trust me. I promised you I would solve Jin's murder, but right now, finding Effy, and keeping you and Stella safe, trumps the dead."

She's standing there, pulling her bottom lip between her teeth and, if she keeps this up, she will chew it raw. “Okay, but you have to promise to keep me informed on anything you find out. What about school?”

“What about it?”

“I have classes to attend. In a very short time, I’m graduating. I’m on track for Summa Cum Laude. I can’t let all that fall by the wayside. I also have a meeting with my computer science professor; no doubt he wants to know what I plan on doing now that Jin is dead. What should I tell him?”

“Let me see your schedule.” She passes me her phone. “Okay, you have two classes today. You can go but you have to take Sal with you. I’ll clear it with the college. As far as the professor, tell him nothing. You will complete the project by the due date. See? I’m willing to compromise.” While I have her phone, I text myself so I have her number.

“I’m going to school with a body guard named Sal and you call that compromise?!”

“Look, Hudson, take it or leave it. Now, get your stuff and I’ll introduce you to him.”

She opens her mouth, no doubt to yell at me, but thinks better of it. While she heads into her room, I let Dad know what’s going on. When she comes back, she slams three composition notebooks into my chest and heads down the steps with me racing behind her. She opens the door and runs smack dab into Sal.

“Hudson, say hello to Sal.” I swear I could see flames shooting out the top of her head. “Sal, she has two classes today at John Jay. I’ll clear it with the college; stay close to her. When she’s done, bring her right back here. I’ve got to run. Don’t worry, my mom’s not going anywhere and my dad is here with her.” I look back as I cut through the alley towards home and I can’t help but laugh. Poor Sal; Hudson has her finger pointed at his chest and looks to be giving him a piece of her mind. I keep a tight grip on the notebooks.

Hopefully Olivia can figure out what's in these books.

When I get through the alley, Kyle is in the same place I left him. I race up the steps and slam right into Andy. I really need to get him alone for awhile but now is not the time.

"Hey, you're early; our appointment isn't for another four hours."

"I needed to drop these books off. Olivia?"

"She's upstairs with Stella and MJ. They are playing beauty parlor. They should be down any time now. Do you have any leads on Effy?"

"I might. Listen, before anyone comes down here, I want you to promise me you won't make any rash decisions or do anything stupid when it comes to Stephen. I promise you we will figure it all out."

He's rocking back and forth along with a look of dread on his face that tells me something else has happened. Andy's always been the one to act first and think later. He leads with his heart and, in some cases, that's great, but not with something like this. Before I can say anything, Stella runs into the kitchen followed by MJ and Olivia. MJ looks at me and back to Andy but says nothing.

"Olivia, these notebooks belonged to Jin. They are written in Chinese. I'm not sure whether it's Mandarin or not but I'm hoping you can make some sense out of it."

She flips open one of the books. "Good news; it's Mandarin. I'll get started on these right away. I'll let you know what I come up with." She takes the books and heads into the living room.

"I'll be back later. Thanks, Olivia!" I call out as I race out the door.

Chapter Fifteen

I HAVE LEADS—LOTS OF THEM, actually—but I have very few people I can trust with this information. It's like I'm looking at the pieces of a giant jigsaw puzzle. Most people start at the corners and work their way in, not me. I start with what sucks me in and work my way out from there.

This time of day the Belt Parkway is not so bad. MJ made me a special playlist for when I'm driving Wanda. She knows getting lost in the music while I'm riding along the coastline helps me clear all the clutter. She made sure to start it off with Creed's "With Eyes Wide Open." I begin and end my days thinking about MJ and the baby. It's a very diverse list from Creed to Journey and everything else in-between.

The lab is in Queens. I get there in just under forty minutes. Hopefully, Travis has come up with something. I try to pull up front, but the entire building is on lockdown. It's like mass chaos out here. I can't get anywhere near the place.

Me: I'm outside the lab. The place is on lockdown, WTF?

Travis: I thought we were meeting back at your house? Did something happen?

Me: Never mind that, why is this place on lockdown?

Travis: A bomb threat was called in. They have us out back with the dogs sniffing us while the bomb squad is inside. After that fire last month, I guess they are taking it very seriously.

Me: What about the chip?

Travis: It's locked up. Stacey already processed it. She was not able to get into anything. It is password protected and it's got an encryption code lock. Sweet lady but it's above her pay grade."

Me: So, what did you find on it?

Travis: Most of the data was corrupted from sitting in her digestive track for an extended period of time. What little I could get off it was the same as was on the drive that Hudson gave you. Do you think the bomb scare is a ruse to get to the chip?

Me: Right now, nothing would surprise me.

Travis: The bomb squad just gave the all clear. I'll meet you out front.

While I'm not-so-patiently waiting for him, I keep reminding myself not to get sucked up in Jin's wild theory but, as time goes on, I'm finding it more and more difficult not to. Travis pulls his Harley up next to mine. "Did you find anything useful from the bottle?" I ask.

"She's bonded, so her prints are on file. I have no clue why she changed her name. All I know is it was not that long ago. Did you find out anything else from her?"

"Yeah, I'll fill you in later. Right now, I want to go to the pizza parlor."

"Fitz, I don't think you should go alone."

"Awe, Travis, are you worried about me?" He rolls his eyes and I can't help but laugh.

"Actually, I don't think you should go at all. I should go since no one knows me. Let's face it, I definitely don't look like a cop."

He has a point. I give him a quick rundown on what Hudson told me and about Jin's books. "Okay, be careful. I'll meet you at the diner in an hour." He takes off and now that the bomb squad gave the all clear, they are letting people back inside. I need to talk to Stacey. I find her in her usual spot: in her lab—lost in her work. "Hey, sunshine, what are you working on? Something for me I hope."

"Hey, Fitz, what are you doing here?"

"You know me; when I have stuff pending, I can't wait."

She looks at me like a deer in the headlights of a tractor-trailer. "I don't have anything of yours pending."

"What about the blood from Effy's kidnapping and the drug that was in the syringe?"

"Oh, I thought that was Brad's case? At least that's what he told me. Anyway, I gave a full copy of the report from the scene to him. Do you need a copy of it too?"

I wish I could tell her not to give that bastard anything but I need to play my cards close to my chest right now. The last thing I want to do is tip him off. "Yes, please." A few clicks on her computer and it's already in my email.

"Did you get any hits on the blood?"

"I did. The blood belongs to Thomas Petrov. He was in Rikers for ten years for breaking and entering. It's very odd; he did his full stretch on a B&E charge. Usually, they can get time off on those charges, especially since it was his first offense, but who knows what kind of prisoner he was. Anyway, do you want this sent to your email too or should I print it for you?"

"Both, please." She passes me his rap sheet. I pull up my sketch on my phone and compare the two. It's actually pretty close. "Damn."

"Fitz, you okay?"

"Yeah, I've gotta run. Thanks for everything." I'm running out the door before she could even say goodbye. I've got to get this dirt bag's picture to the feds.

The lab is not that far from the station and when I get there, I see the mob of reporters out front like a pack of vultures. I park around back and head inside. Brad is at his desk and it takes all of my will not to call him out right now. That's not going to help Effy.

"Hey, where are the feds?" I glance at the file in front of him and he quickly closes it. It's the missing girls. No doubt he's looking to see what he can cover up.

"They set up camp upstairs."

"Do you know if they got a ransom call yet?" I know they haven't and probably never will. I want him to think that he's keeping us all in the dark.

"No, do you think she's still alive?"

"No clue." I race upstairs, cutting off all conversation while resisting the urge to kick him in the ass. When I step in the office, I see a giant whiteboard with pictures of all six girls. They are trying to map out a time line. They are following the standard rules for investigation, and then there's me.

When they realize I'm in the room, they stop speaking and all heads turn toward me. Finally, Simmons, one of the feds, gets up and walks towards me. "Fitz, we're busy in here; is there something you need?"

I pass him the printout of Thomas Petrov. "That's the guy that kidnapped Effy." He quickly looks at the picture and then passes it to the others.

"How the hell did you find this out?"

"I'm sure that whatever you're doing in here makes sense to you, but for me it's like a spinning top that never gets anywhere. Good old-fashioned police work. There was blood at Effy's house. The lab processed it and got a hit."

"What else did you find out?" Now here's the hardest part for me. I have to lie and that's not something I'm good at.

"Nothing yet. Look. I gather you never got a ransom call."

He looks to the group, they all nod in unison and then turns his attention back to me. "No, nothing. The more we look at these cases, the more we are inclined to think they are related, we just don't know how. What are your thoughts?"

So now what I think is meaningful. "Your group took the files so I don't have access to any of the other girls' information. My main priority right now is getting Effy back. I'm going to stay focused on that. If I come up with anything more, I'll let you know right away." I'm standing there waiting, more like expecting one of them to ask about Stella. . . *nothing.* I head out to meet Travis and leave them spinning their wheels.

Chapter Sixteen

Effy

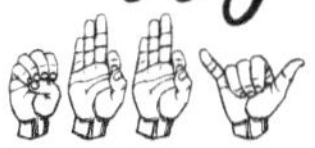

Time seems to stand still. Except for those girls; for them, hell has just begun. When I watched that plane taxing down the runway, I knew I would never see them again. I'm the mother of a young girl. I understand the hell their parents are going through right now. I'm praying for Stella. They said she is stashed with a policeman. I'm surprised my dad hasn't taken her. Then again, he only used her to get a bill passed and for a photo op. She's just a thing to him, a means to an end . . . someone to further his career, nothing more.

He was the same way with me growing up. When I was twelve, my mom was diagnosed with breast cancer. He told her he was investing in his career because investing in her was a waste of time. My mom died with only me by her side. After that, there was no happy life for me; I was passed around from one caretaker to the next. When I turned eighteen, he told me it was time to figure out life on my own. He literally opened the door while I stood there in shock. I think that's when it finally hit me: he was only in it for himself. Even when my mom was alive.

Every night I pray that Jay is watching over us. That he's proud of the mom I've become. My mind wanders to that day. The day I have blocked out for the past six years. The day the best part of me died. We were supposed to meet outside the Justice of the Peace after work but I was running late. I didn't think Jay would mind since he was always late. He picked our wedding day to show up on time. When I finally got to the courthouse, the police where already there. There was a shooting. Just hearing the word *shooting* makes me break out in a cold sweat. A man pulled a gun, determined to stop his ex-wife from remarrying, but Jay stepped in the way. He died instantly, and I was left on the steps of the courthouse, heartbroken and pregnant. I blame myself. He asked me so many times to marry him and I kept saying no. I didn't want to feel like he was marrying me because I was pregnant. I was near the end of my pregnancy and scared. He finally wore me down and I said yes. The night before the wedding, he went to speak to my father. When he came home, he was rattled. I asked him what was wrong. All he ever said was "Our family starts with us. We don't need or want for anyone else, just us." He was in the wrong place at the wrong time. My life was never the same again. If only wishes could really come true. I'd wish for him to know his daughter and for Stella to be safe.

I always wanted her to have a large family. I never wanted her to be an only child. Unfortunately, Stella has no one except me. My father smiles for the cameras and tells the voters what they want to hear. In reality, he's just as bad as the rest of the politicians. Maybe worse; he's a puppet on a string with no heart. I've spent the past six years trying to keep him away from Stella and me. I can't let my daughter fall into his hands now. I've got to get out of here.

I walk around the room, taking stock of my surroundings. I'm being held in a small bedroom equipped with an en-suite. The windows are boarded up. There is a small hole in the wood and, when I look through, I can see bars. The bathroom is well supplied. There is a stack of clothes on a chair in the corner of the room. Ironically, they are my size. This is a lot different than the cage and shackle from before. There is a light knock on the door and then I hear the lock turn. When it opens, a small woman, possibly of Middle Eastern decent, steps inside. "You need to shower and get dressed for dinner. I will be back in one hour." She backs out of the room and locks the door behind her.

I have two choices here. Do nothing and see if they push back, or go along with their demands and find out what they want. I choose the latter. Unlike the other girls, I'm still in the U.S. I still have a faint glimmer of hope. I shower, being careful of the huge lump on my head. The clothes are simple: jeans, t-shirt, and converse. If they are looking to sell me, they better come up with something better for me to wear. The light tap on the door snaps me back to reality. The same lady from earlier steps into the room. "Follow me."

"Where are you taking me?" She doesn't answer. She turns and walks out of the room. I'm quietly following her down a long hallway. The clicking of her heels on the wood floor is the only sound I hear. I count the number of doors as we pass them. I'm not sure it will help me, but I have to do something.

We finally enter a dining room with a long table set for two. Seated at the head of the table is the same man that took me from the airport.. He gets up and pulls out my chair. What the fuck is this all about?

"Thank you, Diana, that will be all."

She scurries out of the room leaving us alone.

"I'm sure at this point you have many questions. Eat and then we will talk." He reaches over and lifts the silver dome off my dish. It's a simple dinner of roasted chicken, rice, and vegetables. I'm not sure what I'm supposed to feel. Should I be happy that I'm no longer in a cage with a shackle around my ankle? Or should I be impressed with his false kindness. Either way, I want to get out of here and find my daughter.

I have no appetite; my stomach is in knots. He can't expect me to feel anything but fear, fear for my daughter. He steeples his fingers and rests them against his lips. He cocks his head to the side and raises one eyebrow. "You must eat to keep up your strength. I can assure you that, for now, you're safe."

Safe? I pull my eyes away from his and focus on my meal. The only sort of weapon I could see on the table is my fork and butter knife. I grip them tightly and with my head bowed, I glance around the room. I don't see an out; all I see is a guard by the doorway. I take a deep breath and pick at my food.

"I can assure you I won't starve. Please tell me why I'm here."

He pours us each a glass of wine. His stare is fixed on me as he lifts his glass. "You are a means to an end. If your father cooperates, you can be home with you daughter soon."

I bite the inside of my cheek trying to calm the rage inside of me. *My father.* I should have known this had to do with him. I despise him. I'm nothing to him, so if this guy is expecting to get something for me, then we are all doomed, especially Stella. I slowly let my breath out.

"What exactly are you expecting from my father?"

"For now, nothing. If he wants you back safely and wants to insure the safety of his only granddaughter, then he will follow my instructions."

"And if he doesn't?"

"Do you have reason to believe he won't?"

I'm not about to tell him what I really think of my father. I don't need to cut my chances short. "No, I'm just wondering. When can I go home? I'm a single parent and I need to know that my daughter is safe."

"I can assure you that your daughter is being well taken care of. I will keep you updated on the progress with your father. Diana will remain outside your door at all times. If you need anything, let her know."

"Do I have to stay in that bedroom all the time?"

He gets up and tosses his napkin on the table. He bends down, his face only inches from mine. "You should be thankful you are no longer in that cage." He turns and walks out as Diana steps into the room.

I have to figure out a way to get out of here. I have no time for a pity party. I toss my napkin over my plate. I could very easily palm the fork or knife and slip it into my pocket but, once they see it is gone, I'm screwed. Instead, I fill my glass with more wine and take it with me to my room. Diana doesn't object. Maybe it will come in handy later on.

Fitz

I head across the street to the diner. Travis is already waiting for me. "Hey, I got the name of the guy that kidnapped Effy—Thomas Petrov. He has a record." I pull his photo up on my phone and pass it to him.

"Wow, it's pretty damn close to my sketch. What was he in for?"

"B&E, and he did the full stretch so no parole check-ins. I have his last known address but I doubt that will be good. What did you find out at the pizza parlor?"

"The pizza sucks. I saw a guy go in the back but he never came out. I was able to snap a picture of him. Not the best, but it's better than nothing. I can tweak it. While I was there, a bunch of school kids came in. It seems to be a neighborhood hangout. Maybe that's how he is getting these kids. He makes them comfortable in their surroundings. They let their guard down and he snatches them."

"Yeah, but none of them were taken from the pizza parlor. They were all taken from random places. Effy was taken out of her house. Jin was snatched off the street when she was on her way to see me. We know Jin was taken because she knew too much. Effy, she's the anomaly." Manny comes by and drops off coffee. He knows, at this time of day, I'm just here to work.

"Maybe she's not an anomaly. Maybe there is some truth to Jin's theory."

"Don't tell me you're buying into the whole tinfoil hat brigade thing."

"Fitz, I don't know what the hell to think. Every rock we turn over leaves us with more questions than answers, like why did a guy go from B&E to kidnapping?"

"Yeah, that's bothering me too. Have you been able to find out who owns the pizza joint?"

"Not yet, but maybe there is something in Jin's journals."

An alert goes off on my phone reminding me about the doctor appointment. "Let's head back to the house. We can check and see if Olivia has found anything before I have to take MJ to her doctor's appointment."

I leave a twenty on the table even though Manny doesn't want it. I call it booth rental. As we head out the door, there is a news flash on the TV that stops us both in our tracks. The President of the United States just announced that he wants Senator Sidney McPhee from Virginia to fill the position of Vice President. "Come on, Travis, time is not on our side."

As we hop on our bikes and head toward home, I silently pray to God for Effy's safety.

Chapter Seventeen

Aafii

I have a Darknet website that only my buyers can access using the TOR software and an Onion Router. It's a safe place for me to conduct my business. I'm the enemy without a face. When Vadik sends me the pictures of the current shipment, I create a buyer's package. I keep the posts very simple. I put the pictures, along with the age and health of each of the girls, on the site. I give the buyers a date and time that the bidding will start. The bidding is open for twenty-four hours. By the time the plane has wheels up, all the girls are already sold. We were on our third shipment when Vadik said an Asian girl showed up at his place asking questions. How the hell did she even find out about the pizza parlor? I sent one of my men to find her and bring her to me so I could question her, however, Vadik got to her first and told me he would get the information. The only thing he got was a dead girl that needed to be disposed of. He's becoming a liability, leaving too many loose ends for me to deal with. Vadik said his contact at the police department told him the Medical Examiner found a chip from a USB drive that the girl swallowed. I told Vadik if the girl was willing to swallow a chip and then die for it, it must have some incriminating stuff on it. All he could find out is that it was heavily encrypted. That information makes me wonder if the girl was able to hack into my site. I don't understand how since once the auction is over, I pull everything down. The whole thing is done within twenty-four hours. The girl swallowing the chip kept nagging me. I decided to have my men toss her apartment. The only thing they came up with is her parents owning a dry cleaners and she had a roommate. They had no time to search the parent's place, so I had them do the next best thing—torch it. The roommate is in the wind, but I have my men out looking for her. Maybe I should have Vadik find her, then he can smash her skull in like the other one.

Now I get word that the plane the girls left on had engine trouble and had to divert to Logan Airport in Boston. They are working on the repair now and will be cleared to leave tomorrow. I know I'll feel better when all this is over. I should probably take this as a sign: close up shop and move to another location. But now, I have the ultimate prize—Effy McPhee. I would have loved to have her daughter too, but for now, she will do. All my sources tell me that Senator McPhee is going to be named the next Vice President. When I see it for myself, I'll believe it. Maybe while I'm waiting I should try to get the child. Imagine what kind of leverage I could have over him then. I shake those thoughts from my head. Right now, I need to prepare Effy for her video debut.

Effy

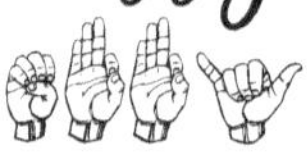

I'm sitting on the bed, staring into nothingness. I keep replaying that night in my head. What could I have done different? A mother is supposed to protect her child, but all I see, over and over again, is the look of fear on Stella's face. She never knew her father and now it doesn't look too promising for me. Will she forget about me? Will she hate me for leaving her? I'm a single parent with a child who has a disability. I'm trying to do it all. I thought I was doing all the right things. Teaching her it's okay to be different. Even though people will look at her as imperfect, love and accept others as they are and they will accept you. But now, I realize my biggest failure is I have no will. The only reason I have a life insurance policy is because Jay insisted we both have one before Stella was born. After Jay died, I changed the beneficiary to my father. I had no choice, he's all I have. In the event of my death, I have no one assigned as Stella's guardian. Dear God, I thought I was being so responsible but, in reality, I was irresponsible. No one ever thinks they are going to die, least of all me. In the event of my death, what will my father do? He wanted me to abort her from the day I found out I was pregnant. After Jay died, I thought my dad would want to help me. He wanted nothing to do with us. When I found out Stella was deaf, I did what any daughter would do; I ran to my father for comfort and guidance. All he did was tell his assistant to give me a list of agencies that might help me. The only time he wanted to be around Stella was for a photo-op. She was going to further his career. I'll be dead and he will probably use her for sympathy and votes.

There is a light tap on the door, snapping me back to reality. Diana steps in and informs me that I'm needed in the study. I step into the hall and take note of my surroundings. I don't know if it's night or day. All the windows are boarded up, just like my room. When we step into the study, my captor dismisses Diana.

"Please, have a seat." He waves his hand in the direction of a small love seat.

"Not until you at least tell me your name."

"My name should be the least of your concerns. What you should be concerned about is convincing your father to meet my demands."

I take a deep breath to try and steady my nerves. Making sure I never take my eyes off him. "What if I don't, then what?"

"Then I will go for your daughter. I can get a lot of money for her on the black market. The choice is yours."

My stomach instantly knots and I'm fighting to stop the shaking. "What do you need me to do?" I barely squeak out.

"See now, that's more like it. I have note for you to read. Do not waver off it."

He presses a piece of paper into my hand. I'm trying to read what it says but my hands are shaking so bad, I can hardly focus on it. He passes me a glass of water and waits for me to compose myself. I look at the paper and back up toward him. "Is this true?"

"Stick to the script. I'll count down and then you can start reading. Three, two, one." He presses record.

"Daddy, this is your proof of life. I'm safe and as long as you do what you are told, I will remain that way. If you don't, they are going for Stella. Don't contact the authorities. They will be in touch soon. Daddy, please keep her safe." He stops recording. He's typing and then there is that familiar sound when a text goes through. He places the phone on the desk and smashes it with a hammer until it's in a million pieces. He takes all the pieces and sweeps them into some sort of pouch.

"Now what happens?"

"That's none of your concern. Diana will take you back to your room."

Out of nowhere, Diana appears and, just like that, she leads me back to my room. Once again, I'm left staring at the four walls. Except, this time I'm even more confused. Why didn't he ask my dad for a ransom? What do they want him to do for them? Hell, if they think he's going to comply they are sadly mistaken. My father doesn't give two shits about me and even less about Stella. All he cares about is his career. I'm pacing around my room like a caged animal. This is no different than the cage I was in before, only now I'm not part of some human trafficking ring. I'm a pawn in something much bigger. I drop to my knees and beg God to please have mercy and protect Stella.

Aafii

It's understandable that she wears her heart on her sleeve when it comes to her daughter. But when she talks about her father, it's like she turns to stone. It makes me wonder if he's going to do what I want. Maybe it's a waste of time and too much exposure. Maybe I'd be better off cutting my losses now. I sent the video with a text saying I'd be contacting him soon. In the meantime, I'll have Diana prepare her so I can put together a packet for a buyer.

My phone chimes with a notification, it's a news alert. *The President announces Senator McPhee has been chosen to fill the VP slot.* Well, well, well, how do you like that? And to think dumb luck dumped his daughter in my lap. If I could get my hands on his granddaughter, it would be like winning the lottery. I think it's time to try.

Me: Did you find the roommate yet?

Vadik: No, she ran after your men torched the dry cleaners. She's got to show her face sooner or later. Do you want my men to grab her or what?

Me: I want her alive. I need to know what she knows.

Vadik: Ok, I'll keep you posted.

Me: Find out where the kid is being held.

Vadik: I told you she's at a cop's house. Are you sure you want to dip into that pool?

Vadik is good for muscle and very little brain. If he was able to rub two nickels together to make a dime, he would realize how much America's enemies would pay for that double package.

Me: Just get me the address, I'll have my men handle it.

Vadik: I know she's in Bay Ridge Brooklyn. I'll find out the exact address and text you. Good luck.

I don't reply. It's not luck; it careful planning and leaving nothing to chance. Next up, finding that roommate. My men, along with Vadik's, better come up with the girl.

Chapter Eighteen

Fitz

I decide to stop at Mom's while Travis heads to my house. She has come to every one of MJ's doctor's appointments. Andy usually comes, too. Needless to say, our appointments are like a convention of the crazies. My dad lets them do their thing and swears he'll show up at the hospital when it's time. He's always been like that, swooping in at the very end to save the day. Well, at least he's always done that for me. When I pull up, Sal's not there. Hudson only had two classes; why the hell is she not back yet?

Me: Where are you?

Hudson: Who is this?

Me: Fitz. Were you expecting someone else?

Hudson: How did you get my number?

Me: I texted myself when I had your phone this morning.

Hudson: Well, the least you could have done is put your name in there too.

Me: So, where are you?

Hudson: We are on our way back to my place to get some clothes. Remember I told you I needed some stuff. I figured since I have a constant bodyguard it wouldn't be a problem.

Me: Did everything go okay at school today?

Hudson: You know you're acting like a dad. Everything went fine. I have to turn in my final project next week. I hope you've come up with a plan.

Me: I'm working on it. Stay close to Sal and I will talk to you later.

Hudson: Okay.

Truth is, I don't have a plan. If what she says is true, there is no way she can turn that project in. Besides, my priority is to find Effy and those five other girls. I head upstairs. The smell in the air tells me my mom has been baking. By the time MJ has this baby, I'm going to be forty pounds heavier.

"Hey, Mom. What have you been up to?"

"I've been baking all day. Your father has been glued to that computer you gave him. I swear it's either the TV or the computer. He's going to go blind from all those rays."

"Ma, he'll be fine." I slice off a piece of warm Irish Soda bread and spread a little bit of Kerry Gold butter on it. Sheer heaven.

"I was giving you a few more minutes to come and get me, otherwise I was calling Andy." Stubborn woman.

"You know we wouldn't leave without you. Until this case is over, you are not to go anywhere without Sal. He should be back soon." She waves me off like I'm some sort of mosquito. I leave her mumbling under her breath while I check and see what dad's been up to.

"Hey, Dad, you need to keep mom from leaving this house by herself." I insist.

He finally pulls his gaze away from his laptop and towards me.

"What do you propose I do, shoot her? You of all people know how stubborn she can be. Besides, you know your mother, if anyone decided to kidnap her, they would end up paying me to take her back." He gives a half smile . . . more to himself, I think. "Speaking of," he continues, "I thought Sal would be back by now. The kid only had two classes; how long could that take?"

"She went home to get some of her things. They should be back soon. What did you do today?"

"I started doing some research on the increase of Human Trafficking. Until Hudson brought it to my attention, I didn't know how bad it had gotten. I also tried to dig into who owns the pizza parlor, but I only got one holding company after another. I really believe you need to focus on that place."

"Travis went there today. He said it's a hangout for teenagers. He thinks that's how the kidnappers are getting the kids. The kids aren't afraid of anyone from there because they aren't strangers to them. He was going to dig into who owns it along with trying to find out more on the VP. I'm still not buying the VP angle. I don't usually believe in coincidences; I think his death was just that—a coincidence."

"So then why take Effy? You said she is older than the others. If not because of the VP, then why?"

I get up and walk over to the window, trying to dig deep into my mind to slow down everything and process it. "I honestly have no idea. I found out the guy that kidnapped her did time for B&E. First offense and he did the full stretch."

"Well, that's odd. Where did he do his time?"

"Rikers."

"Leave me the info on him and let me reach out to Dustin. He's one guy who can't be turned."

I text him everything I have which, in reality, is not much. "Didn't Dustin hit his twenty and retire last year?" His phone pings with a text notification. He pulls it up and is staring at Petrov's rap sheet, totally ignoring my question. "Dad, did I lose you?"

"Sorry, son, the thought of this guy anywhere near Stella makes my skin crawl. Dustin put his papers in last year after they had him take over the women's side of Rikers. He said they were worse than the men. After working there for twenty years, I'm sure he knows a lot of what went on behind the scenes. I'll reach out to him today. Don't worry; like I said, we can trust him."

No matter what happens in life, the job never leaves you and my dad is a prime example of that. After being injured on the job more than ten years ago, he still has the contacts and he will always be my mentor.

"Alright, I'll be back after the doctor. Hopefully you'll have something for me." He waves me off and when I turn around, Mom is standing in the doorway with her coat on and her purse clutched to her chest, waiting.

"We have to cut through the alley since I came here on Wanda."

"If I was twenty years younger, I would have you drive me around on that thing to see what all the hoopla is about Wanda," she states with a sigh as she follows me out of the house. I try to stifle a laugh as I envision my mom cruising down Fifth Avenue. "Was the Chen's dry cleaners totally destroyed?"

"I'm waiting for a call back from the fire marshal later this afternoon. I'm hoping some of their personal belongings can be salvaged." We are almost out of the alley but she stops and squeezes my arm.

"Fitz, they already lost their greatest gift, their daughter. Everything else is just stuff. Yes, that stuff holds memories, but they'll never hold that child in their arms again. There is no greater loss than that." Her grip on my arm tightens even more. "Every day that you walk out that door, I pray that it's not the last time." Her words are barely above a whisper. I pull her into a hug.

"Mom, I can't tell you not to worry because that would be a waste of time for both of us. All I can do is promise you that I will always be careful." What else can I possibly say to ease her fears? We both know the truth, I have one of the most dangerous jobs. Not just physically but emotionally. I see humanity's lowest of the low. However, sometimes, I get to see the best of the best. I get to make a difference and that's what matters most. The blind scales of lady justice do win every now and again.

We walk the rest of the way in silence. When we come out of the alley, everyone is already outside and climbing into MJ's car.

"MJ, you could have at least waited for us to get here."

"Dad called and said you were on your way. I didn't think you wanted Stella to come with us so Travis and Olivia are upstairs with her."

I pull her aside while everyone is getting in the car. "Hey, is everything okay?"

"I'm just a little nervous today; I'm not sure why."

"We are in this together and you have nothing to worry about." I pull her into my arms and do my best to try and calm her nerves. She pulls back and steps away from the car.

"Okay, I don't want you to think I'm losing my mind but I've had a bad feeling all day and it has nothing to do with the baby. I'm having a problem leaving Stella here today."

If there is one thing I've always believed in, it's my gut feeling. "Never discount your gut, babe. I'll run up and get her." I let Kyle know he's coming with us, and I race upstairs for Stella. It's probably better this way; Travis and Olivia can stay focused on Jin's books.

I fought MJ tooth and nail when she wanted me to trade in Wanda for a big car. She finally gave up and traded in her BMW for this huge Infinity QX 60, but I'm realizing now she was the smart one. I put Mom up front with Kyle so she can talk his ear off. Andy puts Stella in a car seat that seemed to materialize overnight.

I'm about to ask but MJ squeezes my hand. Something else seems to be bothering her but I can't figure out what. Finally, we are all situated and on our way.

Hudson

Surprisingly, the meeting with my professor went better than I expected. Thankfully, Sal waited outside his office so I didn't have to explain who he was. When we get back to my place, it's just as I left it. I don't know what I was expecting; it's not like Mr. Clean was going to walk through the door and put everything back to normal. The living room window has a street view and that's where Sal has taken up residency. While he focuses on what's going on outside, I throw some stuff in an overnight bag. I'm not sure how long I'm going to be gone, but this will have to be enough for now. I throw the mail in my bag to deal with later. Before we leave, I pick up a broken picture frame with mine and Jin's picture in it. I gave it to her on National Friendship day and had her favorite quote about friendship engraved on the frame. *Friendship is a gift. It's the gift of family. It's the gift of love and gratitude. I fight to preserve that gift every day.* She was more than my best friend, she was the sister I never had.

"Is there a back way out of here?" He's been so quiet that his voice startles me.

"Yes, it leads to the yard. There is a gate that will let you out into the street, why?" I'm trying to act cool but then he pulls out a gun and my heart nearly leaps out of my chest.

"We need to go now. Make sure you do exactly what I tell you." He doesn't wait for me to answer, he grabs my hand and we are running out the door. Just as we are about to go out the back door, I catch a glimpse of two men coming into my building. Before they go into my apartment, one man turns and locks eyes with me. He raises his gun and yells something that I don't understand. I freeze, my body begins to shake. It's so bad, I can't move. Sal is trying to pull me but my feet won't budge. The man fires a shot that I literately can hear whiz past me. He starts running toward us. Before I know what's happening, Sal throws me over his shoulder and is sprinting through the yard. He tosses me into the car and we are off. Through all of this, I at least have the presence of mind to hold onto my overnight bag. It takes about five blocks before reality hits me that someone was trying to shoot me.

"What the hell?!" I smack him in the arm so hard my hand instantly hurts and turns red.

"Why are you smacking me? I got us out of there alive, didn't I?"

"I don't know. I'm scared and frustrated. Besides, you're a big enough target! Why are they after me?"

"For the same reason they killed Jin. As far as they're concerned, you know just as much as she did."

It feels like we are driving in circles instead of heading back towards Bay Ridge. "I thought we were going back to Fitz's parent's house?"

"We are, I'm just making sure we're not being followed."

"Bad guys shooting at me. Being chased through the streets of Brooklyn. Driving around in circles to make sure we're not followed. Buildings burning down. My best friend getting killed. Kids getting kidnapped. How much more is one person supposed to take? Now I'm hiding out in a man's parent's house that I hardly even know, and all

this is starting to sound normal to me. I thought I was getting away from all the crazies, instead I'm on board the Looney Tunes express train!" I'm sitting in the seat, rocking back and forth with my arms tightly wrapped around myself.

"Am I supposed to answer you or were you just venting out loud?"

His eyes are on the road but he has a smirk on his face. In my mind's eye, I'm shooting flaming daggers at him for being such a smart ass. "No, I was venting out loud. I do that sometimes. I'll tell you when you need to answer."

We finally get back to Fitz's parent's house, but rather than stay outside, Sal follows me inside. "I can manage this on my own." I try to wrestle my bag away from him but he's got a death grip on it.

"I know you can. I want to let Pat know what happened."

"Oh, I didn't realize that you knew him."

"Fitz, Lucas, and I graduated from the academy together. We were inseparable and spent many nights here going over our cases with Pat. When Lucas was shot, he decided to open a private security agency and asked me to go partners with him. I jumped at the chance."

He puts my bag down and heads towards the sound of the TV. I look around at my surroundings. Right now, my world seems surreal. Sal and Pat are chatting away like this is everyday life. A life I didn't sign up for. It's not like I'm chained to the chair, unable to leave. But where would I go? I could go to my parent's house, even though they're dead. Technically, to me, it's still my parent's home. Realistically right now, the safest place for me to be is here. I push my bag aside and put up a pot of coffee. Something tells me I'm going to be here for the long haul.

CHAPTER NINETEEN

Effy

I WASN'T IN MY ROOM for too long before Diana came back in. She made me strip and then took some pictures of me. Finally, she wrapped me in some purple material, posed me the way she wanted and told me not to look to scared. How do I not look too scared when, I'm scared to death? I asked her what the pictures were for but she ignored me. I wonder if I'm going to be up on the auction block like I'm sure the rest of the girls are?

I pray that my father might want to step up and be a real man for once in his life. I need him to do whatever these people want, otherwise, they are going to go after Stella. The problem is, he really doesn't give a shit about either of us. To him, I'm nothing more than a single parent with a damaged child. He's reminded me of that on many occasions, so I'm sure now, when I need him the most, he won't come through. He never did for my mom and he won't for me. A leopard never changes its spots.

There is so much I still need to teach Stella. Last year, she was in a private kindergarten. Her teacher felt, with an interpreter to accompany her, she would do great in public school. This year, she started first grade in public school. I was so worried, but she is doing great! I'm so proud of her progress. She is trying so hard to fit in with the other kids. After the first week of school, she started to question me about her daddy, and why some people had two daddies and she didn't even have one. As much as it hurt me to talk about him, I knew she was ready and needed to learn about her dad. I had to explain to a six-year-old about heaven and death. I told her that her daddy is an angel watching over both of us. So many words left unspoken. Now I might not have the chance.

I curl up into a ball and cry. My tears are unending. I've lost so much in my short life and now everything hinges upon one man—*my father.*

Fitz

Even though we practically fill up the entire waiting room, the doctor's visit was uneventful. She wants to see us every week until the baby comes. I was surprised today when the doctor asked me how I feel. Usually it's all about MJ. I told her I feel like I'm in an airplane and the air traffic controller has us in a holding pattern. Our classes are done, and the room is all set up. I just want this to be done. The look she gave me tells me that was probably the wrong answer. She also asked us if we still don't want to know what we are having. She said sometimes, when it gets closer to the due date, people change their minds. When she first asked, I told her it didn't matter, cause we can just keep having them. That earned me a punch in the gut from MJ and the doctor rolling her eyes. After that, I try to keep my mouth shut. MJ thanked her and told her we would rather wait.

We head out of there and drop Mom off first. I see Sal's car is back. I'll check in with him later. At least, for now, I don't have to worry about Hudson. When we turn down our street, I notice two cop cars parked by our house. "Kyle, pull over and let me out here. Take everyone to my parent's house." Andy is keeping Stella distracted while I pull MJ closer to me.

"I'm sure it's nothing but stay at Mom's house. I'll call you later." I give her a quick kiss and head out.

When I get to my house, I pull one of the cops aside and show him my badge. "What's going on here?"

"One of your neighbors called it in. They said strangers were trying to break into your house. Turns out they're Feds that are friends of yours."

"Don't tell me Mrs. Stillwater called it in." The good and the bad about a close-knit neighborhood.

"Yeah, when we heard it was a cop's, house we raced over here. Sorry if we scared you."

"Thanks." I slap him on the shoulder. They leave and I head upstairs. Travis is sitting at the kitchen table with an ice pack on the side of his head.

"What the hell happened?"

"While Livy was working on the books, I decided to go out and get some healthy food. When I came back, two guys jumped me from behind."

"Wait, the cop said Mrs. Stillwater called in someone trying to break in."

Olivia comes over and changes his ice pack. "Those new video cameras you installed outside just paid for themselves. I saw what was happening and hit the panic button on the alarm, which scared the shit out of the guys and they ran. When Mrs. Stillwater called the police, the only ones left outside were me and Travis. I was helping him inside when the cops showed."

"Who hit you?"

"Not sure, but I think they were speaking Russian or Albanian."

"Shit, they know we've got Stella here."

Travis pulls his ice pack away from his head and focuses on me. "Fitz, it's safe to say that we need to move everyone out of here. Where are they now?"

"My parent's house, but that will be the next place they look."

"Look, Fitz, I know you and Travis think everyone should move, but I don't think that's the best thing. Besides, where would we move? I think we should beef up security around this house. If we need to call in reinforcements from outside, that's not a problem. Plus, with Andy's house right across the street, we can have a lot of round the clock coverage."

"Damn it, I almost forgot I have a new camera on the front of Andy's house that is aimed at my front door." I quickly pull up the app on my phone and we review the footage.

"It looks like they came out of that black car. I'll email this footage to you and maybe you can enhance it. I think Olivia is right, this is still the safest place for my family. We can bring in more people, but I want them cleared by Lucas. If he doesn't know them inside and out, then I don't want them here."

"Okay, that can be arranged. Now, I made some progress with Jin's books. Have a seat and I'll go through them with you."

I grab a bottle of water and have a seat. She spreads out the notes books but I have no idea what I'm looking at.

"Jin was obsessed with the VP angle. She listed all the different Chinese herbs that could mimic a heart attack. She went so far as to obtain a copy of all his medical records. The girl was really good, Fitz. She was using TOR software so she could stay anonymous while she was digging around.

"Her thoughts were that these kids were being sold to fund a sleeper cell. She actually found a girl that went missing two years ago. She said it was easier to track the girl from the past than the girls that were currently missing. Every step of the way, she wrote down her thoughts—why she believed what she was doing and her feelings. This is some really intense stuff."

"So, what happened with the kid from two years ago?"

"She was sold on the black market to a man in the Ukraine. Somehow, she was able to hack into a website on the Darknet. Apparently, the site only goes live for twenty-four hours and only when there is something to sell."

"How do they get these kids out of the country?"

"Reading her notes, she thought they might be using a private plane to take them abroad. Once they get them out of the US, it's very easy to get papers and bounce from country to country."

"What do you think the chances are that Effy is still alive?"

"Well, if Jin is right, then her chances are good."

"And if she's wrong?"

"Then she's already dead."

I get up and pitch my water bottle into the recycling bin while I try to process everything I've just learned. "What about Hudson? Have you figured out what her real story is?"

Travis gets up and puts the ice pack back in the freezer. "I told you earlier her prints came back clean. I got her DNA back and there were no hits on that, either. While Livy was working on Jin's books, I pulled up the sealed files from her name change. I figured if I had her real name then maybe I could find out why. She is an only child; her real name is Ginger Townes. Apparently, her parents died in a car accident."

I don't ever question him on the hows, only on the information he obtains. "Apparently?"

"Yeah, her father was an international banker. He was the mastermind behind a large money-laundering scheme involving Bitcoin. I say *apparently* because there was no reason for the accident. Mechanically, the car was fine and there was no one on the road. The officer on the scene said that maybe he swerved to miss a deer. Except, there weren't any skid marks—nothing. The car exploded when it went over the embankment. They had to use dental records to identify them."

"What was the scheme?"

"Layman's terms. First, you have to set up a virtual wallet, which functions the same as a bank account. Then, you buy your Bitcoins using a bank transfer. They go into your account and, at that point, the money is clean. Then, you can buy and sell to other people using your Bitcoins. He was skimming money off of his clients' accounts and transferring it into different wallets."

"Didn't his clients see they were short money?"

"No, and I have to say it was pretty inventive. He created an algorithm that skimmed pennies off of their accounts. When you have millions, you don't really notice a few pennies missing."

"How much did he get away with?"

"Eight million dollars before he was caught."

"In pennies?!"

"Fitz, you have to remember he was skimming from all his accounts from all over the world. Yeah, pennies add up really quick when you do that."

"Did it say why she changed her name?"

"Yes, even though his crime wasn't broadcasted like Bernie Madoff's was she didn't want to be affiliated with anything her father did. The IRS seized all the parent's bank accounts. The house in Westchester is paid off and in Hudson's name, so they could not take that. They also couldn't touch the life insurance policies that her father had. Everything else was fair game."

"I'm just throwing this out there. Do you think any of this could be because of her father?"

"I don't think so but I can't say for sure. I think these girls stumbled upon something that got Jin killed and now everyone is going to be gunning for Hudson. But, we also need to look at the accounts that the father stole from. Now don't go off on me and start making me a tin hat, but I think that there could be some validity to Jin's theory on the VP death."

I roll my eyes at the thought of where my own mind is going. "The more I think about it, the more I think you might be right. I don't believe in coincidences. The sad part is, if they think they are going to get McPhee to do their bidding to save his daughter, they are sadly mistaken. The man is a total bastard and only out for himself."

"What's our next step?"

"I'll call Lucas and see who he has that we can bring in. While I do that you need to follow the money. Not just from what Jin was following but also Hudson's parents. We also need to find out who owns the pizza parlor. Is it possible that this website will come back on again? If so, can we monitor it?"

"I'm already on that. I'll work on the other stuff while you call Lucas. And Livy can get back to Jin's notebooks."

"Okay, I'm going to my parent's house. I'll call Lucas along the way. I'll keep you posted."

I cut through the alley and before I can call Lucas, the phone rings and it's him. "Hey, I was just getting ready to call you."

"We have a problem. Sal took Hudson back to her place to get her clothes and, when they were leaving, two guys showed up. They took a couple of shots at Hudson but Sal got her out of there. They are back at your parent's house but I'm not sure if you want to keep her there."

"Two people also showed up at my house. Travis and Olivia

were able to fight them off." I stop at the end of the alley and I can see Sal sitting in his car. "I think I need to move everyone."

"Where are you going to move them to?"

"I'll move Stella and Hudson to the safe house with the captain. Everyone else can stay at my parent's house. Start working on the extra security for my parents. I want Kyle to stay there but I'll have Sal go with the girls. I'll call the captain while you round up the additional security. Lucas, I don't need to remind you of this, but it has to be a crew that you would leave your family with."

"Fitz, I understand. Maybe you should let Brad know that you are moving Stella and Hudson. We just won't tell him where they are being moved to. Without them at the house, your family will be safe. We will still have added security on everyone, but they won't have any reason to go after them."

"Unless they want to get to me. I'll call the captain and check back with you." Before I get to the house, I need to run everything by Hart. I much rather bounce things off him in person but the phone will have to do.

Me: Hey can you talk?

He calls me right away; no doubt he's going stir crazy. I bring him up to speed on everything. "Did you get the picture I texted you of Tommy Petrov?"

"Yes, I can't image the fear Stella must have endured at the hands of that man. Fitz, yesterday I moved all of us out of the safe house. I went to my mom's house and took her car since she's at my sister's house in Arizona for six weeks. I figured she wouldn't need it. I took everyone to my cabin."

"What about work?"

"I called in and told them my mom was ill, and I needed to take care of her. If anyone drives by her house, my car is in the driveway."

"Well, I was going to move Stella and Hudson to the safe house with you."

"That's okay, just bring them here. Better yet, bring MJ and Andy too."

"Are you sure there is enough of room for everyone?"

"You haven't seen it since I built a new addition. When the housing market tanked, I was able to pick up the land that was next to me. If you're worried about everyone's safety, you're the only one who's ever been here. Fitz, only you and my mom know about this place. Also, Twilight Park added a full-time guard at the entrance. You know the way the roads are in here, so try to get here before it gets dark, otherwise, shoot for first thing in the morning."

Twilight Park is built into the side of a mountain in the Catskill Mountain range. You take your life into your hands just driving in there. If someone wanted to try and get to the cabin on foot, chances are, they wouldn't make it.

"Lucas suggested we should pass information on to Brad. What's your thought about that?"

"I agree with Lucas. Let's feed Brad the information we want him to pass along. It's about time we get ahead of this. Have Lucas put guards on your house and your parent's house, too. Even though everyone will be with me, we still need to keep up appearances.

"Great idea. Okay, when I get there, we can figure out what we want Brad to know. Even though the cell service where you are sucks, I'll still shoot you a text when we are on our way."

I shoot Lucas a quick text about the guards. Now I have to go over all of this with everyone. The hardest part of this plan is convincing MJ to go. She is a city girl who hates everything about the country.

CHAPTER TWENTY

WHEN I GET TO MY parent's house, Sal and Kyle are sitting in the car. Sal gets out and stops me before I head in. "Did Lucas tell you what happened today?"

"Yeah, how is Hudson holding up?"

"As you can expect; it got to her bad. I'm not sure how much more of this she can take. She has no more classes until Monday, which means she doesn't have to go anywhere. At this point, I'm not sure if that's a good thing or a bad thing. The more free time she has to think, the worse it could be."

"Okay, thanks. I'll talk to her."

I quickly head inside and find Stella in the kitchen playing cards with my mom. Everyone else is in the living room where the noise level is on high. MJ's voice rises above all of them. "Look little girl, I don't give a shit who you are or why you're hiding behind that one name bullshit. All I know is, you helped create one big cluster fuck that we are all dealing with now. This is not a game; it's a fucking life or death situation. My home is cordoned off with police tape. There is a little girl inside whose whole existence depends on what information you might have about the people who took her mother. My parents are going out of their way to protect you and, to top that off, my husband is putting his life on the line for you! In case you didn't realize it, he has a family and a baby on the way. This is my family you're fucking with, so you can't just sit there and say none of this is your fault and you just want out. Grow the fuck up, get your head out of your fucking ass, and start helping them with this investigation!"

I can't have everyone at each other's throats and I especially can't have MJ getting this upset. "Hey, everyone, I'm back. MJ, I gather you met Hudson." If looks could kill, I know I'd be in Hell right now with a flaming pitchfork up my ass.

"What happened at our house? Don't even think of telling me *nothing*. Andy already spoke to Mrs. Stillwater. Are Travis and Olivia okay?" I should have known that the Mrs. Kravitz of the neighborhood, as I like to call her, would have Andy on speed dial.

"Some people tried to get Stella. No doubt they are the same people that took a shot at Hudson today. Travis has a bump on his head and Olivia is fine." Hudson gets up, picks her bag up off the ground and heads toward the door. Before I can say a word, MJ steps in front of her, blocking the way.

"Where the hell do you think you're going? You started all of this and now you want to leave? I don't think so."

"I don't want to put anyone else in danger. I'll go to my parent's house in Westchester. I can lay low until all of this is over."

MJ is not budging and there's no way Hudson is going to get around her. "Okay, now I think everyone should calm down. I have a plan on how to keep everyone safe until this is over. Since Hart already has the Chen's in protective custody, I'm going to bring everyone to him to look after." MJ's face is flushed and I swear every one of her freckles has come to the surface. Before anyone can say a word, my dad puts his hand out to MJ. As she grips it, I notice that her hand is shaking.

"You need to go with Stella and Hudson. I agree with Fitz; you won't be safe here. The people that are after these two won't know that they've been moved. I'm afraid if they come back again for them, which I'm sure they will, you will be hurt. It's not just about you anymore; you have a child to protect. Andy will go with you. I'm sure he will want to stay close to you." I look over at Andy and he nods his head in agreement, knowing it's not a suggestion.

I pull her into my arms and rub her back. I can feel her heart racing. "MJ, I promise it's for the best. I'll be careful. Just knowing that you're safely tucked away, I can give my all to this case."

She pulls back and wipes away a tear. "I'm warning you, Fitz, nothing better happen to you while I'm gone, or else." I don't need to ask or else what. I know better.

"Dad, Lucas is sending over a guard to stay out front. I want to keep up appearances. Besides, if Mom needs to go anywhere, he takes her." He nods in silent agreement.

"Andy, take everyone in to the kitchen and pack up all that food your mother's been cooking." He gives Andy a quick nod and shoos everyone away. He always gets his point across without saying much and, right now, I'm sure Dad wants to talk to me alone. Andy herds everyone into the kitchen.

"What's up, Dad?"

"I spoke to my friend at the prison. He said when Petrov first showed up, he was very meek. Then, two years into his stretch, he had Lasik surgery, courtesy of the United States taxpayers. After that, he started hanging out with some Albanian mob guys. He got into some trouble, mostly bullshit stuff inside. Every time he would come up for parole he would act up. He idolized the group he was hanging out with and, basically, didn't want to leave. The gang became his family."

"Did you find out the name of the gang?"

"He said he thought the gang could be a part of The Rudaj Organization called "The Corporation" but there was no proof.

Did Travis find out who owns the pizza parlor?"

"No, not yet, but maybe this information will lead him in the right direction. Thanks, Dad. And thanks for helping me with MJ."

"You know with her it's all in how you put it. If you demand her to do something, she will fight you tooth and nail. Where are you taking them?"

"Hart has a place in Haines Falls. It's secluded and no one knows where it is but me."

"Okay, keep it that way. Text me and let me know she got there okay."

While everyone begins making their goodbyes, I head outside and let Sal and Kyle know there's a change of plans. Kyle will remain outside my parent's house. Lucas will have a new guy stay at my house. Sal will go with everyone to Hart's place. After stopping at home, so I can get Wanda and Stella's bear Sam, MJ and Andy pack a bag, and we are finally on our way.

Travis

Now that everyone's off to the safe house, I can't stop thinking about Jin. The world will never know what they lost. Her talent, at such a young age, was amazing. Now the only thing left is what's in these books and on her thumb drive.

While Livy is deep in thought, trying to translate Jin's books, I'm going to try and tweak the code Jin used to follow the money. Livy jumps out of her chair, sending it crashing to the ground and my heart nearly leaps out of my chest.

"I found something! Jin knew the code was wrong and she was messing around with changing one strand of it. She says here that it did the trick and she found what she was looking for. Since she was only in possession of one of the thumb drives at the time, she was only able to update that one. She did however make a note to update the other two." She writes out what it should be and passes it to me.

"She also found out who that large wire in Queens went to. He's the same guy that owns that site on the Darknet she was talking about earlier."

"What's his name?"

"It's not in here. It's probably on the drive that she updated."

"What about the VP?"

"Nothing, damn it. She would make these little notes in-between everything. Almost like she had a thought and didn't want to lose it." She quickly flips through the pages.

"Like this one: *People are like snowflakes. No two are alike, yet all of them are beautiful in their own way.*

Then, she would go back to what she was doing. It's like she was working on her computer and jotting stuff in the books at the same time. I'll keep digging through here." She picks up the chair and becomes lost again in Jin's books.

I don't know how much time has passed but the pounding in my head is back with a vengeance. I get up and retrieve the ice pack when all of a sudden, my computer bings. Livy stops what she's doing and I sit back down to see what we've found.

"Oh my God, I've got the name of the pizza parlor owner: Vadik Stasevich. Hold on, I need to open another search for more on him," I say as I frantically type,. Livy moves her chair closer to me so we can both impatiently watch the blank page loading. "Okay, here we go. His parents are from Albania. He came into the United States on a student visa and never left. He's not even legal, Livy. His holding company has owned the pizza parlor for six years. Shit, how many girls has he gotten through that place?" I ask aloud. Livy squeezes my arm.

"You need to keep it together and stay focused. Time is running out for Effy, if it hasn't already. Keep following the money; I'll get a hold of Fitz."

"He's still on the road. You keep digging in the books and I'll try to find out more on the other wires."

"Do you have any clue as to how Petrov knows Vadik?"

"No, I have no idea. Maybe Fitz will."

MJ

Speeding into the night, trying to protect an innocent child is not how I thought I would be spending my last trimester. There is stress and sadness all around me when this time should be filled with the love and excitement of a new life. It was almost dark when we got here. Hart's house is so secluded, I have no idea how Fitz was able to find it. I try to comfort Mr. & Mrs. Chen but every time they see me, they must be reminded of all they lost. I can tell they like Hudson but, again, she is a constant reminder that she is here and their daughter is not. Finally, they retire to their room.

Andy is playing a card game with Stella, while Fitz is going over everything with Hart before he leaves. I need to try and play nice with Hudson. Especially if I'm going to be stuck here with her.

I waddle over and take a seat next to her on the sofa. "Look, I'm sorry I lost it on you back at the house. I could say it's the hormones but that would be a lie. My husband was supposed to be on vacation right now. It was supposed to be just us, enjoying ourselves, before the baby gets here. Instead, he's mixed up in this mess and, right now, I don't see a way out." I frantically wave my hand around as if something will magically appear.

"Look, MJ, I get that this isn't what you were planning. None of us were. I was just working on a final project when all hell broke loose. On top of everything else, today I was shot at! I can't even begin to explain to you what it feels like to be running for your life while bullets are whizzing past you. This is shit you see on TV; this is not real life. At least, it wasn't my life until today. You can't possibly understand the fear, no one can."

I take a deep calming breath and let it out. "Hudson, I understand more than you know. I know how real the fear is. It climbs up into your throat and you fight to keep it down. You can feel the fear reaching up, trying to strangle the life out of you. It becomes hard to breath. You can feel your heart pounding in your chest and it's so loud, you think everyone will hear it. And then, they will know. They will know that you're on the verge of breaking. You want to find a corner and make yourself so small that no one else will see you. But then the uncontrollable shaking starts because you realize you might never see your family again. This could finally be the end. You worry if tomorrow never comes, did you tell the people you hold so dear that you love them? In your mind, you think of all that was left unsaid, and those are the thoughts that may finally break you. *You* think you're going to break. You begin praying for that tiny sliver of hope then, you dig deep down into your soul and find the courage to hold on just a little bit longer."

Her hand covers her mouth as she gasps. "Jesus, how the hell could you know what I'm feeling?"

"I know because I lived it. I was kidnapped by a madman, who made it his business to kill women who looked like me. It was Fitz who finally saved me. So, when I tell you I understand your fear—trust me—I really do."

"I can't look at Mr. & Mrs. Chen without feeling guilt." Her voice cracks.

"What do you have to feel guilty about?"

She quickly averts her eyes from mine. "I should have gone with Jin to bring everything to Fitz. She asked me to go with her but I was studying for a journalism test. I told her to wait and I would go with her after class the next day. She insisted she would be fine and left." She begins to cry. I turn toward her, as best as my belly will let me, and wipe away her tears.

"Listen to me, you had no way of knowing what was going to happen. I'm sure Mr. & Mrs. Chen know that Jin was a strong-willed person and nothing was going to stop her from doing what she wanted to do. You can't blame yourself and I'm sure they don't blame you," I say. She gets up, grabs a box of Kleenex, and sits back down next to me. "So, can I ask you about your name?" She rolls her eyes and I try not to laugh. "You don't have to tell me why you changed it. I've been researching baby names and I'm just curious as to how you came up with the name Hudson." Truth is, Fitz and I already have our names picked out, but maybe I can get her to tell me more about herself before her name change.

"My parents had just died in a car accident and I needed a new beginning. I was heading to the court to change my name, but I still couldn't decide on what name to choose. I wasn't sure what I wanted. I was sitting on a bus on Hudson River Line. At first, I was thinking River but when I walked into the court house, I heard that classic Billy Joel song "New York State of Mind," and I knew it had to be Hudson."

"I'm sorry about your parents. How old were you when they died?"

"I was twenty. Too young to understand the enormity of it all. I'm an only child and after that, I had to grow up really fast. My father was pretty organized, so at least I wasn't scrambling to figure out numerous financial stuff."

I pull a Kleenex from the box. "Now you have me crying, but at least I can blame the hormones."

"Do you know what you are having?"

"No, I didn't want to know. Fitz said he didn't care just as long as we can keep making babies."

"When are you due?"

"I still have six weeks." Fitz comes out of the kitchen with Hart and they head over to us.

"Hey, I've got to get going. You'll be safe here with the captain. MJ, walk me out, please." He helps me up off the sofa and I walk with him out front. "Everything okay with you and Hudson?"

"Yes, I'm playing nice with others. She said she changed her name when her parents died. The name has no meaning other than she was on the Hudson River Line headed towards the city." I take in a deep breath, then reveal the rest of the info she just gave me.

"You're amazing and I love you. I didn't want to say anything in the car ride over here but Travis found out that her parents were in an accident. Her father was a thief and it looks like she probably wanted to separate herself from anything having to do with him. We don't think it has anything to do with this case. Now, I don't want you to worry about me. I promise I'll be careful."

"I love you, Fitz."

He kisses me and then bends down and kisses my belly. I watch him leave and I have an uneasy feeling that the worst is yet to come. I push down those thoughts and head inside to make myself something to eat.

Travis

Time seems to tick by so slowly. Just when I think I'm going to catch a break, I hit another dead end. The doorbell goes off and Livy nearly jumps out of her skin. Fitz has a monitor on the kitchen counter that is about the size of an iPad. It automatically comes on and shows who's at the door, even before they ring the bell. It's Lucas. I was going to buzz him in but Livy's already up and she goes downstairs to get him.

"Hey, stranger how the hell are you?" I call out as I hear him coming up the stairs.

"I'm good. Is Fitz back, yet?" he asks as he walks into the room.

Before I can answer him, the monitor lights up again—Fitz is home. As he's coming up the steps, I yell out to him that we're all in the kitchen.

"Well, you look like shit. When was the last time you ate?" Lucas tells Fitz.

"Thanks, Lucas, I love you, too. I'm sure Andy left some food here for me."

"Sit down. I'll get you both something to eat while Travis brings everyone up to speed." Olivia starts rummaging through the kitchen.

"Okay, so first off, I found out that a Vadik Stasevich owns the pizza parlor for six years. He came over on a student visa from Albania and never left. Jin realized her code needed a few tweaks. Earlier in one of her books, she talked about a guy with a site on the

Darknet. The wire that went to Queens went to that guy. She was only able to update her thumb drive since she didn't have the other two. She put the changes to the code in one of her books but not the name. I'm trying to find out who that is. I can't figure out how Petrov and Vadik know each other."

Lucas reaches into his pocket and pulls out a small notepad. I smile at his old school ways. "I might be able to help you with that one. I did some digging while I was waiting for Fitz to get back. Turns out that Brad's sister Debbie is married to Stanley Hirsch. Stanley and Tommy Petrov grew up together. They are all from the same neighborhood. There's your connection."

Fitz finally finishes his food, gets up and gets a beer.

"Lucas, can you send me all the info on Stanley, please?"

"I already emailed it to you along with his picture. Are you going to pick him up?"

"Yeah, but I'm going for Brad first."

Lucas holds his hand up, stopping Fitz in mid thought. "I checked Brad's schedule; he's doing the 4 to 12 shift. He's still there for two more hours. I wish there was a way I could help you."

"Actually Lucas, you can. I need a car."

"I can do that. I have two spares at the office."

"I don't have time for that. Can you take Wanda and meet me at the station?" He passes him a set of keys.

"Wow, you're trusting me with Wanda, why?"

"Instead of going for Brad first, I want to parade Stanley and Debbie in front of Brad right before I arrest him."

"Okay, just so you know, Kyle is still on your parent's house and I put Johnny Azure on your house. He should be here soon. Anyone driving by will think it's business as usual."

"Great, thanks. My dad talked to a friend of his that just retired from Rikers. He knew Petrov and said that he got in with an Albanian gang. He made it his business not to get paroled. That's why he did the full stretch. The gang was his family and he didn't want to leave them. Travis, were you able to get a picture of Vadik?"

"Nothing recent. Do you know which gang Petrov is in? Maybe Vadik is also in the gang."

"Dad said possibly part of The Rudaj Organization called "The Corporation" but there was no proof." My computer chimes and a picture pops up . . . Vadik.

"Hold on, Fitz, I've got a current picture of Vadik." I show everyone and then send it to their phones.

"Okay, Travis, you and Olivia keep working here. Lucas, can you send someone to sit on the pizza parlor? If Vadik shows up, just have them follow, not engage."

"I can have Benny sit on the place, but are you sure you don't want to try for Vadik first?"

"No, I think Vadik is in the wind right now. Maybe we can get another location for him from Brad. Travis, I'll have Lucas text you when we have everyone in custody. We need to hurry, I don't think Effy has much time left."

They race out the door while Livy and I dig back into our work. My goal: find the owner of the site on the Darknet before it's too late. Hang on, Effy.

CHAPTER TWENTY-ONE

Fitz

When I got to Stanley's house, him and his wife were just sitting around, watching an episode of *Storage Wars*. They were acting like they didn't have a care in the world. Meanwhile, I'm racing against the clock to try and save Effy's life. They didn't even put up a fight. No doubt they think Brad will help them out. Little do they know, that he's next on my list.

Lucas's car is loaded with lights and sirens. I hit them all and race to the station. I don't want Brad to leave before I get there. I told Lucas if Brad gets any calls before I get there, then he needs to step in. I get inside, and Lucas is standing in the doorway watching every move Brad makes. I make a show of parading Stanley and Debbie past him. Debbie tries to wiggle free of my grasp and run towards her brother; no such luck. Brad looks at me and then back to the door. Lucas is blocking anyone from getting in or out. He was a middle linebacker in college before he joined the force. He was going to turn pro but his real dream was to be a cop. That dream got sidelined when he took a bullet meant for Andy. He's as wide as he is tall; there's no getting around him. My eyes lock with Brad's and, in that instant, by the look of dread on his face, he realizes this game is over. I ask Marjorie, the desk clerk, to come over and help me. "Please put them in separate rooms."

Once she has them secured, I head to Brad's desk. It takes all of me not to shoot him right there.

"Fitz, why do you have my sister in lockup?" His face is red and he is fidgeting.

"You can either make this hard or easy on yourself, the choice is yours."

"What the hell are you talking about?"

"Look, the jig is up. I know about the wires you've been getting, and I know you're the leak. I'd like to hear your side of the story before I talk to your sister and brother in-law." I step to the side and he begins walking towards the interrogation rooms. As luck would have it, Marjorie put them in the front rooms so Brad would have to walk past his family before we get to an open room. I give her a nod as we walk by.

"I want my union rep."

"You can have whatever you want, but first, you have to tell me where Effy is?"

"I have no idea what you're talking about. I want my union rep. You can't question me without my rep."

I pull a chair out for him to sit. "You're right. You asked for your rep, so now I can't talk to you." I head towards the door and right before I leave, I drop the bait. "I'm going to talk to Stanley and then your sister. Whomever gives me the information I want first gets the deal." He lets me walk out without saying a word. That means he thinks he is the only one who has any information that I could use. Then again, I don't think like everyone else, I never have.

The Feds and Senator McPhee are waiting for me outside the room.

"Officer, what's going on? Do any of these people know where my daughter is?"

"I'll share mine if you share yours." I'm bluffing but by the senator's fidgety movements, and his inability to look me in the eye, tells me something happened.

"I got a video."

"And you had no intention on sharing it with me. Do you understand I'm trying to help you find your daughter?!"

"All it said was it was proof of life and if I didn't do what they wanted, they were going to go after Stella. They said they would be in touch and don't contact the authorities. I've already violated their terms by working with the FBI. I decided to broadcast the photo of my daughter along with the mug shot of Tommy Petrov. I'm offering a $250,000 reward for her safe return."

"Don't you think you should have said something to me?! For Christ's sake, I've got your granddaughter stashed at my home with my very pregnant wife. Someone tried to break in to my house today. You can rest assure they weren't there selling fucking Avon!" I want to punch him in the face hard, but that's not going to get Effy back, and it sure won't keep my family safe.

"Is everyone okay?"

"No thanks to you. Please make me understand what would possess you to go live with a reward when you were told not to?" He really could care less about Effy and Stella.

"Money talks, detective."

"And, it will also get people killed. At least let me see the video before you broadcast your reward, or question anyone." I head into Hart's office with everyone quickly following behind me. The senator hands me a tablet and I hit play. I watch it a couple of times. There's no natural light coming into the room. It could be a basement or the windows could be boarded up. There really is not much to go on. "Send this to Travis, maybe he can figure something out." I pass the tablet to Simmons. He seems to be the lead federal investigator on this case.

"Now, what did you find out?"

"As you know, Hart called me in to look at that case with the missing girls. There were six girls missing and one of them turned up dead. The clues to all of this are with Jin Chen, the girl that was murdered. The express version is that Jin was working on a final for her Political Science class. She stumbled upon the human trafficking ring and that's what got her killed. Brad, his sister Debbie and her husband Stanley are also involved. They grew up with Petrov and now he's part of the Albanian Mob. There are still a lot of loose ends that I'm trying to tie together, but my main focus has been, *and will always be,* finding Effy. I made a promise to Stella and I damn well aim to keep it. Now, I need to question Stanley." I get up to leave but Simmons blocks the doorway.

"This is not a one-man crusade, detective. What else did Jin Chen have?"

"Whatever she had was bits and pieces. As soon as I find out anything else, I will let you know." He steps aside and I'm out of there. Now I need to find out how Stanley and Debbie fit into this mess.

I watch Stanley through the mirror so I can see just how I want to play this. He's sitting in the chair with his feet up on the table. He has on military boots. He seems to not have a care in the world. Well, that's about to change.

When I head into the room I nonchalantly look at the bottom of his boots. I remember Gail said there was a logo from the bottom of a military boot on Jin's body. I committed that logo to memory and it's the same one on his boot. "You have one chance to help yourself. Your brother in-law is going away for a very long time.

Your wife is not too far behind him. If you want to see the light of day, I'm your only chance."

"I didn't do nothin."

I open my folder and pull out pictures of all the girls, including Effy. I lay them out, one by one in front of him with Jin's autopsy photo last. "You kidnapped all these girls. But this last one, here, her name was Jin. You bashed her head in. You left the imprint from your boot on her body." He slowly slides his feet off the table. His face pales as reality hits him. He just got royally fucked.

"What are you offering?"

"It depends on what you have."

"I didn't take this one, but I know who did." He pushes Effy's picture toward me.

"You're going to have to do better than that. I already know your friend Tommy Petrov took her. I know he was not alone. You were there, so cut the bullshit." He jerks his head back and his body stiffens. I just hit the nail on the head. "Where are these girls?"

"All of them are gone but her." Again, he points to Effy.

"This is bullshit. I need more. Last chance, where are these girls?" He's not budging. I make a show of gathering up the pictures and putting them away. "You had your chance." I get up to leave and he jumps out of his chair.

"Wait, I can tell you where we drop them off."

"I need more than that."

"I need a deal."

"What do you mean they're gone?"

"They've been bought, paid for, and shipped out."

My stomach is in knots. I pass him Effy's picture. "What about her?"

"Craziest thing about that broad. Tommy mixed up the address and we ended up grabbing the wrong girl. Plus, Tommy got hurt on that job, so we thought for sure it was lights out for us. But, as it turns out, the buyer wanted that girl. He even wanted her kid that we left behind. Tommy thought she was dead but I told him those deaf people they have super powers. We were told to go back for the kid but when we went back, she was gone."

"Who has Effy?"

"See now this is the part when you offer me a deal. No deal and I'm not saying another word."

I grab the picture and leave him to wonder whether I'll come back. When I step outside the door, everyone is waiting for me.

The senator grabs me. "You need to press him further. He knows where she is. Let me talk to him."

I pull my arm free of him. "Sir, I know what I'm doing. Please let me do my job." I'm about to leave when Simmons steps in front of me.

"Detective Fitzgerald, wait, the Federal government is prepared to offer him immunity if he can lead us to Effy."

"He's a killer and a kidnapper. I know you guys make deals all the time, but I don't. Let's not forget—his boot print matches the ones on Jin's body. Let me work on Brad and then we can see where we're at. At least give me that."

"Okay. But after that, we need to put a plan together."

"Have you gotten anything back from Travis on the video?"

"No, not yet."

Brad's union rep has finally showed up along with a high-priced suit. When I step into the room, the tension is so thick, you can cut it with a knife.

"I'll be representing Brandon Johnson. As per my advice, he has nothing to say. Either charge him or let him go." The suit passes me his card.

"Oh, don't worry, I'm charging him. Seven counts of kidnapping. One count of murder. One count of attempted murder. And since you participated in illegal wires, that crossed not only state lines but also international waters, you are being charged with Federal Wire Fraud. The wire charge alone is punishable up to twenty years in prison. Add up all the other charges and you'll never see the light of day. So, Brad, do you still want to take the suit's advice and keep quiet or would you like to try and make a deal. Oh, and I have to tell you, Stanley is very talkative." With every charge I read off, his face gets paler.

"What's on the table?" The suit tries to speak but Brad stops him. "At least let me hear what he has to offer."

"It would help you if we can get Effy back alive. But, I have to be honest with you, there is a shit load of charges here and these are just for the girls we know of. Right now, I have a team of forensic accountants going over your finances for the last ten years. They are going to crawl so far up your ass that not even your prostrate will be smiling." What I have going for me is Brad knows me. He knows I don't bullshit and he knows I'm like a dog with a bone. I'll never give up until I see him get what he deserves. He's starting to look a little uneasy. He's fidgeting and looking from his attorney to his union rep, like a drowning man looking for a lifeline. Unfortunately for him, I'm it.

"Fitz, please, you've got to help me out here. I won't survive a day in prison."

"Well, now that depends what you've got for me. I want Effy, and I want her alive. But, I've got to tell you; this is out of my hands. The feds have you by the balls and they're slowly twisting them. Give me something to go to them with, you know . . . to show good faith. You messed with kids, Brad, you know what they do to people like you in prison. You better pray that they put you in solitary confinement for the rest of your life. Otherwise, being someone's bitch will be the least of your problems," I remind him. His body becomes rigid and he's rubbing the back of his neck. He's biting his bottom lip almost like he's having and internal debate with himself.

"I can tell you who Stanley and Tommy collect the girls for."

I hold up my hand stopping him. "Don't waste your time with that one, I know it's Vadik. I also know he owns the pizza parlor on Nostrand Ave and Shore Pkwy. Tell me where I can find him and the girls right now and that will go a long way towards '*good faith*.'" He keeps glancing around the room like someone is going to run in and save the day. There is no one, only me—nailing his ass to the cross.

"I'll give you Vadik's home address. It's where he and his wife Inga keep the girls before they are shipped out. But, I need an agreement in writing or you get nothing."

It's a fucking family affair . . . Jesus. "I need more than that. I want the buyer or no deal." His attorney and his union rep tell him to take a deal.

"Call in the feds. I'm ready to deal."

The words barely left his mouth as the door flies open, and Simmons is there to deal. While they start their negotiations, I head into the room next door to meet with Debbie. Looking at Brad and Debbie, you would never know they were related. Brad is always well groomed and dressed to the nines. Debbie looks like she's had a very hard life. Her yellowed nails and constant hacking, no doubt, is from long-term smoking.

"I think it's only fair to let you know your brother and husband are trying to get a deal. A deal that does not include you. They are selling you out."

"I don't believe you. Neither one of them would ever do that. Besides, I was not a part of anything."

"Come on, see for yourself." I lead her out of the room and into the observation room attached to Brad's. I leave the sound off. She doesn't need to hear anything, just the sight of him talking to the feds rattles her.

"Would you like to see what your husband is up to?"

"I've seen enough. Like I said, I was not a part of anything, so I have nothing to worry about." We head back into her room. She's smirking. I hate smirking.

"Debbie, let me tell you a story. You really should brush up on the law. A simple Google search would have helped you out. Every state is different. You're in New York where you can be charged with aiding and abetting in a crime even if you weren't there during the commission of the crime. Depending upon the crime, it could be a misdemeanor or a felony. But, you see, here is your problem. The laws change when it involves children. So, Debbie, you're fucked . . . royally." While I'm waiting for that to sink in, I pull out all the photos of the children and line them up.

"I want a deal. I'm not about to go down for something I had nothing to do with."

"You have to have something to deal."

She leans in and the lingering smell of smoke is so intense I can almost taste it.

"I have more then you bargained for. I handle the investments for my brother and his partner."

I try to not let the shock I'm feeling show on my face. This woman looks like she could be sleeping in a cardboard box on a street corner, not handling investments.

"You're very quiet, detective. I guess that's not what you expected to hear."

I have two ways I can go here. I can try to pretend I knew all of this or give in to my shock. I decide to choose the latter. "I won't lie to you. You're right; you're not what I expected. So, give me something to prove you're not lying."

"I keep a very detailed log. Every time Stan and Tom deliver a child, I note her name, the date she was delivered and to whom she was delivered to. Stan and Tom get paid via wire transfer when they deliver the child. Brad gets paid to keep the operation going without police interruption. I invest Brad's money for him along with Tom's and his partner. You know, I'm like the Monday morning quarterback of investing. I've made everyone millions. Is that enough?"

Is that enough? Fuck this is not a fly by night operation. "It's a start. Who pays Brad?" What I really want to know is who pays Vadik, but I need to work up to that.

"Detective, let's talk deal and I will give you everything, including who ordered everything."

Now she said the magic words. "I'll be back." I head out the door and check on Stanley. No one is talking with him. Next up, Brad. The feds are still in with him. I step in the room and they are dotting their I's and crossing their T's. They never even bothered to hear what Debbie has to say. "Excuse me." Nothing. "EXCUSE ME!" Finally, everyone shuts up and all heads turn towards me. "Now that I have your attention, before you finish this, you need to step outside." Simmons closes his file and they all head out of the room.

"Detective, this better be good; we are close to finalizing this deal. Hopefully, we're not too late to save Effy."

"You're putting all your eggs in one basket. You never even bothered to hear what his sister Debbie had to say."

"Debbie Hirsch is married to Stanley Hirsch. Stanley is the lowest man on the totem pole. Now, if you're done here, we are fighting the clock." Simmons turns to leave and that's when I drop my bombshell.

"Debbie Hirsch does all the investing for her brother and his partner. She keeps a very detailed list of every child that was ever taken. She's also willing to give up the name of the man who ordered everything. What's Brad going to give you? Vadik? We know about him already. The one we really want is the man who ordered all of this. Chances are, he's the one who has Effy."

"Are you sure she can deliver?"

"The bookkeeper always knows all the dirty secrets."

He steps to the side and waves his hand. "Lead the way, detective, and I hope for Effy's sake, you're right. However, McPhee is still going to offer a reward." When I look down the hall, I can see McPhee holding court with the press.

Chapter Twenty-Two

Hudson

It's late, really late. Everyone finally went to sleep but I can't. I've tried the usual, but I can't seem to shut my mind off. When I cozied up to the fireplace, my tea was hot and the fire was roaring. Now my tea is cold and the fire is just hot embers. There's a storm raging outside. I don't usually mind them but tonight is different. I hear him clear his throat. I'm sure he is being kind and not wanting to scare the bejesus out of me. "It's okay, Sal, I know you're there. The creaking of the floor boards gave you away." He hands me a hot cup of tea, puts another on the table that I'm assuming is for him, and then tends to the fire. He's huge and looks menacing, but he's really an oversized Teddy bear.

"I didn't want to scare you. Want to talk?"

"I need a distraction; tell me about yourself." He takes a seat on the other end of the couch, faces me, and covers his feet with the rest of my blanket.

"Not much to tell. I was a cop and now I work security with Lucas."

"Why are you no longer on the force?" He hasn't been a man of many words, so I don't think this is going to be easy.

"I wanted my degree more than the job. It took me doing the job for me to realize that. I still love law enforcement but from a different perspective."

"Did you get your degree or are you still in school?" He's smiling and, for the first time, I notice he has dimples.

"I graduated from John Jay. I have a Masters of Science in Protection Management."

I nudge him with my foot and his smile gets bigger. "Why didn't you tell me when we were there today that you're an alum?"

"I was going to, but then we were shot at; it didn't seem so important anymore." He gets up and stokes the fire. When he gets back on the couch, he stretches his legs out a little more, pulling the blanket toward him.

"Sorry, but my toes are cold and there's only one blanket."

"So, why are you babysitting me when you could be doing so much more with your degree?"

"Lucas and I own The Cooper Agency. When he called and said Fitz needed help, I jumped at the chance."

"I don't know Fitz very well, but it seems that everyone runs to help him out." I stare intently at him. He's running his finger around the rim of his cup. I'm watching it go around and round. It's hypnotic.

"Fitz will go to hell and back to right the wrongs in this world. Trust rings supreme with him. It's like his mind works differently than everyone else's. He'll get to the bottom of this."

It sounds like his faith in Fitz is unwavering. I wish I could say the same. We're both quiet but his stare is intense. "I wish I had the same faith you have. I've lost so many people I love in such a short time. Now I'm in a fight to save my own life and, frankly, I'm not sure how much fight I have left in me." I quickly look away and wipe a tear that has escaped. I feel a nudge from his foot, and when

I look at him, he has his arms open wide. I quickly crawl into them. I can't explain why, but it feels right and I feel safe.

"Tell me what you want to do when you finish school."

"Are you trying to distract me?"

"Is it working?" He's smiling and those dimples are a major distraction.

"I'm not sure what I want to do. I wanted to go into forensic accounting, but after all of this, I'm not sure. What about you? When you're not helping your friends out, what do you do?"

"Lucas runs the day to day operation. Most of my work is on the research end of things. Neither of us usually goes out into the field. The only time we do is if it's an emergency. Like I said, when Fitz called, we didn't hesitate. Don't let everything that is going on distract you from what you really want to do. If you want to go into forensic accounting, then do it."

"Maybe everything is happening to me because I'm not supposed to be on this path. Maybe there is something else I'm supposed to be doing. How did you know you weren't supposed to be a cop?"

He gets real quiet as he stares into the fire. I hardly know him; here I am, prying into his personal life. Maybe his decision is too personal to share. "My dad was a cop. He died on 911," he finally says. While a lot of my friends joined the military, I joined the force. I thought it was my passion, but I soon realized I joined for all the wrong reasons."

"I don't understand."

"Look, I was following in my father's footsteps. Being a cop was his dream, not mine. I realized that everyone has a passion in life and sometimes the hardest thing is finding out what that passion is. Some people live their whole life and never know what that is. That's a life that's unfulfilled."

"It still doesn't help me."

"Tell me why you thought forensic accounting was the way to go?"

My whole body stiffens and it doesn't seem to go unnoticed by him. He tugs at my hair, sort of urging me to tell him. How much do I really want to share? How much should I? After all, I hardly know him. "My parents died in an automobile accident. My father was in international banking. He was accused of doing some bad stuff. I guess I wanted to try and prove that he didn't do it."

"So, you are doing it for him, not for you. Maybe that's your answer."

I turn around so I can face him. I need to see his face for this. "You didn't ask me what he did. Do you already know?" His face gives nothing away.

"No, Lucas told me I needed to protect a possible witness. Fitz said your life could be in danger. He asked me to stay close to you at all times. I'm also supposed to keep eyes on MJ and Stella. That's everything I know. It's not my case. I'm just helping out my friend. After this, if you want me to look into your father, I can. You will have to be honest with me, though. You can't keep secrets."

I take a deep breath and begin to tell him what I already know. "I'm an only child and when my parents died, I realized I knew nothing about their past. There were never any family gatherings—no aunts or uncles—nothing. I changed my name on a whim. I was pissed off and, in my irrational mind, I thought if I changed it, I could wipe out the past. Afterwards, I realized changing my name didn't change who I am or where I came from. When push comes to shove, I'm still Ginger Townes."

"It's a beautiful name but if you can't live with it, then you did the right thing. What about your mom?"

"My mom, bless her heart, she was like a typical 1950s stay-at-home wife. That's what my father wanted from her and that's what she gave him." I shift and now I'm sitting cross-legged between his legs. He takes both my hands off his thighs and I realize I was squeezing them.

"Let me help you find the information you're looking for. I promise you total confidentiality. Maybe it will give you closure and lead you in the direction you should be going in."

"What if I don't like what you find?" I ask. He throws his head back and lets out a big belly laugh. "Shh, you're going to wake everyone up!"

"I'm sorry, but I can tell you right now, you're not going to like what you find out."

"How do you know?" Maybe he does know more than he's telling me.

"Every girl puts her daddy on a pedestal. He was knocked off that pedestal in the worst possible way: doing something illegal. You never had a chance to ask him about it and, on top of that, your mother died in that car accident. Do you blame him for her death?"

Boy he's not pulling any punches. "At first, I didn't. As time went on, though, I found out what he was being accused of; I changed my mind," I barely whisper the words out. He lifts my chin so our eyes lock.

"Hudson, tell me what he's been accused of. It might not be as bad as you think."

My hands are shaking and he takes them in his. "He stole millions of dollars from his clients' accounts."

"Like a Bernie Madoff type of stealing?"

"Oh God, no. He skimmed money off their accounts. After the accident, all those alphabet government agencies came in and seized everything but the house and their life insurance policies. Apparently, my father put the house in my name and paid it off."

"When did you move to the apartment?"

"Not too long after I settled their estate. I just couldn't stay there anymore. The memories were eating me alive. Right after that, Jin moved in with me. It was her first adventure away from home. Little did we know it would be her last."

"Do you blame yourself for her death?"

"Boy, you just go right for the jugular." He's got his hands on my shoulders. I try to pull back a little from him but his grasp on me is very tight.

"You're the one who is carrying around the weight of the world on your shoulders. You can't be responsible for the decisions of others. After this is over, accept the help I'm offering you. Or sit around and have a pity party, the choice is yours."

"Okay, but you have to keep me alive, so the pressure is on you." He rolls his eyes, gets up, and offers me his hand.

"Deal, now let's get some sleep."

We head down the hallway to our rooms and for the first time in a long time, I have hope.

Travis

The ticking of the clock on the wall is driving me crazy. Every minute that passes makes me fear the worst for Effy. I keep tweaking Jin's program, but it keeps falling short.

"Livy, maybe we should call Fitz and get an update."

"Oh my God! I found an address for Vadik. Jin found it when she was checking housing records. Quick—call Fitz!" She turns to me.

I call Fitz. "Hey, we got an address on Vadik. Hold on, I'm passing you to Livy." I put my cell on speaker and hand it to her.

"Fitz, he purchased a house not too far from the pizza parlor. He put it in the name of Inga Romanoff. Inga Romanoff is now Inga Stasevich. She changed her name after they were married. I'm texting you the info now."

"How did you find it?"

"When Jin got frustrated that she couldn't find anything she started thinking outside the box. She figured he had to live someplace and he wouldn't want to rent if he wanted his privacy. She was very thorough in her searches. Any luck on your end as to who the head of this whole thing is?"

"Not yet. But I've got a good lead. Apparently, Brad's sister was the bookkeeper and investor for everyone. We're in the process of making a deal now. I'll keep you posted."

"Okay, be safe and good luck."

She hangs up and something Livy said is gnawing at me. "Investments!" I leap out of the chair yelling and I scare the bejesus out of Livy.

"Travis, did you find something?"

"No, Fitz just gave it to us. Debbie, is doing the investing for them. If she is doing that she has to have a license! All I need to do is get into her trading accounts. I need Fitz, again." I quickly dial and put him back on speaker.

"Hey, did you confiscate any computers from Stanley and Debbie's house?"

"I only picked up Stanley and Debbie, but the FBI is on their way over there now to see what they could find. They are bringing everything back here. If she can prove what she said, they will make a deal. Why?"

"Give me first crack at it. I know I can get into her computer. If I can find the information, we won't have to give her anything.

I'd rather see her rot in prison."

"Okay, but hurry. I'm not sure how much more time Effy has, if any."

"We're on our way." I hang up and Livy has already gathered up her stuff, grabs me and we're racing out the door.

Chapter Twenty-Three

Vadik

No matter how many times I check my phone, nothing changes. My text messages from Tommy are going unanswered. I need him to get that kid. I know Aafii wants her, but the more I think about it, the more I want her dead. She might not be able to talk but she can still pick Tommy out in a lineup. Aafii's greed is going to get us all busted. He's got the senator's daughter, why does he need the granddaughter too? Maybe Inga heard from him.

Me: Tommy's still not answering my texts. Have you heard from him?

Inga: Yes, he's at the Howard Johnson's in Saugerties. A friend he went to school with is a veterinarian up there. He said he could fix his arm without any questions. I told him to lay low for a while. Did you have any luck with the kid?

Me: No, Brad said they put added protection on her. I think Aafii is going after her himself. I really want Tommy to go

after her. Did he say how long he is staying away?

Inga: No, better off he stays away for a while. I've got a bad feeling about all of this. We have more money than we could ever want. Why don't we cut our losses and get out of here?

Me: You worry too much. Brad's got our back. I'm leaving now. I'll see you in a bit. I need you to send Tommy a message since he's checked in with you. Tell him I want him to find that kid before Aafii's people do. She's a loose end that needs to be taken care of—now.

I keep thinking about what Inga said. Maybe she's right. We have more than enough to live off of for the rest of our lives. Thanks to Debbie, my portfolio would make even the best financial advisor drool. That's it—decision made! This place doesn't close for another two hours. I'm about to head out when the news catches my eye. I turn up the volume and there's a picture of Tommy; the senator is offering a reward, a big one. I flip the channels and Tommy's face is plastered everywhere. This is bad, really bad. With his face on every news channel, it's a bad time for him to go after the kid.

Me: We might have a problem.

Aafii: I don't do problems. What's wrong?

Me: Turn on the news. The senator is offering a 250k reward for the return of his daughter. They've got a picture of my guy that took the daughter, plastered all over the news.

Aafii: It looks like you've got the problem. Your guy got made. Now I suggest you find him and fix this before the feds do. I still want the kid, no matter what happens.

Me: I'll handle it.

He doesn't answer me back. Decision made; I grab my keys and head out back. There's no way I'm going after Tommy, that's like stepping into the lions' den. I need to get Inga and take the first plane out of town to a destination that has no extradition. I race out the back door, down the alley, and hop into my car. No one is the wiser that I'm gone.

Aafii

I'm watching the news over and over again. No matter what channel I put on, there it is. Fuck, I wanted to have the vice president of one of the most powerful countries in my pocket. He's making a grandstand about offering a reward, but he really could care less about his daughter or his granddaughter, otherwise, he would have kept his mouth shut. That's got to be why Effy was shaking so much. Not so much her fear of me and what I can do, but her knowledge that her father couldn't care less about her and her daughter. I still want to get my hands on that kid. If I have both of them, then maybe I can get the new vice president in line with my plans. Or I could make a show of killing Effy while I keep the kid for leverage. Everything rests on getting that kid. While I have some of my men out searching for the kid, I send my two best enforcers to tie up loose ends with Vadik.

Vadik

Our house is at the end of a dead-end street. It's quiet and that works out great for us. Inga is a creature of habit. She always leaves a small light on in the front window. That's how I know something is wrong . . . no light. Rather than go through the front door, I pull my piece out and work my way around back.

There are no lights on at all. When I try the back door, it's unlocked. Slowly, I make my way from the mudroom into the kitchen. No sign of Inga and nothing is disturbed. Quietly, I step into the living room and that's when I feel a cold barrel on the back of my head. I close my eyes and take a deep breath. Many years ago, my uncle told me that if you die a violent death, the last thing you see is what you will see over and over again, where ever you end up. He said that's what hell really is, reliving your worst nightmare day after day. I hear a click and when I slowly open my eyes, the small light in the window is now on. Inga is sitting in her favorite chair, except, she's not moving. Her eyes are open wide and her face looks to be frozen in fear. Her neck is slit from ear to ear. My poor, beautiful Inga.

He takes the gun from my hand and pushes me further into the room. "Have a seat."

"What do you want from me? Why did you do this to my wife?" He pushes me into the chair directly across from Inga. I avert my eyes not wanting to have the look on her face be the last thing I see.

"It's nothing personal, Aafii just wants to clean house. Dead men can't talk."

I don't have a chance to try and fight back. One of the men grabs my hair and pulls my head back, holding it in place. I feel the steel tip digging into my neck. I close my eyes, not wanting to see her in my last moments.

"Open your eyes!"

At the sound of his roaring voice my instinct is to open them and when I do I feel the blade race across my throat. I feel the blood, but I don't see it. All I see is Inga.

"Is he dead, yet?"

"No, fucker is taking forever to die"

"Can't we speed this up, we have to go help find the kid."

"Should we take their phones and computers?"

"Our orders were to kill them and find the kid. That's what we are getting paid to do. We do that and we get a bonus. If we get caught, we get nothing."

It's so cold. I wonder if this is how Inga felt right before the end? I feel my life slipping away.

Fitz

While the Feds are working on which dirt bag is going to get the deal, I take a team and head to Inga's house. Hopefully Vadik is there and maybe, just maybe, Effy. We find the house at the end of a dead-end street, those are rare in Brooklyn. There's a small light on in the front window. There's a walkway that leads towards the back of the house. I send two officers around back and I take the other two with me in the front. The door is unlocked and we step into a small living room. I'm prepared for a fight. I wouldn't think he would go easily. Before my eyes can adjust, the familiar metallic smell hits me first—*blood.* For the smell to permeate that strongly, it must be bad. Finally, my eyes adjust. Two dead, and it's a blood bath. I wave the others on while I check to see if anyone is alive. The woman, who I'm assuming is Inga, is sitting in a chair. Her eyes wide open along with her mouth. The wound is so deep she's practically decapitated. The man, I'm assuming, is Vadik. His wound doesn't look as deep as the other one but his hair is sticking up, like someone fisted it. Maybe they held his head in place. I'll leave that up to the medical examiner.

I get back to checking the house and all is clear. I'm coming down from the upstairs when one of the officers comes running out of the basement. He just barely makes it to the kitchen sink and pukes.

"What's the problem?"

"Sick." Is all he can say.

I've seen the worst of mankind but nothing prepares me for what I find in that basement. Cages, eight of them. Cuffs that you would see in medieval times on chains that are bolted into the ground. Flimsy cots with buckets under them. The windows are all boarded up. In the very back of the room, nailed to the wall, is a Saint Andrew's Cross and I'm instantly reminded of Mystik. I push those thoughts of the past out of my head and continue to look around. It's like a torture chamber with all types of restraints. When I get closer to the cross, I shine my light and it's covered in spider webs. A shiver runs up my spin. It looks like it hasn't been used in a while, that's good at least for the girls that were being held here. I was praying I would have found Effy. Now I have to hope I can find the answers I need with Debbie. I really believe she is the one who knows all the secrets.

When I head back upstairs, one of the officers informs me they found a laptop and two cell phones. Unfortunately, everything is password protected. There is nothing else here that's going to help me find her. I leave everyone here to process the scene while I race the electronics back to Travis.

It's too late to check on MJ. Besides, service there is minimal. I race back to the station house and the mob has grown to a ridiculous size. I find Travis in Hart's office, working on a laptop and Olivia curled into a chair with the Jin's books.

"Hey, please tell me you got into her computer and found a lead."

"Nothing yet, I just got in. I heard the call come in on Vadik. The guys said they were keeping the girls in the basement. Did you find anything useful?"

"I found phones and a laptop, all password protected. Maybe there is something on them that can help us find Effy." Olivia puts the book she's reading down and closes her eyes.

"Olivia, you okay?"

"Fitz, it's very hard to read such personal stuff that was never meant to be read by anyone but the author. I feel like I'm invading her privacy. We'll never know what great things she might have accomplished in her lifetime." She picks up the book and flips the page she was reading back and forth. She leaps out of the chair, nearly giving Travis a heart attack.

"Fitz, Jin has the name Teterboro in bold letters and six question marks after it. What's Teterboro?"

"It's a smaller airport that is used by private planes. Travis, do you think the girls are being flown out of the country on a private plane?"

"Whomever is buying and selling these girls has to have a lot of money. It's very likely that's how they are getting the girls out of the country. Get Teterboro on the phone and see if they can pull any flight plans that were filed for flights going out of the country since Effy went missing. They would have to notify customs of the destination country that they were going to so they could clear them."

"I'll call them, but filing a flight plan is a five possibly a ten-minute phone call; not a big deal. Let's face it, I'm sure they've paid off a lot of people along the way."

After wasting five minutes in phone loop hell, I finally get the head of Teterboro on the line. He confirms that there have been three international flights out of there since Effy went missing. One of them is a prominent businessman from New York whose celebrity wife is always on page six of The Post. I think I can safely rule them out. Another one left the same day that Effy was taken, but very early in the morning. That leaves one more owned by a company call Jibril.

"Hey, Travis, is there anything in her computer that mentions a company called Jibril?"

"Hold on." He's furiously banging away on those keys.

"No nothing yet that I can see. Did Teterboro give you that?"

"They gave me information on three flights. I've ruled out two of them. That leaves me with a flight that left last night. It was supposed to go to Heathrow but it experienced engine problems and was diverted to Boston Logan Airport. It took off today and should be landing in the UK in about forty-five minutes."

Olivia stops what she's doing and turns her attention to mine and Travis's conversation. "Fitz, Jibril is an Arabic variant of the name Gabriel. Which in Hebrew tradition, Gabriel was one of the seven archangels. I think you should try and get the authorities to meet the plane when it lands."

"I'm on it!"

After five phone calls and being transferred a half dozen times, I finally convinced them to meet the plane and hold the occupants. I don't believe Effy is going to be on the plane. With the announcement of the VP and the reward, she has become a hot commodity.

"I'm going to let the feds know what we've got." I get up to leave, but Travis starts slamming the keys really hard. He's looking from the phone to the computer and he keeps saying "Oh my God."

"Travis, please tell me you've got something."

"I do, Vadik's text messages. His buyer is a guy named Aafii. I don't have a last name yet. I'll run it through INTERPOL and if something hits, I'll let you know." I don't need to remind him that time is not on our side.

I step into the hallway and find McPhee and Simmons's crew waiting for me. I quickly fill them in on what we've got so far. We head into one of the empty rooms and set it up like a war room. McPhee's pacing at a frantic pace. For once, he's showing some concern for his daughter. Finally, the screen comes to life and a plane comes into view. It is taxiing down the runway flanked by British Police. For security purposes, the police inform us that the plane will be guided to a hanger away from the main airport. It feels like everything is happening in slow motion but, in reality, it's all very quick. Finally, the plane is secured and the door opens. The police race up the steps and my heart is in my throat. I know Effy is not on this plane, but for the other families, I'm praying that my hunch was correct.

Finally, we see some movement. The police are escorting the pilot and the first officer along with a woman in handcuffs down the steps. We can see and hear everything that is going on. We are all moving closer to the screen as if that will make us see more. Suddenly, there is a crackling noise and a voice comes booming through. "We have five girls. They are alive. Effy McPhee is not on the plane. I repeat—Effy McPhee is not on the plane."

For the first time, the senator actually looks upset, even the feds look defeated. "Captain, this is detective Fitzgerald. Did any of the girls say anything about Effy or about where they were being held?"

"Only that she tried to comfort them."

The captain informs us that the girls will receive medical care and then they will be brought to The Embassy of the United States in London. From there, they will be reunited with their families.

The screen goes black and everyone is sitting there looking lost and deflated. "Hey, snap out of it. This is far from over. Travis has a lead on the man who has been purchasing these girls. Where are you at with Debbie?"

Agent Simmons keeps glancing from his notes to the other agents. "She wants no time. We can't do that. She was a part of numerous crimes; she can't just get a pass."

"Well, while Travis keeps working on her computer, I'm going to take another crack at her."

"I appreciate your enthusiasm but I think, for my daughter, there are no more tomorrows."

I get up and head toward the door. It takes all of me not to lose it on him. Before I step out the door, I take a deep breath and turn towards him. "That, sir, is where we differ. I will never stop—*ever.*"

Chapter Twenty-Four

Travis still hasn't gotten anything back from INTERPOL on Aafii. That leaves me with Debbie. She either voluntarily gives me what I need or I will rip it out of her. When I step into the room, I mentally tell myself to keep calm. She's sitting there with a smug look on her face and it takes all of my control not to slap the living shit out of her.

"Look, Debbie, if you want to deal I'm willing to put in a good word for you with the feds."

"Now, why would you do that? Oh, let me guess, you need something from me that you can't find in my computer. I'm not an idiot, detective. I know you probably have someone going through my computer and my phone. Unfortunately for you, what you are looking for is not in there. You see, it's kind of like the rules of investing. You would never put all your money into one fund . . . *diversification*. That, detective, should be your word of the day. See, I've got a little here and a little there. I had to make sure I was prepared, should this day ever come. My husband is nothing but a good fuck. Given the chance my brother would sell his mother up to the highest bidder, I had to make sure I had an ace in the hole."

The feds can continue to work out a deal with Brad, however, for me all the answers lie right here with Debbie. "Well, to start negotiating, you need to give me something in good faith. Something that's not in your computer."

"The wires come from a man in the middle east. He sends them to a holding company that was owned by an international banker right here in New York. The banker would then send them to Brad, Vadik, and his partner Aafii. Once the funds were available, everyone would wire them into their brokerage accounts. I would get a notice that the funds were available and I would start investing them. Everything was going smoothly until the banker got greedy and wanted a bigger cut. Next thing I know, he turned up dead. This was going to be the last load until things quieted down."

Jesus, this is a lot bigger than I thought. "What's Aafii's last name and where can I find him?"

"For that, you are going to have to give me a deal."

"Who was the dead banker, and what was the name of the holding company?"

"I don't mind giving you that one; dead men tell no tales. Consider this a gift. His name was Leland Townes and he was the sole owner of Crypto Holding."

I'm trying not to show any shock by the name she just dropped, instead, I need to show her I don't really give a shit about it. "While we wait for the feds to work out a deal, tell me what you know about Aafii?"

"Stan said his father was thrilled to learn that he had the senator's daughter. He really wanted the granddaughter, but Aafii was having a hard time finding her. Brad was going to have Stan go out tonight and try to find her. He wanted Tommy to go with him but he's off the grid right now getting his arm fixed up. No doubt he'll eventually have Tommy find her. He's a vicious animal and unfortunately, for me, my husband's nothing but a useless pussy. I told you he's a good fuck with no brains."

"Who's the father?" She throws her head back and lets out such a sinister laugh that I feel a chill run up my spine.

"I told you, first we deal and then you get the rest of the information. Now, I think I gave you enough information to prove to you that I'm the keeper of all the secrets. Right now, I would like a smoke and a coffee."

"There's no smoking in a government building." I get up and head out the door and find Simmons waiting for me.

"Detective, only one of them is getting a deal. Who do you think will have the information we need to find Effy?"

"I think Brad and Stan only have part of the information. I think Debbie has it all. But you need to do this quickly if Effy stands a chance to survive."

"For Effy's sake, I hope you're right."

While they go in and finalize everything, I head into Hart's office to give Travis the information I got from her.

"Hey, was Hudson's fathers name Leland Townes?"

"That's out of left field. Hold on, I'll pull up that case." He looks from his computer and then back to me with his mouth hanging open.

"I never told you his name how could you possibly know that?"

"The Townes's case just collided with this one. Debbie said the wires come from Aafii's father in the Middle East, and go to a holding company in New York City. The owner of that holding company distributes them to Aafii, Vadik, and Brad The name of that company is Crypto Holding Inc. Hudson's father was the owner of that company. She said he got greedy and that's why he was killed."

"Do you think Hudson knew what her father did?"

"I don't know what to think. Before we jump to any conclusions, we need to make sure that it was her father who was wiring the money. Besides, I thought the father was involved in the penny scheme, why would he get involved in this?"

"After he died and the IRS got everything they wanted, the feds dropped the case. The holding company was listed among his assets, but not what it was used for. There was no reason for them to pursue this anymore since he was dead. Let me dig a little bit more on this. What else did you find out from Debbie?"

"Apparently, Effy was taken by mistake, but Aafii's father was happy to have the next vice president's daughter. What he really wants, though, is Stella. Maybe it was just a coincidence that Aafii's father decided to capitalize on. Either way, we need to find Aafii. I'm sure he is holding Effy." I close my eyes for a moment and rub my temples, trying to fight off the headache I feel coming on. When I open my eyes, Olivia tosses me a protein bar.

"Eat, we can't have you less than one hundred percent. Now, what else did you get from Debbie?"

"She said she doesn't keep everything in her computer. She likened it to diversification in investing. What about Vadik and Inga? Travis, were you able to find out anything from their laptop and phones?"

"Vadik only referred to Aafii by his first name. There is nothing in INTERPOL. I have an idea. I'll run a search on anyone entering the United States for the past ten years with the name Aafii. It's not a common name; how many could there be?" Travis furrows his brows, shrugging his shoulders.

While he works on that, I want to check in with MJ. I know it's late, but I really need to hear her voice, it grounds me. I try calling and texting, nothing works. I know cell service in Haines Falls is bad. Hart has a landline but I don't want to wake up the whole house. I hate not being able to talk to my wife. I'll try again later.

Travis leaps up, fist pumping the air, "Yes! Fitz, I got it. There was a total of seven men with the name Aafii. If I narrow it down to the east coast, that gives me three. One is in New York, his name is Aafii EL-Hashem. I've got an address on him but not sure how valid it is. I'm sending it to your phone now. Fitz, take backup on this one, please."

I wave at him as I'm heading out the door. I find Simmons in the hallway talking to the senator. "Simmons, I have a lead on Aafii's location. It could be a bust but I need backup."

"Say no more, detective."

We head out and I'm praying that we have the right man.

Aafii

I keep watching the video of the senator offering up a reward for his daughter. What a fucking idiot. On top of that, he's a really bad actor and better not quit his day job. It really is a joke, if he would have followed my instructions this might have turned out differently, at least for Effy. My dad is pressuring me to find the kid. Vadik had nothing on where she is stashed. My men checked the cop's house and it's quiet. Maybe I can get something out of Effy. "Diana, bring Effy in here now," I call out to her and she quickly scurries off.

Finally, Effy steps into the room and Diana stays just outside the door. Judging by Effy's red, swollen eyes, I would say she has spent her time here crying.

"Effy, please have a seat." She takes seat in a chair furthest away from me. "I think I'm a pretty reasonable man. I gave your father every opportunity to play by the rules, but he ignored them. Tell me something, does your father hate you?" Her hands are clasped in her lap and she's rocking back and forth. Sweat begins to bead on her upper lip. Sure signs of fear. Fear of me? Fear of her father? Or both?

"He doesn't hate me, he's just not a very loving person. Please, let me speak to him. I know I can persuade him to do whatever it is you want."

She's so naive. "Can you persuade him to give me your daughter?" She leaps up and charges towards me. I grab her and in one quick move, I spin her around, her back against my front. My hand wrapped around her throat. "You don't get it. You were a mistake but now that I have you, I want it all. What that means is—I want your daughter. It's clear you don't mean that much to your father. He couldn't follow my instructions. Instead, he offered up a reward for your return. Do you know what he valued you at? Two hundred fifty thousand dollars. In the grand scheme of things, Effy, that's not really a lot of money. Not for a man in his position. Now your daughter, that's a different story. I can get a lot on the black market for a little deaf girl. Some men will pay extra just because she can't hear." Her whole body stiffens at the mention of her daughter being sold. She reaches up and tries to pry my hand off her throat. Such a foolish girl.

"Please, do whatever you want with me but please, I'm begging you, leave my daughter alone." She's trying to sound so convincing, however, I want the child more than I want her. My father wants her so he can control the second in command of the most powerful country in the world. Me, I know what I can get for that type of child on the black market. My hand tightening around her throat sends a jolt to my cock. I haven't had relief in days. Maybe—shit, alarms start going off. Effy is struggling to break free of my grasp. Diana is screaming. I hear gunshots and they are getting closer. I grab my switchblade off my desk and put it to Effy's neck. She's screaming uncontrollably.

"Shut the fuck up." In an instant, someone tosses Diana across the room. She hits the wall and lands on the floor. Two men enter the room with guns drawn on me. I have no problem using Effy as my shield. She's a woman; she's useless.

"Police, put the knife down now!"

My grip on Effy gets tighter "Put your guns down or I'll slice her throat."

"Look, Aafii, put the knife down and we can all get out of here in one piece."

I squeeze her throat, slowly cutting off her air supply. "Lower your guns!"

"Okay, keep calm. I'm lowering my gun. Simmons, lower your weapon."

Once they start to lower their guns, I will kill her. Their instinct will be to save her. That will give me my opportunity to run. As they begin to lower their guns, I slice her throat. She slides from my grasp and as she hits the floor, I try to bolt from the room. I hear the shot and then feel the burn. Everything around me is fading out.

Fitz

Everything happened in slow motion. Aafii is lying dead and Effy is bleeding out. "Effy, please hang on, Stella needs you." She's trying to talk but it's nothing but gurgling. Blood is everywhere and I'm trying to apply pressure to her neck. The paramedics show up and take over. By the grim look on their faces, it doesn't look good. The tears are rolling down her cheeks. She lifts her hands and signs to me. "Please take care of Stella. She has no one. Don't let her end up with my father. Tell her I love her and I will be with her always." Through my own tears, I watch as her hands begin moving slower. I watch the life slowly fade from her, and all I can do is promise to protect Stella for the rest of her life.

Chapter Twenty-Five

She's gone. Up until the very end, the only thing she cared about was Stella. Jesus, how am I going to explain to her that I failed her . . . that her mother is dead? I'm numb, unable to move or speak. I drop to my knees and pray for some sort of guidance. I've won some cases and lost some, but this one has hit me hard. I haven't felt this lost since the day my mom died. Maybe because I was the same age as Stella and I also witnessed her losing her life to violence. I hear talking but it sounds like garbled voices. I look up and Simmons is handing me something. "What is this?"

"Effy was being held in one of the bedrooms. She left a letter for Stella. I figured you would want to be the one to read it to her."

"One sec," I say to him before I step into the kitchen to wash the blood off my hands before I even think of touching the letter. Even if I can't see it, I still feel it. I should have tried harder. I've always told MJ I'm nobody's hero and this just proved it. I take the letter and stare at it for a long time. I'm having an internal debate with myself. Do I read it or just put it away for her? I feel like I'm invading her privacy, but I know she would want me to relay her message to Stella. I try to stop my hands from shaking as I read the letter.

Stella

I'm never really gone.

I carried you for every second of your life. Now, you will carry me in your heart forever.

I will be by your side through good times and bad. With angel wings wrapped around you in this turbulent storm called life.

The memories of us will be etched in your heart forever.

I love you. Mommy

I get up, fold up the letter and put it in my pocket. I need to keep moving. I need to stay focused. The sun is rising and the threat is still not over. Tommy is still out there—somewhere. And that means he's still a threat to Stella.

"Fitz, the crime scene unit is here now. I've instructed them to bring all the electronics back to the station. Maybe Travis can get more information from them. I've got to get back to the station. I think the senator will want to hear what happened in person."

"I'll go with you. Maybe Travis has found something else on the other computers he was working on. Maybe he can find out where Aafii's father is."

MJ

Ever since we were kids, Fitz has loved coming up here. He said the mountains calm him and clear out the clutter in his head. We are polar opposites. Personally, I don't understand it. Fitz hates bugs and, sweet baby Jesus, there are huge bugs that I've never seen before. Noisy, too! How do people get any sleep? I have never liked the country. Put me in the city and I thrive. I feed off the hustle and bustle. The good thing about the seclusion here is that Stella can enjoy running around outside.

She has been up since the crack of dawn. Right now, I'm glad she's outside with Andy. Hart has the news on and every station is covering the rescue of the five missing girls. They keep playing the same clip of them at Heathrow on a continuous loop. I'm about to shut it off when they interrupt with breaking news. Effy McPhee was murdered. My heart sinks. I keep trying to call Fitz and text him but nothing goes through. "Captain, how do you stay here with such crappy service?"

"That's why I love it here. I can truly disconnect from the outside world. I have a landline but last night's storm knocked it out. If you want, we can go into town, maybe Woodstock. I don't know all the details, but it sounds like it will be safe for us to head back to the city."

"Okay, maybe then I can get a call in to Fitz. I'm going to go get Stella, please shut that off."

"Are you going to tell her about her mother?"

"No, I'm going to wait until Fitz can be there." I'm just staring out the big picture window, watching Stella and Andy throwing all the leaves in the air. I want my brother to be happy; family means everything to him. The fact that Stephen doesn't want one is breaking Andy's heart. Now, we have to explain to this little girl that her mother is gone. The one person that was her whole world will never be there again.

"MJ, what's wrong?"

"I'm worried not only about this sweet little girl, but Fitz. This could be what breaks him."

"Fitz's love for you is very powerful. Effy's death will hit him hard, but he has you and his family and that's what keeps him going. Come on, let's gather everyone up and head into town. It will do us all a world of good."

He's right, all I can do is be there for Fitz, support him. Mr. And Mrs. Chen didn't want to go out so Hudson and Sal offered to stay behind, too. We load up my car and Hart drives us into town. A nice, sleepy, country town will do us all some good.

Fitz

We drive in silence. It seems to take forever but really it's only twenty minutes. Simmons pulls up front and there is a mob of reporters. I can't face them, not now. "Don't stop here; pull around back."

We get inside and I find Travis and Olivia still hard at work. Olivia sees me and wraps me in her arms. "Fitz, you did all you could." I know she means well, but right now I need my wife. She is the only one who can help me.

"This isn't over. Travis, where are we at with Tommy's location?"

"I got into Inga's phone. Apparently, he is hold up in upstate New York at a hotel. He went up there to get his arm fixed up and to lay low. Vadik wanted him to find Stella before Aafii's men did."

I freeze, his words swirling around in my head. "Upstate? Where upstate? Exactly what did he say?!" I slam my fist down on the desk and everything rattles.

"He's in a Howard Johnson's in a place called Saugerties. I've never heard of it. Fitz, what's wrong?"

I pull out my phone and try to call MJ but it goes right to voice mail. “MJ is upstate.” I’m running out the door with Travis and Olivia following closely behind me. When we get into the car, I toss Olivia my phone. “Keep trying to get MJ or Andy on the phone.”

I hit the lights and sirens; my heart is in my throat. Travis has a knuckle grip on the dash. “Fitz, I thought they were in the safe house with Hart?”

“Hart didn’t know who to trust. We knew Brad was the leak but what if there were others. It would be too easy for someone on the inside to find the safe house. We decided to move them to his house in Haines Falls, just outside of Saugerties. But, if Hart saw the news he might think it’s safe to go out.”

“Andy? Andy? Can you hear me?” Olivia has the phone on speaker. She’s yelling and I’m praying Andy can hear her.

“You’re breaking up, Olivia. Why are you calling me from Fitz’s phone? Is he okay?”

“He’s fine, Andy, where are you?”

“We saw the news, we figured it was safe and we could go out for a bit. We’re in Woodstock, tooling around the town. We are just going into Candle Stock. We’re trying to keep Stella busy. Are you on your way up here? If you are, Mr. And Mrs. Chen didn’t want to go out so Sal and Hudson are still at the house with them, they can let you in.”

“Andy, shut up and listen. Get everyone and go right back to Hart’s place. Tommy is in Saugerties and he’s looking for Stella. We’re on our way. Andy? Andy? Can you hear me?! Ugh, fucking technology. The call dropped. I don’t know if he heard me.”

“Olivia, try Hudson and Sal, for God’s sake—try everyone!” This is the longest one hundred twenty-five miles of my life. “Travis, what else did you find out?” I glance over at him and he loosens his death grip on the dash. He pulls out a pad from his bag.

“Please, Fitz, keep your eyes on the road. I’ve got most of the pieces of this puzzle together. It seems that Jin really did stumble upon a sleeper cell. I checked and none of the other agencies knew anything about it. I'm still getting information on Hudson's father. I'm not sure if he got greedy or if he wanted out. Either way, we now know his death was not an accident. We know he owned the holding company that the wires went to. Remember he was the head of an international bank? Well, that was the same bank that Hudson did her internship with."

"Are you fucking kidding me?! She's with my family, Travis!"

"Calm down, Fitz. I'm willing to bet that she didn't know what her father was doing. The girls were working on their final project for months. I think her father wanted her to do her internship at his bank. He was able to keep close tabs on her. If she got too close, he could steer her in a different direction. It wasn't until after her father died that she found the wires. Maybe if she would have found them before he died, things would be different. Maybe he planned it that way. It's something he took to the grave with him."

"What about the father stealing the money, was that just a diversion or something?"

"Once I started to put all the pieces together, I realized that some of the money he stole was from Aafii's father's account. He got caught and that's how he got sucked into this whole mess. From the research I've done, I found that Leland Townes was not involved with these people for long, just long enough to get himself killed. Hudson's parents have been dead for about eight months. She moved into her apartment six months ago. Right after that, Jin moved in and Hudson found the wires."

"But according to Debbie, they've been selling girls on the black market for years. So how did they get the money wired out if Leland Townes only just recently got mixed up with them?"

"I'm sure they have a lot of different sources that they use. That's why I think the deal should be made with Debbie. I feel like she has the most useful information. She's been keeping the books for a long time. Follow the money and cut off the money—that's what's going to work on these people. I need time to dig around Aafii's computer. Hopefully, that will lead me to his father and the sleeper cell."

"I agree, Debbie should get the deal and the others should rot in hell. Let's hope the feds listen to us for a change."

"Do you know where this Howard Johnson's Hotel is that Tommy's hold up at?"

"Yeah, it's right off the thruway. I've stayed there before. We still have two more exits to go. We'll stop at the hotel first. With any luck, he'll still be there." I press further on the gas pedal. Hold on, MJ, I'm coming.

MJ

Messing around in Woodstock is a welcome break from the solitude of Hart's house. Honestly, I love the man but he can be overbearing at times. Fitz and Andy would come up here every chance they could. Even after Andy had to give up driving, Fitz always made it a point to bring him here whenever he wanted.

"Andy, after we hit the candle store let's take Stella for ice cream."

"MJ, trying to bribe me with ice cream is not going to get me out of my favorite store any faster," he informs me.

I continue waddling up the steps of the shop and make my way inside. This store was an old house, so the rooms are very small. In the center of the store is a giant wax sculpture that they have been burning since I was a kid. It goes from the floor to the ceiling. They just keep sticking more candles on it. Add to that all the shelves and tables everywhere and it's a nightmare to move around. Either my ass or my belly is going to do some damage in this place.

"Have you tried calling Fitz back, again? I tried on my phone but I have no service at all. Honestly, I don't know how anyone can live up here." I groan. Hart laughs—no doubt—at my frustration. I'm the poster child for city girl.

"MJ, I'll go outside and try calling Fitz. He was probably trying to let us know what happened. You and Andy can take your time in here. Give me your packages, too. It's hard enough to navigate around in here, let alone being pregnant with lots of shopping bags."

"Okay, let me know if you get a hold of him."

Thankfully, it's not that crowded in here so we decide to start upstairs and then work our way back down. The music is a little too loud and the scented candles are a little too much for me, but my brother loves this place, so I'm trying to enjoy it too. Half way up the steps, Stella stops, her eyes following all the colors from the floor to the ceiling wax statue. She's got the most beautiful smile. We head the rest of the way up and into the first room. Andy and I are looking up at a design on the ceiling when Stella grabs my hand and starts to violently shake. Andy and I crouch down in front of her and try to calm her, but nothing is helping. We look around the room to scc what could have possibly scared her, but there is no one here.

"Stella, you're safe baby. No one is here. Andy, we need to get her out of here. Something has spooked her."

I hear a car engine backfire and then the place gets really quiet. No music, no noise at all. I look up at Andy and he is deathly silent, his eyes are wide and he's not moving. When I look over my shoulder to see what has caught Andy's attention, I see him. The man from Stella's sketch. He's got a gun pointed at me at and he's bleeding. I realize that wasn't a car backfiring, it was a gunshot.

"Get up, bitch, now!"

As I slowly rise I pull Stella close to me, her face hidden from his. "What do you want from us?" I'm next to the window and when I glance out I can see cop cars and Hart in the middle of the street, looking up.

"Back away from the window. I want you to stop this bleeding and then I want the kid."

He moves his jacket aside with the butt of his gun to show me where he's bleeding from. "I'm not a doctor, I don't know what to do with that."

"Well, I guess you're going to have to learn real quick and, if you do, you just might make it out of this alive."

"Andy, take Stella."

"MJ, no," he states sternly to me then turns back to this guy, "I'll stop the bleeding, just let them go. Look, the last thing you need is a pregnant lady and a kid. Not if you expect to get out of here in one piece."

He's quiet and the color is draining from his face, a face of pure evil. He takes the butt of his gun again and looks at his shoulder. He swings the gun towards Andy and then lowers it towards Stella. In an instant, I know if I don't do something, she is going to die. In one quick sweep, I pick up a mirrored, round candleholder and pitch it right at his head. He stumbles when he tries to block it. His hand with the gun goes up, too. He gets a shot off anyway just as I step in front of Andy and Stella.

Chapter Twenty-Six

Fitz

We finally get to the exit and my heart is racing. Something bad has happened, I can feel it. My heart is in my throat and the feeling of dread is coursing through my veins.

The hotel is right off the exit and this time of year, it's filled with people who are leaf peeping. When I get inside, I find the manager staring at the TV with his mouth hanging open. When I look up, I see the police have surrounded the Candle Stock store. Tommy's picture is also on the screen. They are saying he has hostages. Fuck!

I run out just as Travis is getting out of the car. "Fitz, I turned on the police scanner and there is a hostage situation in Woodstock, it's Tommy."

"I know I saw it on the TV. Get in we've got to get there."

"Do you know where it is?"

"Yeah, it's Andy's favorite store here." We get as close as we can to the store but all the streets surrounding the store are closed off. We get out and hit the ground running. I'm not a fast runner but today, I could win a gold medal. Travis and Olivia are following close behind me. The police are trying to hold us back. I show them my badge and they don't give a shit. That is, until Travis and Olivia show their FBI credentials. All doors open, then. When we get closer, I see Captain Hart by an ambulance.

"Fitz, Andy told me that Olivia called but he couldn't make out anything she said. MJ tried to call you too, but the service was so bad, so I told them I would go outside and try to get a hold of you to see what you wanted. The store wasn't that busy and everyone was already heading upstairs. I told them I would meet them out front when they were done. I was trying to call you and when I turned around, I saw him in the window of the store. He must have been in one of the little rooms. I went back inside and he was headed up the steps. I began quietly getting the few people that were downstairs out of the store. I looked up at the landing and that's when he saw me. He pulled out a gun. I got my shot off first and I nailed him in the shoulder. His shot only grazed me. I think the only ones left in the store are MJ, Andy, and Stella, but I can't be sure. Fitz, there was another shot fired."

My heart is in my throat and it sounds like a freight train is running through my head. "What's the plan? Has anyone made contact with him?"

"I'm Sargent Lewis, I'm in charge here. We've tried to make contact with him, but, as of yet, he hasn't picked up the phone. The plan is we let them sit for a bit and then we shut off the electric. After that, we wait. It's getting dark; eventually he'll want to talk to us."

"Wait! Wait! Are you fucking kidding me? My family is being held at gunpoint by a derange murderer. A man who thought nothing of drugging a six-year-old. Hell, he thought he killed her, and your bright idea is to freeze him out?!"

"You need to stay back and let me do my job. I assure you, I know what I'm doing."

Do his job? I'm not about to leave my family in his hands. Travis nudges me and then walks back towards Hart. I follow his lead. "Travis, tell me you have a plan, please."

"I do. There is an exit behind the building that leads into a parking lot. I'm going to go in the front door. I don't look anything like a fed or even a cop. While I do that, you go in the back door. I'll cause some sort of distraction that should buy you enough time to get in without being noticed," Travis relays his plan.

He takes off his jacket off and rips the sleeves off his shirt. Travis has some of the most extensive artwork I've ever seen. "How are you going to get this past Sargent Lewis?"

He pulls out his FBI credentials and flashes them to me before he goes up to Lewis and tells him that the FBI has just taken over. After a minute or so, he walks back over to us. "He's not happy, but he is offering his help, if we need it. Lewis gave me these ear buds. At least we can stay in contact. Olivia will go in with me. We are just a couple, messing around Woodstock." I'm about to leave when he grabs my arm, holding me back. "Fitz, are you sure you can do this?"

"No one is going to stop me."

"Okay, then let's do this."

I head around back, staying close to the wall. I try the door, it's unlocked, but I can't remember if there is a bell on the back door or if it's just on the front. I try to look up and see but it's too dark. One wrong decision could cost everyone their lives. I've got a clear line of sight from the back door to the front. I've got to wait for Travis's distraction. My heart is pounding so hard, I can hear it in my ears. I can finally see Travis start to open the door and I open mine at the same time. I glance up and notice the chimes over the back door. I silently thank God that I waited. There is only one staircase and it faces the front door. I'm tucked up against the wall, right below the landing. I make sure I'm staying out of Tommy's sight. I'm watching Olivia, she is still by the front door with Travis. I'm hoping she can, at least, give me some sort of sign as to what she's seeing. It's still deathly silent and that silence is playing into my biggest fear—losing my family. Finally, I hear the creaking of floorboards and then I hear Tommy. "Get out there and get rid of them. If you make one wrong move I swear I'll shoot the bitch right in her belly and then the kid." It comes out like a growl but I can hear him clear as day. I lean out just a little and I can see Andy's feet but nothing else.

"Sorry, guys, we had to close up early. Big inventory came in and we need to restock everything before another storm hits."

"Well, the door was open and we're already inside. Man, it's cold outside, can't we just look around a little? I promise we'll buy something."

"I'm really sorry but I've got to follow the boss's orders. I can't afford to lose my job." I see Andy take a few steps forward, out of the view of the doorway. He must be signing to Olivia, knowing that he can sign very fast and she will get it. Her eyes grow wide and her face turns white. Dear God, please protect my family.

Travis holds his hands up, "Okay, we get it. I wouldn't want you to lose your job over us. Thanks anyway." I watch them leave, unsure what Andy said to Olivia. I have to somehow lure him away from that room.

"I did what you said, now keep your part of the bargain. She's bleeding bad, let me bring her downstairs so she can get some help."

Either Stella or MJ has been shot. The sweat begins running down my spine.

"I don't give a fuck about her, and if you don't shut up, the next bullet will be in you. Now where the hell is the first aid kit?"

"I don't know. I don't work here. Maybe somewhere downstairs.

Do you want me to go look for it?"

"Let go of me!"

Oh my God, MJ. *Hold on, baby.*

"Leave her alone. I'll find the kit. It's got to be downstairs, either under the counter or maybe the bathroom. Just let me go look for it."

"Fine, do it now and make it fast."

I hear the creaking of the floorboards and then Andy comes down the steps. He looks up and then waves his hand directing me towards the bathroom.

"Andy, what's the status up there?" My voice barely above a whisper.

"MJ's been shot and has lost a lot of blood. Stella is in shock, on the floor rocking back and forth. Tommy's been shot in the shoulder and he's also lost a lot of blood."

"What's taking you so long? You've got two minutes to get back up here or I start shooting again!"

Andy begins banging some stuff around making some noise. "I'm looking for it damn it!"

I find the kit and pass it to him. "Go, do whatever he says. We need him to stay calm."

I grab a small, wooden chair and pass it to him. "Take that, too. Get him to try and sit in the chair and get everyone away from him."

"Make if fast, Fitz, and you better not fucking miss."

I grab a mirrored plate that a candle is sitting on and follow him up the steps, making sure I stay against the wall. I stop just one step before the landing and watch Andy go inside. At least now I'm closer.

"What's the chair for?"

"You're bleeding like a dead pig. I need to stop it. I can't do that with you standing up. You're a good foot taller than me. I also need you to take off your jacket. Look if you don't want to sit then fine,

MJ can sit."

"Forget about her."

"MJ, there's some absorbent compresses in the kit. Take one and start applying pressure on your wound."

"I told you forget about her. Give me that chair."

"If you want my help to stop the bleeding, you need to do what I tell you. Now, take off your jacket and have a seat."

"What if I shoot you?"

"Then you'll die for sure."

It's quiet and I'm praying that Andy's ploy works. Finally, I hear the creaking of the chair.

"You better not try anything."

"You're the one with the gun, I'm just a man with the bandages."

I'm trying to angle the mirror so I can see into the room but it's not big enough. I hear the floor creaking again.

"Where are you going?"

"It looks like the bullet when right through. I need to get the antiseptic from the first aid kit. Or would you rather die from an infection?"

If this is going to happen, it needs to happen now. It's getting dark and the electric is off. Andy's making a lot of noise and for me, it's now or never. I take that last step and swing around into the room. Tommy has his gun pointed at MJ. Andy is crouched on the floor next to her and Stella. There's a lot of blood and when Andy sees me, he covers them with his body. I take the shot. In that split second, I see my whole life laid out before me.

Chapter Twenty-Seven

I got my shot off before Tommy had a chance to react. He fell out of the chair with my shot going right through his neck. I'm yelling for Travis to send up the paramedics. "MJ, please be okay." Andy gets up, keeping Stella wrapped up in his arms. He's trying to shield her from the gruesome scene.

"Fitz, she's lost a lot of blood. She took the fucking bullet for me! What the hell was she thinking?"

The paramedics are working on her as we're running out the door. Everything is a blur. The lights and sirens sound like background noise. Finally, her eyes flutter open.

"Fitz?"

"I'm here, baby. You need to fight, for you and our baby. MJ, fight hard."

She grabs a handful of my hair and yanks me towards her. "Fitz, no matter what happens, save our baby—*please*."

"Stop talking like that. You need to fight hard, MJ."

"Promise me, Fitz. Now!"

"Stubborn pig-headed woman. Fine—I promise, but so help me, MJ, you better fight like hell." She's out again. I've got a grip on her hand and I press it to my heart. Willing hers to keep beating.

We pull into the ambulance bay and it's like controlled chaos. One of the nurses pulls me away from MJ. "You need to let them work on her. The more information you can give me, the better it is for her. When is the baby due?"

"I need to be with her."

"Not yet. Now focus. When is the baby due?"

"We just went to the doctor and she said we were on schedule; six more weeks."

"Is she on any medications besides pre-natal vitamins?"

"No, nothing." I pull out my phone, bring up the doctor's information and pass it to her. "That's our OBGYN, you can get whatever you need from her. I need to be with my wife." I'm about to push past her when another nurse comes running over to us. "Mr. Rodriguez, you need to come with me now."

As we get to the area where they have MJ, a doctor steps out and pulls me aside.

"Your wife has lost a lot of blood. We are trying to stabilize her but the baby is in distress. We need to do a C-section now. Once the baby is out, we can repair the damage that the bullet caused and find out where she's bleeding from. The nurse will have you sign some papers and get you ready to be there when your baby is born." I don't have a second to ask anything. The clipboard is thrust in front of me and with the sweep of my pen we are running towards the operating room.

I'm following every direction, knowing that MJ and our baby's life is in the hands of complete strangers. MJ is in and out of it. I'm not sure if it's from the blood loss or something they gave her. They let me stay by her side. I lift her hand and place it on my heart. Willing her heart to keep beating with mine. I'm running through every prayer I've had committed to memory since I was an altar boy. *"Dear God, please, I'm begging you, please don't let this be another unanswered prayer. She's all that's good in me. She keeps me whole and humble. She's always been my true hero in a bitter life."*

"You need to move faster; her blood pressure is dropping!"

I hear a small cry and the doctor passes my baby to a nurse. "It's a boy." They have a team that begins working on him. I'm praying for him and for MJ, but time seems to stand still. The nurses put him in an incubator and I catch a glimpse of him as they take him out.

"MJ, it's a boy." Her grip on my hand goes soft, too soft. "MJ, please, baby. I can't do this without you." A nurse pulls me away and out of the room.

"You need to let them work on your wife. Come on, I'll take you to the neonatal unit and you can check on your son."

I don't know what to do? I've never been this lost. For the first time today, I'm not racing around. It's the doctors who are racing to save MJ and my son. He's asking me something but I can't concentrate on what he's saying. He's doing his best to distract me, but it's not working. All I can see is her delicate hand slipping from mine.

"Mr. Rodriguez, we're here. The doctors know that you are here and as soon as your wife is out of surgery, someone will come and get you. In the meantime, this is your son's nurse Emily, she will explain everything they are doing to help your little guy."

"Hi, Mr. Rodriguez, let's get you ready to meet your son."

She gives me all kinds of clean cover-ups to wear along with a mask. "You can call me Fitz."

"Okay, Fitz, most parents of preemies are overwhelmed when they first see their baby. There will be a whole bunch of different tubes and monitors. It's common to feel helpless. I'm here to guide you through everything. You can ask me anything. There is no such thing as a stupid question. Come on."

As she opens the door, I take a deep, calming breath and follow her inside. When I do, it's like walking into another world. It's warm, very warm. There are all kinds of beeping noises; it's distracting. I don't know where to look first. Nurse Emily pats me on the back and gently nudges me along until I see a sign: Baby Rodriguez. "He's so tiny."

"Actually, at three pounds, four ounces, he's bigger than the other babies in here."

I'm staring at him, watching his little chest move up and down. "Is he in pain?"

"No, not at all. The pediatrician checked him out and baring any complications, once his weight hits four pounds and he's able to eat and breath on his own, he will be moved to the regular nursery. The doctor will meet with you in the morning. For now Fitz, the sound of your voice and your touch will help him."

She passes me gloves to put on. I sit next to the incubator and put my hands through the holes. When I stroke his arm, he tries to wrap his tiny hand around my pinky. "Hey, little man, you need to fight hard, just like your mom is fighting right now." He kicks his tiny feet and then falls back to sleep. The constant beeping, that was originally distracting, is now soothing. The beeps mean life is continuing, in spite of ourselves. I don't know how much time has passed. The only thing I know is, I need MJ. *Please, God, I can't do this alone.*

"Fitz, I just got word that your wife is out of surgery. I've arrange for a volunteer to take you to the waiting room so you can meet with the doctor."

"Hey, little man, I'm going to see your mom. I promise I will be back soon. You just keep fighting." His little hands and feet are moving and his cap slides up just a bit to reveal a little whisper of red hair. Yeah, he'll fight hard, just like MJ will. I pull out my phone and take a quick picture before I go.

I leave the neonatal unit a lot calmer than when I got there. The volunteer is trying to make small talk but she sounds like one of those noise machines. When we get to the waiting room, everyone is there, everyone, that is, except Stephen. My mom has her rosary beads and I'm sure by now she has worn them out.

"Dad, how did everyone get here?"

"Lucas. When he heard what happened, he came and got us."

We're the only ones in the waiting room. When the door opens, out steps a very small lady. She calls out my name and we all quickly converge on her. "Mr. Rodriguez, there is a consult room just through those doors where we can have some privacy."

I hold my hand up stopping her. "You can tell us what's going on right here."

"Okay, I'm doctor Giulia. I operated on Makenna. Your wife was shot in the shoulder with a hollow point bullet. That type of bullet is meant to cause the most tissue damage when it expands inside the victim. It appears that your wife must have been moving or turned her body at the moment she was shot. Therefore, it wasn't a direct hit. That's probably what saved her life and the life of your baby. The bullet missed the brachial artery. It did, however, graze past the brachial plexus, which is the large nerve bundle. That bundle controls her arm function. I was able to remove the bullet and repair the damage to the surrounding area. I won't know if there's any nerve damage until she wakes up. She might have some problems with her shoulder and eventually she might need more surgery. We are going to keep her pretty sedated, so she will be out of it for the rest of thc night."

"When can I see her?"

"She's not out of the woods, yet, but I'm looking at this on a positive side. By all accounts, she's a very strong lady. I'm amazed that with the amount of blood she lost, she was still able to hang on and deliver the baby. She's in recovery now. I'm going to keep her in ICU overnight. If I like what I see, she will be moved to a private room in the morning. When we get her set up in ICU, I'll have someone come and get you. Please keep in mind that she needs rest.

ICU is immediate family and only one at a time." She looks over at everyone surrounding her and shakes her head.

"Thank you."

She leaves and now we are back to waiting again. "Dad, where's Andy?"

"Stella was in shock. The doctors gave her something. Andy is with her."

"Dad, it's going to be a while before we can see her. Maybe you can take everyone to see the baby." He squeezes my arm and pulls me closer to him.

"If you want to talk to Andy alone, the lady at the desk can tell you where he is. I'll take everyone to see my grandson now."

I wait until they all leave before I go in search of Andy. I need to know what happened in that room. I find him sitting on the bed with Stella tucked into his side. He's attached and, when the senator takes that child away, it will break him.

"Hey, what's the news on MJ and the baby?"

"MJ survived the surgery. The baby was in distress, so the doctor had to do a C-section. We have a son. He's in the neonatal unit and he seems to be doing okay. What's going on with Stella?"

"She went into shock. She was shaking so bad. The doctor sedated her and they said to keep her warm."

"Now that I'm calm and focused I need to know exactly what happened in that room? How did MJ get shot?"

"It all happened so fast. Stella saw Tommy before we even knew he was there. She began to violently shake, turning so pale. When Tommy finally entered the room, he was already shot in the shoulder. He wanted MJ to fix it. I tried to tell him to let MJ and Stella go, but he was crazy. He raised his gun. MJ grabbed a mirrored ball and threw it at him. Then stepped in front of Stella and me just has he got a shot off. I keep replaying it all in my mind. It all happened so fast. Right after that, you showed up."

"What the hell would possess her?" I'm pissed at my wife and know I shouldn't take it out on Andy, but he's here and MJ's not.

"Fitz, she's MJ. She is like a mama bear when it comes to her family. Face it, that's one of the things you love about her. Hell, I'm surprised that's all she did."

"You're right. I love that she will go toe to toe with anyone, but at what price?"

"You and I both know that you'll never be able to change her."

"I'm still pissed at her," I grumble under my breath. Andy chuckles lightly.

"How much does Stella know about her mother?" He pulls her a little bit closer, and it doesn't go unnoticed by me.

"She knows nothing. I kept her away from the television. What's going to happen to her?"

Stella begins to stir and her eyes flutter open. I'm not prepared to face her, yet. I don't know if I will ever be ready. "Take care of her, Andy," I whisper right before I hightail it out of the room.

I find the ICU and watch as they bring MJ in. Once she's settled in, the nurse lets me go inside. She's so pale; I feel my heart tighten in my chest. I sit next to the bed, take her hand in mine and press it to my heart. I need to keep the connection.

"MJ, I don't know if you can hear me, but fight hard, babe. Our son needs you. I need you. I can't do this without you. You're what's good in me." I look up and the nurse is wheeling Dad in.

"They will only let one person in at a time. Fitz, can you give me a few minutes with my daughter, please?"

I kiss her, "I love you, MJ, I'll be right outside that door." I don't know if she can hear me but I need her to know that I'm never too far away.

Chapter Twenty-Eight

I find Mom right outside the door and, for the first time, I can see how tired she looks. This case has taken a toll on all of us. I try to keep my work life away from my home life, but sometimes, the two collide.

"Mom, did you see your grandson?" That seems to bring a smile to her face.

"Of course! He's so tiny. Did you get to speak to the pediatrician?"

"Not yet. By the time I got to the neonatal unit, he was already gone. The nurse went over his notes with me and said that he's good. He will probably be moved to the regular nursery soon."

"How did all this happen? You said she would be safe at Hart's house."

Her words make the guilt I'm feeling rise front and center. "Once they saw the news that Effy was dead, they thought it was over and they could go out. They weren't expecting Tommy to be up here, none of us were."

"Please, is it finally over?" Her plea breaks my heart.

"Yes, although, there are some details that I still need to clear up. But, for the most part, the danger is behind us." I don't need to have her worrying over all the details. Especially since I don't have everything resolved yet. She has something else on her mind. I can tell when her wheels are spinning. "Mom, what is it?"

She wraps her arm with mine and pulls me a little bit closer. "What is going to happen to Stella?"

"I have to tell her that her mother is dead. I made a promise to Effy that I would protect her for the rest of her life. As she was dying, she begged me not to let Stella end up with her father. I don't know what I can do about that."

"She's very attached to Andy."

"Right, Mom, as if I didn't notice. Andy's very attached to her, too."

"Maybe I should talk to the senator."

"Maybe you should concentrate on MJ and your new grandson. Leave everything else up to me." Before she can answer me, Dad comes out of the room.

"Annie, I know that look; what are you up to now?"

"Nothing. I'm going to see my daughter now." She leaves in a huff and Dad shakes his head.

"What the hell is she up to?"

"Nothing, Dad. She's worried about Stella, that's all."

"I know your mother . . . she's up to something. I'll try to keep a close eye on her, but I'm not making any promises. The neonatal nurse wouldn't tell us much, even after Travis flashed his creds. What did the doctor say?"

"I won't get to speak to him until tomorrow but the nurse said the doctor checked him out and he's doing good." He turns his wheelchair so that he can see MJ through the glass entrance of the ICU.

"Just so you know, Travis got a call. The senator and the feds are on their way here to pick up Stella. Between your brother and your mother, I don't think they have a snowball's chance in hell of taking her."

"Damn it! I need to be the one to tell Stella what happened. I'm the one who broke a promise."

"For the record, you didn't break a promise. You're only human and what happened today should prove that to you. I'll stay here with MJ, you go handle it. Besides, your mother is probably saying the entire rosary, so she'll be awhile."

I don't know how much time I have left before they take her away, but I have to try and stop them. I already broke one promise, I can't break another. The hospital is a large maze but, by some small miracle, I find Andy and Stella in the emergency room huddled together. Stella is asleep again.

"Fitz, you're out of breath, is everything okay?"

"Listen, I promised Effy before she died that I wouldn't let Stella end up with her father. I just found out that the senator and the feds are on their way here to pick her up. I can't let that happen. What did the doctor say?"

"When she wakes up, she'll be discharged and that she needs to follow up with her regular doctor. They said her doctor can prescribe therapy closer to home. What's your plan?"

"I don't have a plan per se, but I think hiding out at Hart's place will be a good thing. They won't be able to find you right away. It will give me time to talk to the senator and then figure out what I'm going to say to Stella."

I see the nurse heading towards the desk with a wheelchair and I flag her down. I look at her name tag: Nancy. I got this. I put on my biggest "I lost my puppy" look, as MJ calls it, and get ready to charm her.

"Is everything okay in here?"

"Hi, Nancy, we need your help. We were getting ready to leave when I noticed the TV news and all kinds of crowds out front. It's my niece's birthday and I got her a pony that I rescued from the

Animal Sanctuary in Saugerties. She is going to be so excited, but, as you know, she's deaf. I'm afraid with the huge crowd and all the flashing lights, she will be really scared. I don't want her to be upset when she meets her new pony. Is it possible that we can leave by a different exit?" Let's see, I covered animal rescue and protecting a child from the media. If that doesn't tug at her heartstrings, I don't know what else could.

"Well, I was just coming over to let you know that the doctor signed her release papers. I wouldn't want her to be upset when she meets her new pony. There is a back entrance on the east side of the building. If you want you can get your car and meet us there."

"Nancy, you're the best. I'll text her other uncle to meet us there."

Me: Bring the car around back to the east side of the building. Don't let anyone know you're leaving.

Hart: okay.

Andy climbs into the wheelchair with Stella safely in his arms. We head through the different corridors and before we know it, we're out back. "Thank you so much, Nancy."

Andy climbs in the back of the car with Stella still asleep in his arms.

"Fitz, how long do you think you can keep her away from her grandfather?"

"Long enough for me to have a nice talk with the man. Hart, do not leave that house unless you hear it from me." He winces at my words, no doubt they sting. I watch them drive away and take a moment to clear my head. There are still pieces of this puzzle that I need to look into further. Like Hudson's father and his dealings, for one, and Aafii's father, for another. Then, there's the sleeper cell. For now, I want to check on my wife and my son. Then, I'll have a meeting with the senator.

First stop is the neonatal unit. I want to take some more pictures to show MJ. Nurse Emily sees me and comes out to get me. I'm glad security is tight, but I think I'm going to have Lucas put someone here, too. Better safe than sorry.

"He's doing really well. Have you decided on a name for him?"

"My wife and I have a name picked out, but I want her to see him to be sure. I want to take a couple of pictures for her."

"Okay, let me help you. We need to make sure to get one without the cap on. He's got the most gorgeous red hair."

"Yeah, he got that from his mom." I snap a few pictures before he falls fast asleep again.

"Thanks again for all your help. I'm going to show these to his mom."

Me: Hey, can you put someone on baby watch please?

Lucas: Is something wrong? Has there been a threat?

Me: No, but better safe than sorry.

Lucas: Kevin is here; I'll put him on it.

Me: Thanks.

Lucas: Travis is looking for you, the feds want Stella.

Me: Gee, I've been so busy with MJ and the baby, I don't know what happened to Stella.

I'm on my way to ICU when Travis intercepts me. "Hey, Travis, heard you're looking for me, what's up?"

"I've held the senator and the feds off for as long as I could. They want Stella. I checked and she's already checked out."

"I need to check on MJ and then I will sit down with the senator. Can you buy me a little bit more time, please?"

"Okay, but hurry."

The words are barely out of his mouth and I'm already heading down the hall to ICU. When I get there, Mom and Dad are in with her. I swear we are a family of rule breakers. I'm about to go in when the nurse stops me.

"I made an exception for them, but now they need to let her get her rest."

"Thank you. I know how they can be. Has my wife woken up, yet?"

"No, but she should be coming around soon. I'll go in and check her vitals. I'll tell your parents to step out and then you can deal with them." She bites her smile back. They come out of the room and I just shake my head. It doesn't matter what I say, they will do whatever they want.

"When the nurse is finished, I'm going to spend some time with MJ. Did you guys get a hotel, yet?"

"No and we're not leaving here without my daughter and grandson."

"Mom, I swear you are the most stubborn woman I know, well, except for MJ. It's going to be days, maybe even weeks before we can leave here. There is a hotel a couple of blocks from here. Why don't I have Olivia take you? Besides, I know MJ would feel better knowing that you're not sitting here. You don't want her worrying about you and Dad. She needs to put all her energy towards getting better. You know, the longer it takes for her to get better, the longer your grandson is without his mother." Damn I'm good. I can throw out the guilt trip along with the best of them.

"Annie, he's right. We can get a hotel room near here. We can be back here first thing in the morning."

"Okay, but you have to promise that if anything changes, you will call us right away."

"I promise. Olivia is out front. I'll text her that you're on your way."

Me: Hey, can you please do me a favor and take my mom and dad to one of the local hotels?

Olivia: I already have the hotel holding three rooms. When they are ready, I will take them over.

Me: They are on their way to you now. You're the best. Thanks.

When I head into MJ's room, the nurse is just finishing up. I pull the curtain so we can have some privacy. She's starting to stir and, finally, her eyes slowly open. "Hey, beautiful. You're safe and so is the baby."

"I vaguely remember; he is so tiny. Where is he?"

"He's in the Neonatal Unit. I have pictures for you." I quickly bring them up on my phone.

"Oh my God, Fitz. Look at his hair."

"I know, beautiful, right?"

"He's going to get picked on for it. He has your chin. I want to see him."

She's trying to get up and I won't have any of that. "You need to rest. When we get the okay from the doctor, I will bring you to see him. For once in your life, you will follow the rules." Her bottom lip begins to quiver and now I've made her cry. "Shhh come on, babe. Don't cry."

"You don't understand. I'm a terrible mother. I stepped between that man and Andy and Stella. I didn't give any thought to my own child. Now he's a preemie and will be faced with all the complications that go along with it. All because of me."

"Oh, for the love of Pete! Faced with the same situation all over again, you would have done the same thing. It has nothing to do with your skills as a mother. You're a protector—you always have been—and nothing you can do will ever change that. I love you and all your wild ways that make me crazy. Now, we seriously need to give this child a name. I know we have a few picked out and we said we would pick one when we saw him." She takes my phone and flips through the pictures.

"I look at him and all I see is the name, Patrick Fitzgerald Rodriguez. Are you okay with that one?"

"Totally. It's a strong name and he's a strong boy."

"How long will he be in the NICU?"

"When he hits four pounds and can eat and breath on his own. It shouldn't be too long. We are meeting with the pediatrician tomorrow. For now, the best thing you can do is rest."

"Where is Stella and Andy?"

"I had Hart take them back to his place. No one knows where that is, so that bought me some time."

"Time for what?"

"I have unanswered questions."

"Do you want to talk about it?"

"Not yet."

"Okay, what did the doctor say about my shoulder?"

"They don't know if you have any nerve damage and eventually you might need another surgery." She closes her eyes and tries to move it but nothing happens.

"I can't move it or feel anything." Her eyes pool with tears that she's trying to hold back.

"There's a pain blocker in the area. You won't be able to do anything just yet. That's why I said to rest. You are not Wonder Woman and the sooner you realize it, the better this will be for all of us." My words came out harsher than I would have liked. "I'm sorry, I didn't mean to sound like a bully. I love you, MJ. Let me carry the load for a while." I lean in and rest my forehead on hers. Gently tugging at her bottom lip.

"Excuse me, Mr. Rodriguez, there are some people outside to see you. I sent them to the waiting room. I don't care how important they claim to be, Mrs. Rodriguez cannot have all these distractions. She needs to get some rest."

I gently kiss her lips and when I turn to get up, the nurse looks like she's primed for a fight. Both hands on her hips and a stern look on her face. I give her my biggest smile. "Thank you so much for looking after my wife. You are really special." Left her speechless. Now I head out to the waiting room, knowing full well it's the senator that's waiting for me.

This time of night, the only ones in the waiting room are the senator, secret service, and Federal Agent Simmons. "What can I do for you gentlemen tonight?"

"Where is my granddaughter?"

"She's in protective custody until this case is closed, but you know that already."

Senator McPhee's cheeks flush and he looks like he might blow a gasket. "The case is closed detective; my daughter is dead, no thanks to you."

"Me! I did everything I could possibly do to find her with no help from any of you." I wave my hand around as if it would somehow help prove my point. Simmons moves in closer towards me.

"Fitz, what did Effy sign to you as she was dying and where is the letter I gave you?"

"I still have the letter because I have not had a moment to sit down with Stella and tell her what happened. As far as what Effy said, she begged me not to let you, Senator, end up with Stella. That was her dying declaration."

His face was red before; now he's nuclear. "You can't possibly know my relationship with my daughter and you can't keep me from my granddaughter."

"How about we make a compromise? For now, let's leave her in protective custody. This case is not over. There are lose ends that need to be tied up. You're in the middle of the vetting process for your appointment as vice president. The last thing you need is to be caught up in this mess. When all this is done, then we can figure out what you want to do with Stella. She's a special child with special needs. I'm not saying you can't handle it; we all know you can just buy help, but that might not be what's best for Stella. Let the dust settle and after I tie up all the loose ends, we can get together. How does that sound?" Geez talk about laying on the bullshit thick. My only hope is that he will become so busy being a VP that he'll let me keep Stella.

"How long?"

That just proved my point. If he really loved this kid, he would be fighting me tooth and nail. "A couple of weeks. I promise to keep in touch with you on a regular basis."

"Okay, it seems it would be best for Stella. I will be in constant meetings on the hill for the next couple of months. There is no one to take care of her just yet."

He gets up, shakes my hand, and just like that, he's out the door. What a dickhead.

Chapter Twenty-Nine

While MJ slept through the night, I went to check on Patrick. He sleeps a lot. The nurse said that's perfectly normal. She also let me know that the pediatrician will be by at ten to speak to us. It's very early in the morning, but there's a twenty-four-hour diner across the street. When I get inside, I find Sal and Hudson having breakfast. I put my to-go order in and then slide into the booth next to Sal. I want to watch Hudson's reaction when I question her.

"Why are you here?"

"I need to get back to the city. I have classes to go to but I wanted to stop by and see how MJ is doing."

"I can't force you to stay here, but you need to know that your father was involved with this whole mess." Her fork freezes in mid-air.

"What do you mean involved? Why the hell would you think my father was involved in any of this? He died before all of this happened."

"Tell me what you know about your father?"

"He stole money from his clients' accounts. That's it. What the hell do you know about him?" She puts her fork down and pushes her plate of pancakes away from her.

"Your father owned the holding company that all the wires went to."

"No he didn't. Why would my father be involved in any of this? Why would he own a holding company?"

"Until this case is completely wrapped up, I can't go into details. I promise you I will find out everything. But just know that if you go back to the city, back to your everyday life, I can't guarantee your safety. There's still too many unknowns."

"What am I supposed to do, stay hidden in that god forsaken cabin forever?"

"I'm not saying forever, but give me a little bit more time."

"Sal, do you agree with him?"

"I promised you I would look into your father's case. I can take whatever information Fitz has gathered and run with it. I can contact your professors and make arrangements for you to enter your stuff online. It's better to be safe than sorry."

The waitress comes by to top off their coffee and to let me know my order is ready. Hudson closes her eyes and rubs her temples. "Fine, if you can arrange it with my professors, I will stay put. But, you have to tell me everything you find out about my father. I don't care how bad it is, I need the truth."

"Deal. Now, I need to get back inside. As soon as I find out anything, I will let you know." I pick up my order and head back across the street.

When I get to ICU, MJ's bed is empty. I'm about to freak out when the nurse informs me that she has been moved to a private room closer to Patrick. I head out to find her room when something

Hudson said hits me.

Me: Hey, did you get a list from the IRS on what they seized from Leland Townes?

Travis: Let me pull his file, hold on. Okay, got it. Now what are you looking for?

Me: I'm not sure. Can you email it to me?

Travis: Sure, How's MJ and the baby?

Me: They are good. I want to know more about Ginger Townes, and her mom and dad.

Travis: Okay, I'll email you whatever I find. Give MJ a hug from me.

When I finally find MJ's room, she is sitting up in a chair. "Hey, beautiful, how are you feeling?"

"Ready to meet my son. Please tell me you've got some decent coffee in one of those bags."

"Coffee and a full breakfast. After you eat we can go to the nursery."

"I still can't feel anything in my arm. I tried moving it and it's dead. The nurse said the pain block wears off in twenty-four hours, so I should start feeling something soon. She said it starts with a feeling of pins and needles. Fitz, if I can't lift Patrick, how am I going to take care of him?"

"That's what you have Andy and me for. I don't want you worrying about what ifs. We've got this all covered."

"What about Stella?"

"I spoke with the senator and, for now, she is staying with us."

"Does Andy know?"

"Not yet. I haven't told Stella yet that I failed her and her mom is dead."

She reaches for my hand and pulls me closer to her. "You gave it your all. You can't blame yourself that you couldn't save her. Life will go on for her. Now, do you want to tell me what else is going on?

Don't say nothing, because you suck at lying."

"I hate when you are always right. When I found Effy, she was still alive. That bastard slit her throat right in front of me. I tried to stop the bleeding but I couldn't. When the paramedics took over Effy began signing to me. She begged me not to let Stella end up with her grandfather. She pleaded with me to keep her safe. On top of that, Andy has become very attached to her. I see a lot of pain and heartache on the horizon and I don't know how to stop it."

She's real quiet, just sipping her coffee, but I can see the wheels turning. "Isn't there some sort of dying declaration or something that can allow Stella to stay with us as part of Effy's wishes?" she asks.

"I don't know. Simmons and the paramedics were there but I don't know if they understood what she was signing. Maybe Stephen can shed some light on this for us."

"Good luck with that one. He never once tried to get in touch with Andy while we were gone. Not that we had great service up there, but still. I talked to Andy for a bit and he seems to think it's over for them. Stephen did the worst possible thing anyone could do to a person with a disability. He used his disability as a weapon against him. He told him if Andy died, he didn't want to be stuck with a kid. I've watched Andy with Stella; he would make a great father."

This is really a lot worse than I thought. "No one can predict when they are going to die. It sounds to me like the problem is with Stephen and not Andy. Did they discuss having kids before they got married?"

"Yeah, Stephen would always put him off. He would say sometime in the future, or when we get settled more. The reality is, Stephen never wanted children, which is okay, but he should have been honest with Andy before they got married. Then Andy would have to live with whatever decision he made. Stephen took away

Andy's right to make his own decision."

I clean up our breakfast and help MJ into the wheelchair. "Well, my beautiful girl, enough sadness. Right now, you need to meet your son."

When we get outside the Neonatal Unit, MJ holds up her hand to stop me. I look down and realize she's crying. "Hey, what's with the tears?"

"What if I suck at being a mother?"

"Oh, for the love of Pete! You'll be a fantastic mom; now stop crying."

We head inside and I forgot how overwhelming it can be the first time in here. "After a bit, you'll get used to the beeping." When we get to Patrick, he's kicking his little legs and fisting his hands. I put a glove on MJ's good hand and now she's able to touch our son. He grabs her finger and he won't let go.

"See, he knows his mom is here."

"He's so tiny and so beautiful."

"Please tell me those are happy tears." Before she can answer, the pediatrician walks in and makes his way toward us.

"Hi, I'm Dr. Lancaster." He holds out his hand to shake mine. "Your son is doing great. Usually babies lose a little bit of weight when they are first born, but he's gained two ounces. Have you picked out a pediatrician, yet?"

"We actually live in Bay Ridge Brooklyn. We were just getting ready to interview a few but never got around to it."

"Okay, I can give you a list of recommendations in that area for you to choose from, if that will help. When you decide, I will forward everything on your son to his new doctor."

"How long do you think he will remain in here?

"He's really making great progress. I don't like to put a timeline on him but once he can eat and breath on his own and holds his weight above four pounds, he will be good to go."

MJ's listening to him talk but her eyes are focused on Patrick. "Will he go into a regular nursery or will he be able to go home?"

"We will slowly wean him off the NG tube. When he is fully off that, I will have him go into a regular nursery for a few days, just to make sure he maintains the weight. After that, we can send you home."

"Great, thank you." He leaves us and attends to other babies.

"MJ, did you hear what he said? He's doing great." I crouch down next to her and try to get a read on her emotions right now. She should be happy but she seems sad. I can't fix it if I don't understand it.

"I know, I'm just feeling a little bit, I don't know scared, overwhelmed maybe."

"You got this, babe. Give yourself a few days to rest up and you'll be just fine. Now, we need to get you back to your room. I'm sure your doctor will be making his rounds soon." I want to be there when he does so I can talk to him about how emotional she is. I'm sure it's normal but I need to make sure.

Chapter Thirty

We're only back in MJ's room for two minutes when Dr. Giulia shows up. I take a step back and let MJ ask the questions.

"Hi, Makenna, how are you feeling today?"

"The pain blocker has started to wear off. It's kind of hard to move around with only one arm. Plus, I have the incision from the C-section that's adding to the difficulty. When do you think I'll know if I've lost any use of my arm?"

"It's only been twenty-four hours since everything happened. I know you don't want to hear this but time really does heal all wounds. The best thing you can do for yourself and your baby is get as much rest as possible. The less stress you have, the quicker you will heal."

"What about breastfeeding my son? Will I be able to do that since I had surgery and I've had pain medication?"

"Is he eating on his own, yet, or is he still on the NG tube?"

"He still has the tube."

"Okay, that will give us some time. I can change your pain meds to something safer for the baby. The nurse can set you up right now to start pumping your breast milk. They can then feed your son through the NG tube. He will get all the benefits of breast milk. Now, back to your shoulder. Your arm will be kept in a sling. How long depends on how you heal. After that, you will have to have physical therapy three days a week. I'm hoping you will regain most of the use of your arm without having to have another surgery. We'll play this one day at a time. Do you have any other questions for me?"

"When can I shower?"

"You can't get that area wet, so, for now, only sponge baths. I'll be by tomorrow to check on you, again."

"Thank you."

The doctor leaves and MJ is just staring into space. "Hey, what's going through that head of yours?"

"I'm just trying to absorb it all without having a pity party or a meltdown. I want to make everything perfect for, Patrick."

"MJ, whose version of perfect?"

"You know I hate when you're right. Fitz, please sit next to me." She moves over a little in the bed so there's some room for me. "What happened with Effy?"

"You know what happened; she was murdered. Why are you bringing it up now?"

"Because, in some strange way, you're blaming yourself. You did everything you possibly could to find her."

"I know, but I promised Stella I would find her mom, and I wasn't able to keep that promise."

"Andy told me what happened in the candle store. Why did you step in front of them?"

"Fitz, do you blame me for getting shot?"

"Always right to the point, babe. My head says no, but my heart says yes." I don't want to upset her but with her face getting flushed, something tells me I have.

"When Mark Chambers took that shot, you dove in front of it

to save me. I loved you for saving my life and hated you for thinking my life was more important than yours. Just like you, I reacted on instinct. In that instant, I knew that Tommy was going to kill someone and I knew it would be Stella. He looked at her with such evil and contempt. When I threw the mirrored ball at him, it forced him to try and block it. His shot was high and would have hit Andy. I didn't think I just reacted. I hate myself because I should have been thinking of my baby. I turned, thinking I was shielding everyone. It was stupid, but I can't change what happened nor who I am. I'm always going to protect the ones I love. So, Fitz, please don't hate me. I've been doing that enough for both of us."

I reach over and wipe away her tears before I gently put my arms around her. "I don't hate you, I never could. We just need to promise each other that there will be no more crazy shit, okay?"

"Okay, I promise, but the same goes for you. Maybe your long vacation will help you not to bring your work home with you."

"I'll try—promise."

"When you talk to Stella about her mom, I want to be there. She's going to need a lot of love and support from all of us."

"I have a few loose ends to tie up before I do that. I also need to find a lawyer so I can find out what her rights are."

What's your plan for today?"

"I'm going to give my beautiful wife a sponge bath."

"Well, if you're going to do it, you better get started. Oh, and while you're at it, can you wash my hair?"

"Okay, when Mom and Dad get here, I can run to the store and get what we need. I'll text Dad to see where they are at."

Me: What time are you planning to get here?

Dad: We just got here. We'll be up in a minute.

"They are on their way up."

The door opens, Mom and Dad come in, their arms filled with bags and flowers. I help Mom with the flowers while she puts all the bags on the bed. I turn around and MJ is already rummaging through them.

"Did you buy out the store?"

"No, Travis and Olivia went by the Captain's house last night to check on Andy and Stella. While they were there, Olivia grabbed your overnight bag."

"How are they doing?"

"She said they are doing better. She can tell you all about it when she gets here. Now, what do you need me to do for you before I go see my grandson? Did you finally pick a name for him?"

I sit back down on the bed and take MJ's hand. "Yes, we did . . . Patrick Fitzgerald Rodriguez." Dad's eyes grow wide and I can swear I see a tear that he quickly wipes away.

"Thank you, both of you. I'm truly honored."

"Dad, he's a strong boy and he needed a strong name. Now, I'm going to help MJ with a sponge bath. Why don't you go spoil your grandson?"

They head out the door, while mom is reminding him not to let it go to his head.

"Are you up for your sponge bath?"

"There is a chair in the shower. The shower head is on a hose, so you won't get my shoulder wet."

"Wait, I thought I was going to sponge you all over."

"You are so weird. You can sponge me in the shower, happy?"

"Don't burst my bubble; I've been looking forward to this all morning." I scoop her up and carry her into the bathroom.

"I can walk, Fitz. The nurse said walking is good for me."

I kick the door closed behind me. "Let the fun begin!"

After MJ's sponge bath, she was so exhausted that she fell right to sleep. I don't want her to wake up with no one here, so I'll wait for Mom and Dad to come back. There's a light knock on the door and Olivia steps in.

"Oh, she's sleeping. I can come back later."

I wave her in and pull another chair in the room, close to mine. "Have a seat. Thanks for taking my mom and dad to see Andy last night. Tell me the truth, how are they doing?"

"Stella seemed better last night. I'm worried about Andy. He's very attached to her and I don't think he'll give her up without a fight. I asked him what he needs me to do for him and he said to get him a good attorney. I assured him I would. Fitz, what happened to Stephen?"

"Honestly, I'm not sure. I haven't had a minute alone with him since this whole thing started."

"Okay, well, if you need me for anything, you know I'm here for you. By the way, Travis went back to the city early this morning. He said he wanted to get to work on Aafii's computer."

"Did you get anything more from Jin's books?"

"Yeah, the wire that went to the secret service guy in Washington was sent directly from Aafii's father. It had nothing to do with the girls. And, Fitz, the VP was cremated so there is no way to prove or disprove Jin's theory."

"What about McPhee, is he clean in all of this?"

"Yes, there is nothing tying him to any of the girls or Aafii and his father."

"So, he's just your standard dirt bag."

"It would seem that way. Do you want to talk about what happened with Effy?"

"No, you don't need that shit in your head, too. Did Travis say who's getting the deal?"

"I haven't spoken to him since he got there. I'm sure he'll check in with you later. Do you want me to stay here with her while you go see the baby?"

"It's okay, I'm sure Mom and Dad will be back soon."

She's trying to hold in her laughter but she loses that battle. "Your dad is camped outside the NICU. He's got a sign with the baby's name on it. He's telling everyone that comes by that the baby is named after him. Does that sound like he's coming back up here anytime soon?"

"Maybe I should go and rescue my mom."

"Go, I've got a bunch of magazines. If MJ wakes up, I'll tell her you'll be back soon."

"Thanks."

Something Olivia said about the VP is bugging me. It's in the back of my mind but I can't bring it forward. I'm on the way to the NICU when I feel my phone vibrate. It's Travis calling.

"Hey, what's up?"

"Did Livy bring you up to speed on everything?"

"Yeah, have you found out anything new?"

"The feds gave Debbie the deal. You wouldn't believe how much we've gotten from her so far. The feds are hoping that they can find some of these other girls that have been sold over the years. I think it's wishful thinking."

"Did you find anything else about Leland Townes?"

"Debbie didn't have much on him, but Aafii, on the other hand, is another story. Leland has been in bed with Aafii's dad, Haidar EL-Hashem, for quite some time. It appears that prior to Leland opening up Crypto Holding Inc. Haidar sent wires directly to Leland. Once the wires started getting bigger and more frequent, Leland, with the help of Haidar, opened up the holding company. He was Leland's silent partner."

I head outside so I'm out of earshot of anyone. "What about Hudson? Does she know or was she in the dark?"

"She was in the dark. I found an email from Aafii to Leland where he blind copied Haidar. Aafii was worried that too many people knew about the holding company. He was worried that his father could be put in a difficult position if anyone found out that he was an equal partner in the holding company. Leland assured him that everyone was in the dark on who owned the company. According to Aafii's texted messages, it was only after Vadik killed Jin they found out she had a roommate named Hudson. He wasn't aware of her connection to Leland. Ironically, her name change probably kept her safe."

"Are the feds going reopen the case they started on Leland?"

"They already have."

"This means that Hudson can still be in danger. What about Haidar? What are the feds doing about him?"

"He's in the wind. We couldn't keep a lid on Aafii's death because of Effy. The news is all over it. Hudson is definitely still in danger. I think it's good that she's hold up with Sal at Hart's house. But, how long do you think you can keep her there?"

"Not long at all. I'm going to have to head over there to tell her everything we learned and tell Stella her mother is dead."

"Do you want me to come back up there?"

"No, stay where you are and keep doing what it is you do. Olivia is here and can stay with MJ. I'll let you know what happens."

I head back inside to check on my son and MJ is with him. I suit up and head inside. "I left you fast asleep, what happened?"

"I woke up right after you left and I wanted to see my son."

"Hey, how's he doing this afternoon?"

"The nurse said he gained a half an ounce. What's the matter?"

"I need to talk to Hudson and Stella. I know you wanted to be there but I need to go there now. I know the minute she sees me, she's going to ask about her mother."

"Okay. Maybe Andy can bring her here?" Her voice is barely a whisper.

"I know you want to be there when I talk to her, but I don't think bringing her here is a good thing. Olivia will stay with you till I get back. I don't think you're going to be able to pry Mom and Dad away from here."

"Tell her I'm thinking about her."

"Of course."

I take a minute to enjoy all things Patrick, snap a quick picture to show Andy, and then head out.

Chapter Thirty-One

The ride to Haines Falls is about a half an hour. It gives me the time to go over everything Travis came up with. That's when it hits me. I quickly dial Travis.

"Hey, not to long ago, Gail went to a seminar about cremation. I remember she was so excited to share what she learned with me. She said that the remains can be tested for so many different things. One of those things was testing for heavy metal based poisons."

"I heard about this. I'll give Gail a call and find out more."

"Okay, I'm heading up the mountain now so I'm sure I'll lose you. I'll check in later."

I hang up and run through my head what I'm going to tell Hudson. I don't know if she is going to believe me or not, but for her safety, she's going to have to try. The longer I think about it, the more I am dreading this part of my day. I navigate my way to his cabin and find Stella swinging on an old tire swing. Andy is pushing her and her laughter is contagious. Why can't the whole world be like this? Stella sees me, jumps off the swing, and comes running. I lift her up and twirl her around in my arms. I know right here, right now, I can't let her go to her grandfather. I *have to* find a way.

"Hey, Fitz, did you bring me some pictures of my nephew?"

I pass him my phone as we head toward the porch.

"Look at that hair! How's he doing?"

"He's getting stronger every day."

"Great, and MJ?"

"She's being hard on herself but she'll be okay. I need to talk to Hudson, but before I do that, I think it's time I tell Stella what's going on."

"Do you want me to go inside and give you some privacy?"

"No, it's best if she has us both here." I put her down on the bench. Andy takes the seat next to her while I pull the rocking chair in front of her.

"Did you find my mommy?"

How do I tell a six-year-old that her mother was murdered? "Do you know what heaven is?"

"That's where my daddy is. Mommy said he's an angel."

"Your mommy is with your daddy now. They are both angels watching over you."

"My mommy is up there with my daddy? I'm never going to see her again?" She points up to the sky and then begins to cry. "You said you would find her. You said you would bring her home, but you didn't do that. You didn't do what you said you would do. Why? Why? Why?" She's hitting me in the chest and crying.

"I tried but I . . ."

Andy gets up and crouches down in front of her. "Fitz, did everything he could to bring her home. Your mommy is with your daddy now. You will always have us."

I open my arms and she climbs into my lap. She's crying so hard and all I can do is hold her tight so she knows she is safe. My heart is breaking for her. As I rock back and forth, my mind flips back to that awful day when I was lying on the bathroom floor, looking out from under the door, watching my father beat my mother to death. I stayed in that locked bathroom for three days while she laid on the floor dying. Unfortunately, the last memory Stella will have of her mother is violent, as well.

I don't know how much time has passed, but Stella has fallen asleep. "Andy, I need to talk to Hudson, can you take her?" She stirs a little, but Andy takes my seat in the rocker and she falls right back to sleep.

I try to clear my head as I head inside to find her. Everyone is at the dining room table playing cards, except Hudson. She's knee deep in papers, which I'm guessing is her homework, that she has spread all over the living room floor.

"Hey, Captain, I don't mean to interrupt your game, especially since you have a large pile of pennies, but I need to speak to Hudson."

"Hey, Fitz, no problem. How's MJ and the baby?"

"They are both doing well."

Hudson closes her book and comes into the dining room. "Is everything over? Can I go back to my apartment now?"

"Far from it. Why don't we go for a walk out back?" There's a distinct chill in the air and she grabs her jacket as we go.

"This must be bad if you want to talk to me alone."

"How much do you know about your father's business?"

"Look, if you're going to tell me my father stole money from his customers, I told you this morning—I already know that. The IRS told me that when they took everything. The only thing I was left with was the house and two insurance policies."

"There's more, a lot more. I promised you I would find answers and I would keep you safe. Your father was involved in a lot more than you realize. Jin was murdered because she was on the verge of finding everything out. I told you your father was the owner of Crypto Holdings Inc. You didn't believe me, but now I have proof and . . . he had a partner."

"Wait, he had a partner?"

She's a smart girl; I won't be able to shelter her from everything her father did. I do, however, need to make her understand how much danger she is in. "His partner, Haidar EL-Hashem, is the father of Aafii El-Hashem. Aafii was the one who was buying the girls. He's the one who received the large wire in Queens."

Usually she is pointing a finger at me and giving me a piece of her mind. Instead she's staring at me like a deer in the headlights. "Was my father responsible for Jin's death?"

"Everyone who was involved in this played a part in her death."

"Why am I still alive? If what you're saying is true, then I should be dead, too. I mean, I helped Jin put all this together."

"Aafii and Vadik only found out Jin had a roommate after her death. Hudson, your father's involvement with Haidar goes back years."

"What should I do? I mean, if your daughter was in this position, what would you have her do?"

"I would have her stay in protective custody until I can make sure she was safe. Especially since Haidar is in the wind."

"How long?"

"I can't put a date on it."

One hand is on her hip and she's pointing her finger at me. Her face is almost as red as her hair. Her eyes are wide and for the first time I notice how blue they are. I brace myself for what's coming. "You can't put a date on it?! So, I have to give up my freedom indefinitely? Are you out of your fucking mind?! I have a life. I'm almost done with school. The world doesn't stop spinning so you can neatly wrap this case up in a box with a pretty, pink bow on top. I need other options and you need to come up with them."

"Why do I have to come up with them?"

"Why? Because you promised."

"I promised to find the answers and to keep you safe. I did my part. I can't help it that you don't like what I found. I also have a life.

I almost lost my wife and son over all of this!"

"What if I change my name, again?"

"You can't keep changing your name like you change your panties. What if you give the feds more time to find Haidar and go through all of the evidence they collected?"

"What about school?"

"I'm sure they can work with the school to let you turn everything in via email. They might even be able to let you Skype during lectures. Look, Hudson, you need to give it a try. Doing nothing will only get you dead." I'm waiting for her reaction and she begins to cry. Not what I was expecting. For the first time, I notice how young and vulnerable she really is. I pull her into my arms and let her cry.

"I'm sorry."

"There's nothing to be sorry about."

"Yes, there is. I wanted to know more about my father. Sal was going to help me with it. You know that saying 'careful what you wish for?' well, never in my wildest dreams did I think my father would be wrapped up in all of this. I didn't know what he was doing, but he was still my father. My mother and my best friend are dead and he had a hand in it. So, yeah, I'm sorry." She takes a step back and wipes her tears. "Fitz, what would make him do this?"

"Money, and lots of it."

"If I go along with your plan, would I stay here?"

"No, the feds are involved now. It's become a matter of national security."

"Can I force them to let me stay here? I mean, really, it's not like I have anything for them."

"Actually, you do. You are the bait to get Haidar out of hiding. They can spin a story that you found some of your father's papers when you were cleaning out the house. The papers show details about everyone he was involved with."

She gets quiet, looking down and kicking around some leaves.

"Fitz, The house has two separate places for storage. One is a normal attic and the other one is a small storage area behind a panel in the loft. It holds the air conditioners. I found some boxes in there. I haven't been through them, so I don't know what's in them. I thought maybe it was some of my baby stuff that my mom saved. After finding all this out, I can't really be sure."

"Does anyone know about these boxes?"

"No. When the IRS came, they only took stuff of value: paintings, bank accounts, jewelry, stuff like that."

"I need to get in there."

"I go with you or you don't get in."

Tough girl Hudson is back. "Okay, but Sal comes with us. I not going in without back up, and I don't want to babysit you. Get ready and we'll meet you out front."

After quickly filling the captain and Sal in on everything, we head out to Westchester.

Chapter Thirty-Two

I never go to Westchester; I'm a Brooklyn guy. But wow, talk about pompous. This house is huge and pretentious. It's everything Hudson isn't. She heads up the walkway, like it's no big deal, but Sal and I are looking up, our feet frozen in place and our mouths hanging open.

"Are you guys going to just stand there?"

Her voice snaps us back to reality. We quickly follow her inside.

"Guys, this is not me, it never was. Most of my fights with my parents were over all of this." She waves her hand around the vast room. Her face flushed, no doubt with embarrassment.

"Sal, stay down here and keep an eye out. I'll go upstairs with her to get the boxes." He just nods, which seems odd for him. Something's up, but now is not the time to question him. When we get up to the loft she moves a love seat away from the wall and there is a small door. Not one that you can walk through, more like crawl through. If you didn't know it was there, you would never find it on your own. That explains why the IRS didn't find it. There's a light switch on the wall, she flips it and opens the door.

"How many boxes are in there?"

"I'm not sure. It's really for the A/C units. I just figured they ran out of room in the attic."

She starts pulling them out and passing them to me. There are four white cardboard file boxes until she gets to the last one. It's a heavy-duty black plastic tub that's sold at the Home Depot.

"Fitz, I can't move this. I'll crawl in and push it towards you."

I grab it and pull it out. It's so heavy there's no way I can carry this down all those steps by myself. I flip open the lid and the two of us are staring at it. Our mouths hanging open until she yells for Sal. I can hear him running up the steps, but I can't move. Hell, I can't even put two words together to form a sentence.

"Holy shit, is that real?"

"Sal, I lifted it, it's real. The box is completely filled with gold bars."

Hudson drops to her knees and pulls a black pouch out of the box. When she looks inside, she lets out a squeal.

"D-diamonds. Big ass ones. What the hell was my father into? I don't want any of this. This is like blood money." She tosses the pouch into the box.

"Fitz, what's in the other boxes?"

"I didn't look, yet. Hopefully, it's something the feds can use to lure Haidar out of hiding. Let's get this stuff loaded up and then we can figure out what we've got."

Hudson puts the lid back on the tub. "What about this? I don't want any of this stuff."

"I understand, but we still have to take it all with us."

"Fitz, where are we going to bring all of this. You can't exactly walk into the station house with a tub of gold bars and diamonds. Maybe we should bring it back to Hart's house. We can have the feds meet us there."

"No, I don't want anyone outside of us to ever know where that place is. I've got an idea. I'll call Simmons and have him meet us at Federal Plaza in the city. We turn everything over to him. Hudson, just look through these boxes and make sure there is nothing personal in there that you want to keep."

While Sal pulls the car into the garage, I help Hudson flip through the boxes to see if there is anything she wants. Sal takes them two at a time and loads up the car. When Hudson gets to the last box, she begins to cry. Damn it, I was hoping there was nothing in here that she would feel an emotional connection to.

"What is it?"

"It's a box of photographs."

"Okay, do you have some sort of bag you can put them in? I don't want the feds to think we kept any of the boxes. After you get the pictures out, I'll take some of these papers and put them in this box."

While she looks for a bag, Sal and I do our best getting the tub downstairs without killing ourselves. In my lifetime, I never thought I would get the chance to hold a gold bar. They are a lot heavier than I thought. Hudson comes down with the last box and her bag of photographs. She's not saying much. Maybe it's just too emotional for her. After all, she is young. I'm about to close the door when the hair on the back of my neck stands up.

"Hudson, was there anything other than the photos in that box?" Bam, her face just gave it away. "Before you answer, think real hard about who you're talking to."

"Fitz—"

"Sal, don't; this is between Hudson and me."

"There are two letters, one from my mom and one from my dad. I didn't have time to read them, but since they were in the box with the photos, I would think they were personal, but I can't say for sure. Happy now?"

"Did you know about the tub?"

"No, you saw how it was tucked behind the A/C units. I had no idea. I knew the boxes were there, but, honestly, I was sick over what the IRS said my father did. I moved out and put my focus on my final project. Look where that got me."

"Before we get to Federal Plaza, read those letters. If there is anything in it that needs to be turned over, then do it. I'm only looking out for you. You want to wash your hands of everything having to do with your father's business dealings."

While Sal drives, I shoot a text to Simmons.

Me: Can you meet me at Federal Plaza?

Simmons: Why?

Me: I have evidence for you from Leland Townes house that your boys missed.

Simmons: What about Hudson?

Me: I'm hoping what I have can keep her out of all of this.

Simmons: I'm on my way.

I glance back at Hudson and she's crying. I want to help but she needs to face all of this before she can move on with her life.

Hudson

Two letters, one from my mom and one from my dad. I put Dad's to the side, nothing he says could ever change this big cluster fuck that I'm in the middle of. Sal said all girls put their fathers on a pedestal and no matter what happens, I'll be disappointed. I don't think even he expected what we found today. I take a deep breath and open my mother's letter.

My sweetest Ginger,

If you're reading this, then everything worked as planned. Please remember everything isn't always what it seems. It started out innocent enough but then, frankly, we both got greedy. I could blame everything on your father, but I knew what he was doing. So, I guess I'm just as much to blame as he is. Unfortunately, he got in bed with the devil herself, literately. Yes, your father had an affair. She set him up and held over his head a lot of information on him that could have sent him to prison for a very long time. All she wanted was for him to accept some funds that were wired in. It seemed innocent enough, but it wasn't. They wanted more and more and, before we knew it, her father was a full partner in your father's business.

I tried to leave with you, but they threatened to kill you. I stayed and helped your father cover up one crime after another. We knew there was no way out, so we planned an accident. That would be our way of getting out and for you to get out from under everything that was "us."

Her name is Dalal EL-Hashem. I hope you never have to deal with her or her father Haidar EL-Hashem. If you found this letter, then you found the gift we left for you. Use it wisely. Remember nothing is what it seems.

Love always,

Mom and Dad

I quickly rip open the letter from my father and it's just a random set of numbers along with a key. I show it to Fitz. "What are these numbers?"

"If I had to guess, I would say a bank account somewhere. Is that what was in the letters?"

"Along with a key. Fitz, read this letter and tell me what you think." I pass him Mom's letter and quietly wait for his response.

"Holy shit!"

"What is it? Someone tell me, please." Sal begs.

"Sal, I don't think her parents are dead."

He gets off the first exit and pulls into the nearest parking lot. "If they're not dead, then where are they?"

Fitz passes him the letter while I'm digging around in the bag to see if I missed something. Nothing . . .

"This looks like a key to some sort of locker. It's definitely not a bank deposit box. Have you ever seen it before?"

"No, never."

Sal closes the letter and passes it back to me. "Fitz, you already told Simmons we were on our way. Hudson, I think you have two choices. Before we turn over all this evidence, we take as many pictures as we can of everything. There might be some clue in there as to where your parents are. Or we turn everything over and we wash our hands of this whole damn thing. Ultimately, babe, the choice is yours. You have to ask yourself, do you want to look for your parents? Even if they don't want to be found? Or do you want to put this to bed now?"

"Fitz, what would you do?" As much as he royally pisses me off all the time, he's also totally honest and he's the one man who has kept his promise to me.

"I would want to know. You never want to go through life saying, 'what if?' What ifs will drive you crazy. You need to remember, you're not them. You might carry the same DNA but not the same morals. Your friend was murdered because of their actions. What you have to ask yourself is, once you find them, what will you do?"

"I'm not sure what I'd do with them. I can't trust the feds to do this. Will you both take me on as a client and find them?"

"Let's get the pictures and then we can talk about what we can do with all of it."

We each take a box and within minutes, we've got it all. Now I have to explain to the feds how I ended up with all of this stuff.

Chapter Thirty-Three

Fitz

Simmons was in shock when he saw all the gold and diamonds. He was even more thrilled to find the boxes filled with Leland's personal notes and ledgers. I brought Sal and Hudson back to Hart's house. I need to be back with my wife and son. Everything else will have to take a back seat. Before I left, we exchanged photos. Now the three of us are technically in possession of stolen evidence. This is great for my career. I kept the key and told them I'll try and see if Travis can figure out what it belongs to. Hell, I'm already knee deep in the crapper on this one, so what's the big deal?

When I finally get back to the hospital, I find MJ right where I left her this morning, with Patrick. "Hey, did you stay here all day?"

"No, I took turns with Mom and Dad. What happened with Stella?"

"It was gut wrenching, as I expected it would be. I told her that her mommy and daddy are together in heaven. I think she understood as best a six-year-old could. How's little man doing?"

"Good, the nurse said tomorrow they are going to start weaning him off of the tube. I'm nervous, I mean what if it's too soon? What if I suck at the whole damn motherhood thing?"

"MJ, you worry about stuff that hasn't happened and never will. You're a great mom. Let's look at this as a positive. Our son is getting stronger every day and tomorrow will be another big day for him."

"I love you."

"Yeah, I know that, you always have and I always will."

"What else did you do today?"

"I ran an errand with Hudson and Sal."

"You're not ready to talk about it yet."

"God, I love you. No, I'm not, but I need to hire a lawyer. I don't think Stephen is going to be in the picture much longer."

"What the hell happened?"

"Not sure but no one has seen or heard from him since all this started. Last night Andy asked Olivia for a good lawyer. That can't be good. I would have thought Stephen would have come up here when he found out everything that happened. I didn't ask Andy if he heard from him."

"You have that app on your phone to access the security cameras at the house? Maybe you can see if Stephen has even come home."

"I promised you I would never use it to spy on any of us."

"Why do you have to be so right as rain? Fitz, I give you permission, this one time, to spy on us. Now, open the damn thing and look to see if Stephen has been coming home."

I love when she gets fired up. I log in and oh shit this is bad. This is why I don't want to spy. "It looks like Stephen moved out."

"What? Give me that thing!"

I pass her my phone and now she's crying. "See, this is why we should be minding our own business."

"How could he just leave? If I wasn't stuck here, I'd go kick his ass. Maybe you should go kick his ass for me."

"You're like mama bear and someone is messing with her cubs. Listen, they are adults, and I think Andy knew this was coming. They are at an impasse; one of them had to make the move. Better he's gone before Andy gets home."

"He can't just wipe out years of being together overnight."

"If they ask for our help, we can get involved but, for now, can we please let them work it out on their own?" She's trying to stifle a yawn and I think it's time we head back to her room. "Come on, let's get you back to bed. I promise we can come back down here later." For once, she doesn't argue with me. By the time we get back up to her room, she is out cold. I lift her up and put her in bed. Then I crawl in next to her. While she sleeps, I'm trying to do research on the key. After an hour of looking at all kinds of keys, I give up. I take a picture and send it to Travis.

Travis: Okay, I'll bite. Why are you sending me a picture of a key?

Me: I need to find out what it opens. Do you have any clue?

Travis: You must think I'm some sort of genius or something.

Me: Or something. Lol. If you come up with anything, let me know.

Travis: Okay. Give MJ a hug. Later.

Having given up on the key I turn my attention to the files. But I can concentrate, all I keep thinking is these people faked their death. Their child went through the grieving process. I'm a dad now and I can't imagine putting my child through all of that. Why? For money, stuff that they could never use. It's sick.

"Fitz, what's wrong?"

"I thought you were sleeping."

"I felt your whole body tense up. What's going on? Does this have to do with the errand you ran today?"

"Yes, I spoke to Hudson about her options," I start. I then fill her in on everything else that transpired. Her eyes are wide and it's safe to say she's surprised. "That's not even the bad part."

"There's more?"

"Oh, hell yeah. There was a box with photos and two letters. One letter had a key and what appears to be a bank account number."

"And the other one?"

"A letter from her mother, implying their death was staged."

"Wait, they put that kid through hell for some stuff? What the fuck is wrong with these people?"

"She asked Sal and I to help find them. I'm not sure what I want to do."

"Why? You've always helped anyone who needed it."

"First, I'm a cop and I'm in possession of stolen evidence. Second, I'm a dad now. I have to make sure I'm here and I can provide for my family. I have to make wise choices every day. No more dicking around."

"Fitz, you've always righted the wrongs in the world, this is no different. What's really bothering you?"

"You getting shot was a game changer for me. I know how much I love you. I can't live my life without you. When we were in the back of that ambulance, I realized what I must put you through every day that I step out the door. Maybe it's time for a change."

"You can change your job but you can never change your heart. You say you're no one's hero but, reality is, you are everyone's hero. You can never stand by and let all the wrongs in this world win. That's what makes you Fitz."

"I need time to think about it. Time to spend with my family. Maybe then I'll be ready to jump back in."

"Well, you found Effy. It wasn't the conclusion you wanted, but you kept your promise. Now it's time to start your vacation."

"I can't start my vacation until I secure Stella's safety. The only thing I will settle for is either Andy or we adopt her."

"What about her grandfather?"

"I have Effy's dying declaration. That has to count for something. I bought us two weeks with McPhee. In that time, I need to see a lawyer."

"Okay, let's make this happen." She cuddles into me and I know that as long as I have her and Patrick, my life will always be complete.

Chapter Thirty-Four

Andy

It's been almost two weeks since everything happened and I haven't heard one word from Stephen. I've left countless messages but no response. Stella is staying with Hart while I've come home to deal with personal stuff. I have to make sure my home is all set for the social worker to visit. I've already passed the background check and, with the help of Fitz, my private adoption of Stella will be final right after her grandfather is sworn in as the new vice president.

I figured Stephen might be staying at a hotel close to his work. I never expected to walk into my home and find it completely empty. He took everything, even the trash can! The only thing I found was a note from him on the kitchen counter.

Andy,

You want the one thing that I can't give you, a child. Call me a selfish bastard but I don't want to share you with anyone. Most of all, I don't want the responsibility of a child after you're gone. You have become so involved in MJ and Fitz's life that you totally stepped out of ours. You were being held by a madman, he took a shot at you and, when it was finally over, you never even thought to call me. I had to find out on the news what happened. Through eight years of marriage, you have put everyone, including your family, before me. I don't want to be a part of the batshit crazy stuff that surrounds you and your family. It's time I finally put myself first, since you never have.

I did a quick deed on the house and took my name off it. It was yours before we met. As you probably can tell, I have taken all the furniture. I feel I earned it. Call it combat pay for putting up with everything. I filed for an uncontested divorce. Everything has always been divided up between us so the only thing left was the house and the furniture. If you agree it to this, it will be final in three months.

I wish you the best of everything and I hope you get what you really want in life. I'm just sorry that it's not me.

Stephen

I wish I could say I've been sucker punched by all of this but the truth is, I was expecting it. When he decided to dangle my illness in front of me as the reason for everything I can't do, I knew it was the beginning of the end. There is no such thing as perfect. Everyone in this world is carrying some baggage. For some people, it's a carry- on bag and for others, they need a bell hop to carry it all. For me, it's a carry-on. I know there is no cure for my Parkinson's, so, rather than fall into a constant pity party, I choose to make the best of my situation. Fitz always says I'm a glass half full kind of guy and I guess he's right.

In a few days, MJ will be coming home with Patrick. Which means Stella will be coming here, too. On top of that, the social worker can pop in at any time. I can't have an empty house. The quickest way to do anything nowadays in online and, in the course of an hour, I have ordered all kinds of furniture that will be here within forty-eight hours. No one and nothing will get in the way of my dream of becoming a parent.

I'm trying not to get stressed out. I keep reminding myself to tackle any obstacles as they come at me, and never dance around them in fear. If need be, I will have Fitz bring some stuff from his house to sort of fill in the blanks. In the meantime, I have nothing here so, rather than take the time to dwell, I'll go across the street and get MJ's house clean and ready for her return.

Fitz

Today's the big day; we finally got to bring Patrick home. His final weigh in before we left puts him at five pounds two ounces. The doctors are pleased with his progress, and I couldn't ask for more. MJ is getting stronger every day. She starts physical therapy next week. Senator McPhee gets sworn in today as the new vice president. Stella's adoption is also happening, and Andy is a basket case. It's fitting that same day we will be having a celebration of life, honoring Jin Chen. Everything seems to be going according to plan and that has me worried. I'm not usually walking around, waiting for the other shoe to drop, but I've had an uneasy feeling all day. Travis and Olivia are coming up today, maybe I'll feel better when they get here.

While MJ and Patrick are both napping, it's time I finally look at all the stuff from Hudson's house. I've put it off long enough.

The kid deserves answers. I printed out both letters that her parents left. There has got to be some sort of clue. I keep looking at the key. I know it's to some sort of locker, but it could be anywhere. I'm staring at this paper for so long I think I'm going cross-eyed. The doorbell rings and I nearly leap out of my chair. When I look at the monitor, I see Travis and Olivia with their arms full of gifts. I run down to let them in. "Hey, what is all this?" I help them upstairs and try not to drop any of it.

"Olivia is out of control."

"Fitz, I'm not the one who insisted Patrick had to have a mini motorcycle and a train set. I stopped him at the trampoline."

"You realize he's not going to be using any of this for a couple of years, right?" I ask. He waves his hand around quickly dismissing me.

"Never mind that Fitz, what time is the adoption hearing?"

"Noon, and right after that we head to Leif Ericson Park for Jin's celebration." The monitor comes on; Patrick is starting to wake up. Before I can even put all of these packages down, Olivia is on her way to his room.

"You know she's going to be a great aunt to Patrick and Stella."

"I know. it just proves you don't have to be blood relatives to be family. I decided to start looking at the stuff from Hudson's house. I wish she would have gone along with the protective custody, but I have to respect her decision. I checked in with her yesterday, and her and Sal still had nothing more to go on."

"Well, I have some good news in that department. I figured out what the key opens."

"Really? What?"

"Those numbers that Leland left are the coordinates to the place where the locker is. It's right by Penn Station. The fee is $6.95 per day. What's interesting about all this is the fee is being paid monthly."

"So, it's another thing to prove the parents could still be alive."

"Exactly. We need to go see what's in it. Sooner, rather than later."

"Has there been any progress on finding Haidar?"

"No and the files that you found only show how far back Leland was doing business with him."

"We'll have to pick this up later, right now, we need to get to the court."

It's Patrick's first real outing. I'm not sure who is more nervous me or MJ. Patrick, on the other hand, is sleeping through it all. I've never been to an adoption, let alone be a part of one. When the judge comes in, Andy's attorney asks each of us to introduce ourselves to the Judge and give a short testimony as to why Andy should be allowed to adopt Stella. He made sure he emphasized short when he looked at Mom. For this case, they have brought in an interpreter for Stella.

The judge is an older gentleman who looks like he just stepped out of a Norman Rockwell painting. We all share how wonderful Andy is with Stella and what a positive influence he is. When we are finally done, the judge begins riffling through his papers. "I see Vice President McPhee has agreed that this is in the best interest of the child. Stella, do you know why you're here today?"

She stands up and is clutching her teddy bear, Sam. "My mommy went to heaven to be with my daddy. You are going to make Andy my new daddy. Andy has a boo-boo, I have a boo-boo, and Sam does, too, so we need to take care of each other." She holds up Sam to show the judge he has a Band-Aid on his arm.

"Mr. Justice, please bring Stella here and have your camera ready."

The judge puts Stella on his lap as he signs the decree of adoption. The three of them are taking selfies, and there's not a dry eye in the house. The judge hands Stella his gavel. Not needing any direction, she hits the gavel on the block and then gives the judge a big hug. The judge is kind enough to stay for pictures with all of us, including Sam.

When we finally get done, I take Patrick and MJ home while everyone heads to Leif Ericson Park. As much as I know MJ wanted to be there, it's to soon for Patrick to be out that long. After I get them settled I head to the park. When I get there, Hudson and Sal pull up right behind me. Hudson seems very tired. Sal keeps looking around like he's waiting for someone to jump out of the bushes. We find Hart and Mr. and Mrs. Chen in the picnic area. They have a cake for Stella's adoption, and they are passing out balloons.

"Thank you, everyone, for coming here today to celebrate my daughter's life. Rather than dwell on all the things we will miss with our daughter, my wife and I decided to focus on all the wonderful times we had. We are so proud of all she did in her short life. She was instrumental in saving five girls from being sold on the black market. Her research was the key to breaking up a human trafficking ring."

I look around us and more people have gathered. Some look familiar and I realize it is the five girls that were rescued and their families. Mrs. Chen passes them balloons.

"In each balloon, there is a prayer for peace, love, and good health. On the count of three, release them and let them float to the heavens. One, two, three."

We all release them, a rainbow of colors, flooding the sky. There are plenty of hugs, tears, and cake. I finally find a minute to pull

Hudson aside and let her know what I've found.

"So, you think that whatever is in that locker might help with my father's letter?"

"It's the only lead we have. You look tired, how are you holding up?"

"I am tired and scared. Part of me wishes I would have stayed in protective custody, but I don't think anyone else is really looking for the same answers I am."

"What do you mean? Of course they are."

"No, Fitz, they are looking for Haidar and anyone else in the sleeper cell. I'm looking for my parents."

"I guess there's no way of talking you out of this?"

"No. If you give me the key, I can go find out what's in there, and you can be done with all of this."

"I would have thought by now you would know that I never walk away from anything until it's done. Right now, it's time to go home. Meet me back at the house, I'll get the key and we can go see what's in that locker."

Chapter Thirty-Five

After much deliberation, Me, Travis, Hudson, and Sal head out to the locker. When we get to the place, it's not what I was expecting. It's a small convenience store that also sells coffee, beer, and souvenirs. In the back of the store, there are lockers that are rented out. There are all kinds of items for sale that would appeal to the massive amounts of tourist that must come through here. The owner said the locker is paid for on a monthly basis via wire transfer. We find the locker and inside is another journal.

"Are you serious? This is it? How does this help me find my parents?"

"Let's go, we can talk about this later." The last thing I want to do is draw attention to us. When we get in the car, I have Sal drive while Travis and I look more closely at the journal. The spine appears to be re-glued. When I pry it apart I find a safety deposit box key hidden inside. "I'll be damn."

"What? You found something, please tell me you've found something?"

I hold up the key. "This safety deposit box key was in the spine of the journal. Now we need to find out what's in that safety deposit box along with these accounts."

"Fitz, you're not going anywhere. You just had a baby and you're on vacation. Besides, I don't ever want to get on MJ's bad side again. As soon as we find out where the box is I can go myself."

"I would feel better if agent Simmons went with you. You're going to turn everything over to him anyway and at least I'll know you're protected."

"Okay."

We finally get back home. Before we go in, Sal pulls me aside. "I don't want you to worry. I'm going with her, she just doesn't know it, yet. I've been sticking like glue to her since we got back and she might not let anyone know it, but she's really scared. Not just because of Haidar, but she has no clue what to do with her parents if she finds them."

"*If* being the operative word. I don't need to tell you how much danger she is in. I'll send Simmons a text to see if he can go. Please keep her safe."

Me: Hey, Hudson found another journal in a storage locker. Inside is a key to a safety deposit box. We determined that it's to a box in Switzerland. I think her and Sal are leaving tonight. As soon as I can confirm it I'll let you know. I'm thinking it would be best if you went with them.

Simmons: We are still analyzing the stuff she gave us, but text me the flight info and I'll make sure I'm there.

Me: Thanks.

We head upstairs and I put my unease about her going aside. I trust Sal and now that Simmons is going, I feel better about her going. Besides, I know my place is here. I check the monitor and Patrick is asleep. Good food and laughter is flowing. Stella is enjoying all the toys everyone gave her with Sam the bear always by her side. I don't see Hudson or Travis. I make my way around the kitchen and nab a beer before heading into the office. "I thought I would find you in here."

"Pull up a chair, Travis just got us into the accounts. There are four of them that are in the name of Dalal EL-Hashem. Three are in Aafii's name and seventeen are in Haidar's name. There's millions of dollars in each one of them. Sal and I are leaving for Switzerland tonight. After I access the box, I'm turning everything over to agent Simmons. I'm leaving you this journal for safekeeping," Hudson informs me.

"Travis, can you give us a minute alone, please." He leaves and we take a seat on the sofa.

"Tell me what do you plan on doing about your parents?"

"Fitz, every day I wake up and feel like I'm carrying the weight of the world on my shoulders. I'm looking around every corner for the boogieman to get me. You told me that I'm not them and just because I have the same DNA doesn't mean I have the same morals. That really hit home for me. I won't spend my life chasing a ghost. What I will do is give everything I find over to the authorities. Then, I'm walking away. Even if I found them, I want nothing to do with them."

"You don't want to ask them why?"

"They put the love of money and stuff over the love of their daughter. I don't need to know any more."

"I wish I could go with you, but I'm happy you're taking Sal. Promise me you will do exactly what he says. He's a trained professional and I trust him."

"I promise I'll be careful and, much like you, I keep my promises."

"You better get going." We get up and I give her a hug. Sal is in the doorway waiting.

"Explain to MJ for me, please."

"I will. Be safe."

They leave and now it's a waiting game. Is this what it feels like when you give your kid the keys to the car for the first time?

The party is winding down. Andy called it a night. With Stella, asleep in his arms, he went home. Travis and Olivia took Mom and Dad home before they headed back to Virginia. MJ fed Patrick and he's out cold. Finally, it's just the two of us. I head into the living room and find MJ on the couch with her feet propped up on a pillow.

"I think today went great, but you're exhausted. Why don't you go to bed?"

"Soon. Come snuggle with me." I climb in next to her, careful of her arm.

"Where did Hudson and Sal sneak off to?"

She doesn't miss a beat. "Right about now they are wheels up on their way to Switzerland."

"Switzerland, why?"

"She has one more hurdle before she can close the door on her past. Hopefully, she will find enough information to help the feds keep her safe."

"I'm surprised you let her go without you."

"My place is here with you and Patrick." She moves in a little closer and rests her head on my shoulder. These are the moments I live for.

"It was so nice that the other families showed up today for Jin's service."

"Hart let them know how instrumental her work was in rescuing them."

"I'm not sure if you know this, but Mr. and Mrs. Chen decided to rebuild the dry cleaners."

"Wow, I really thought they were done. Did they say why?"

"They went back there yesterday for the first time since it happened. They found their neighbors cleaning the place. When they saw how committed everyone was to helping them, they decided they would rebuild."

"It will give them something to focus on. I'll drop by and offer my help, too."

"Did you talk to Andy about Stephen?"

"Yeah, he said Stephen filed for divorce. It will be final in three months. He doesn't want to dwell on it."

"I tried to talk to him but he wasn't ready to talk to me about it. Probably in time, but, for now, I'm glad he has Stella to focus on."

"She was amazing today in court. I held it together until she talked about boo-boo's."

"Did he tell you that he asked McPhee if he wanted visitation and he said no? I guess Effy really knew what her father was all about. You know, it just goes to show you, no matter how old you are, you must have a will."

"I'm not surprised he didn't want any visitation. McPhee only cares about himself. Oh, and I already made an appointment with a new attorney for next week to update all of our stuff. I figured since Stephen is no longer handling everything, we need to get this done."

"Fitz, I just can't seem to wrap my mind around the fact that Stephen is no longer here. He was a large part of this family for so long and, just like that, he walked away. It makes me wonder, do you ever really know a person?"

"That's probably the same thing Hudson's thinking. I mean, if she finds her parents, which I don't think she will, what does she do with them? Turn them in? Let them off the hook, what?"

"Maybe she just should have walked away from the whole thing."

"She needs to know she gave it everything she could. Then, she will never wonder 'what if.'"

The baby monitor lights up and Patrick is starting to fuss. Cuddle time is over. "The party's over, you go see to our son and I'll finish cleaning up here." There really isn't much left to do. It's too early to check on Hudson's and Sal's flight, so now I have to wait. I know I'm not going to get any sleep.

Hudson

Sal managed to sleep through the entire flight. Simmons cat napped and all I did was toss and turn. Knowing that Fitz has the journal for safekeeping makes me feel a little better. What I can't wrap my mind around is why my parents would put me in so much danger? Does their love of things trump their love for me? So many people have died because of what they have done. I don't know how MJ and Fitz want to be in the same room as me. MJ and her baby almost died because of what my father started. How could I be part of them? Sal ordered room service and all I can do is push it around my plate. I know he means well but I'm having a hard time wrapping my mind around all of this. I don't think I have anything left in me to devote to him.

"Hudson, did you hear anything I said?"

"Sorry, I was lost in thought. Is it time to go?"

"Yes, we have to meet Simmons in the lobby. If we leave now, we can be there when the bank opens."

We get downstairs and, like a good agent, Simmons is waiting for us. "How long do you think this will take?"

"You have to show them your paperwork from your name change. Once we do that, maybe ten minutes. It depends how big of a box they have and what's inside. You'll be okay, I promise."

The cab ride to the bank was very short. Thankfully, the bank manager speaks English. He checks my paperwork and actually smiles when he sees my name change. "Can my friends come in with me?"

"No, I'm sorry but only you can go in. Together we will take the box and bring it into a private room for you. When you are done, just knock on the door. I will come back in and then you and I will return the box."

"Thank you, all this is new to me. I've never had a safety deposit box. I've only seen them on television." I'm nervous and rambling. He doesn't say anything. He's probably thinking *another crazy American.* I follow him into a room that looks like a giant vault. There has got to be hundreds of boxes, all different sizes. He finds my number, puts his key in, turns it, and waits for me to do the same. The box is not the smallest but not the biggest. He carries it for me into a room with a round table. He sets it down and leaves. *Hudson, you are not a baby. Put your big girl panties on and get this shit over with.* I look around to see who's in the room with me and I realize it was me giving myself a pep talk. I take a deep breath and open the box.

The first thing I pull out is a pouch. Inside, there are more diamonds. I read somewhere that diamonds are being used as currency. Next, there is a manila envelope. Inside, there are bonds that were issued in 1979. When I look closer, I realize they are Bearer bonds. They stopped making them in 1982 since they were mostly used for money laundering. Each one has a face value of ten thousand dollars. There has to be north of a million dollars just in bonds. Next, I pull out a photo album. It's filled with pictures of me as a baby. Lastly, I find one more manila envelope. Inside is a birth certificate, an adoption decree, and two letters. The birth certificate is mine. I was adopted. How could this be? Why did my parents hide this from me? My hands are shaking so bad, I can't open them. I gather everything up and bang on the door. The man comes back in and wants me to go with him to put the box back.

"It's empty now. I won't be coming back . . . ever." We get out front, Sal and Simmons are right where I left them.

I pass Simmons the bonds and the diamonds. "Those are for you. The only other thing is my birth certificate and two letters."

"Do the letters give any indication as to where your parents are?"

"I didn't read them but, apparently, I'm adopted. The letters are old. When I read them, if there is any indication as to where they are, I'll let you know."

"Hudson, these are Bearer bonds, do you know what that means?"

"Of course, I do; whoever holds them owns them. I want no part of anything that belonged to them. That includes the house and the insurance policies. With everything I've given you, do you think you can find Haidar?"

"Those accounts from the new journal will be a big help in finding them and shutting them down."

Sal puts his arm around me and pulls me closer to him. For now, it feels good to have someone to lean on. "Come on, guys, I think we have a plane to catch."

CHAPTER THIRTY-SIX

Hudson

I'VE BEEN HOME FOR ALMOST a week and I still haven't opened the letters. Sal checks on me daily, but my focus has been school. I have enough of credits to graduate in December rather than waiting for the spring. I've been carrying the letters in my bag since I left Switzerland. I pull them out and try to smooth out the wrinkles. I know I need to read them, and I know I've given myself every excuse why I shouldn't. Reality is, I'm adopted. Millions of kids are adopted. That's not the part that bothers me; it's the lies. The upside, I'm not related, as Fitz puts, it by DNA, so that might account for my high morals. I open the adoption decree and spread it out on my desk along with my original birth certificate. My adoption was private and, apparently, I was born in Colorado. My birth mother's name is Kelly Walker. My birth father is unknown. Apparently, my name was Chloe Walker. Hell, I'm twenty-one years old and I've already had my name changed two times. It's a pretty generic decree. Next, I open the letter from my birth mother. Along with that is a picture of her holding a baby that I assume is me.

Dear Chloe,

If you're reading this, your parents must have told you that you were adopted. I need you to understand how hard this was for me. I was only fifteen when I found myself pregnant. My own mother was a single parent and knew the hardships I would be facing. She convinced me to do what is best for you and put you up for adoption. Joshua, your daddy, had an uncle who was an attorney. He set up the private adoption for us. We knew we were too young to be parents. We picked Leland and Sandra Townes to be your parents. They seemed to be settled and comfortable. We thought they could give you what we couldn't, stability.

We didn't give you away because we didn't want you. We gave you away because we loved you more than we loved ourselves. I hope you've had a happy life.

Love, Mom

When I opened this letter I wanted to hate her, but how could I? Fifteen? I didn't even know which end was up at fifteen. I can't even imagine having a baby. I'm scared to open the next letter. I pick up Jin's picture and run my finger over it. I wish she were here to tell me what to do. She'd probably would have made me open these up right away. I put her picture down right in front of me and open the next letter.

Ginger,

So, you made it to Switzerland. Now you know you were adopted. Truth be told, it was your mother's doing. I knew I never wanted children, so, at twenty-one, I had a vasectomy. In the end, your mother was right . . . you really were the light in my life.

We've left you enough of money, bonds, gold, and diamonds so that you will be set for life. I've made good choices and bad choices all throughout my life. Having you was a good choice, and I wouldn't change a thing.

I got mixed up with some really bad people. They dangled the bait in front of me and I fell for it hook, line, and sinker. It got to a point that I knew there was not going to be a way out. I had to set it up so that it looked like we died in that car accident.

Don't look for us and we won't look for you. You grieved once for us, let it go at that. Have a happy life.

Love,

Dad

I gather everything up, shove it in my bag, and head out the door. There is only one person who can make me understand it all. He told me if I ever needed him, he would always be there for me. I need him.

The streets of Brooklyn are all set up with Christmas lights and wreaths. It's such a great time of year. I ring the bell and am immediately buzzed in. I'm not even half way up the steps and Annie is there to meet me.

"Oh, child, it's freezing outside. Are your feet wet? Come in and Pat will give you a shot of Irish Whiskey."

"I'm okay. I need to run some stuff by Pat."

"You know where he is planted—in front of that idiot box."

I'm trying not to laugh. He sees me and turns it down. "What brings you out on such a cold night?"

"Did Fitz tell you about Switzerland?"

"Only that you went and you came back safely. As far as I'm concerned, everything else is personal stuff that I don't need to know."

"Well, I've found out a lot of stuff about my parents and none of it was good. Fitz has been helping me deal with it all. I went to Switzerland to access a safety deposit box that they set up for me. There was a lot of diamonds and bearer bonds in it. All stuff that as far as I'm concerned is blood money. They also left me two letters along with my original birth certificate. I turned everything, except the letters and the birth certificate, over to the feds. Pat, I was adopted." I pull out the letters and pass them to him.

"Are you sure you want me to see these? I'm sure they are very personal."

"Yes, I do." He opens the one from my birth mother and when he's done, he puts it back and takes a deep breath.

"That's a beautiful thing she did. Not only for you but also for your adoptive parents. There's nothing wrong with being adopted." He opens the next one and as he's reading, his face becomes flushed. When he's done, he shoves it back in the envelope.

"I hope you are going to listen to him and just let it go."

"Is that what you think I should do?"

"When you have a child, it changes you. You learn to put that child first before anyone. Leland and Sandra didn't do that. They made a show of it, but none of it was real. Leland made it real clear that he was first and too bad so sad for you."

"Do you think I should look for my birth mother?" I barely get the words out and a floodgate opens. I can't wipe the tears away fast enough. He wheels over towards me and pulls me into a hug.

"Shh, stop crying. I can't tell you what to do about that one. It has to come from you. She might not want to know all the stuff that happened to you. It could make her feel really guilty about placing you with them. Give it time and, eventually, you'll know what to do."

He pulls back and hands me some tissues. "Thank you. I think I'll take that shot of Irish Whiskey now."

As if on cue Annie comes in and gives us all a shot. "Have you figured out what you're going to do after graduation?"

"Annie, I haven't been able to think about anything. I just finished my last final. And now that I gave the insurance company back the money from the life insurance policies, I'm going to have to find a job and get a smaller apartment."

"What about the house in Westchester?"

"I turned it over to the IRS. They are going to sell it and use the proceeds to pay back the people Leland stole from."

"That's an honorable thing that you're doing. You know there's plenty of room in this house for you. Most days, it's just Annie and me here. There's also a studio apartment downstairs that used to be Fitz's. Take your time and think about it. But, don't take too long."

"Why don't you stay tonight. It's late and it's dark out. Besides, I made a stew and some fresh bread."

Before I can answer I hear a lot of commotion coming from downstairs. The door opens and everyone comes piling inside. "They have radar when it comes to my wife's stew."

"Hey, Hudson, what are you doing here?"

"Hey, Fitz, I'm here for the stew like everyone else!" He passes Patrick off to Pat and takes me aside.

"You look like you've been crying. Are you sure you're okay?"

"Yeah, I can finally say I'm okay and mean it. Pat helped me see what was right before my eyes. Love and friendship can be family, too."

"Wow, my Dad's good, but I knew that already. Are you all set for graduation?"

"Yep, last final today. Will you be able to come?"

"We are all coming, even Dad."

I give him a big hug and then poke him in the chest for old time's sake.

EPILOGUE

Fitz

Three Months Later

MY VACATION IS QUICKLY COMING to an end. I'm supposed to go back tomorrow. Patrick is growing by leaps and bounds. The pediatrician is impressed with the progress he is making. MJ was so worried about if she would be a good mom. Turns out—she's a great mom, but I knew that already.

While MJ's still sleeping, I'm going through a box that came from Shutterfly. She put together some photo books. The first one is for Andy and Stella. It was her first Christmas without her mom but she pulled through it like a real trouper. Olivia and Travis came up and took her ice-skating for the first time. Travis spent most of the time on his ass, which of course left us all in hysterics. It seems like Stella has always been with us. When she gets older, I will give her all the letters from Effy along with the article about her father. She will know that she was always loved, no matter what.

Andy's divorce became final. He's had very little contact with Stephen, if any. Andy made sure his attorney handled everything. The hardest part was stopping MJ from kicking Stephen's ass all over New York.

I can't believe how many books MJ made. There's even one for Hudson. Right after graduation, she moved into my old apartment at my parent's house. She gave back every penny that her parents left her. She's still a pain in my ass, but I wouldn't have it any other way.

I head into the kitchen to get some more coffee and find MJ feeding Patrick. He started oatmeal and enjoys flicking it everywhere. "Good Morning. What flavor is he tossing around now?"

"Peach, I don't think he likes this one. He keeps making that 'oh crap, what the hell are you giving me now?' face."

"Can't blame him . . . peach? Really?" She just rolls her eyes and goes back to feeding him.

"Andy, called earlier. He got the results back from Stella's ENT about the cochlear implant. The doctor said she's not a candidate for it."

"What about getting a second opinion?"

"He's thinking about it."

Patrick is still fighting her on the oatmeal, and by the mess that's everywhere, I think it's a win for him.

"Tomorrow is D-day for you. Are you excited to go back to work?"

"Yeah, about that. I'm going to put my papers in tomorrow."

She's staring at me like a deer in the headlights, while Patrick takes a fist of oatmeal and tosses it at her head. I want to laugh but I know when I better just shut it down. Now is one of those times. "Don't even. Don't you think before you make a life altering decision, that affects all of us, you should talk to me about it?"

"I thought you would be happy that I'm retiring."

"What the hell will you do all day?"

"Well, gee, I thought you would be happy to have me around more."

"It has nothing to do with that. We should have discussed this like a family. Have you thought about what you might want to do with the rest of your life?"

I toss her a wet washcloth for her hair while I take another one and clean up Patrick.

"Lucas and Sal are expanding the business. They asked me if I wanted to be a partner. It's a thirty thousand dollar buy in."

"Do you want to do that? What would you be doing?"

"They are expanding their security business to include private investigation services. They are looking to rent a small office space not too far from here."

"It sounds like you're already in."

"No, you have to be on board for this before I even consider it."

"Well, we can't both stay home or one of us is going to end up on the news. And not in a good way."

"Do you want to go back to work? If you do, I have no problem being a kept man." That earned me a smack in the face with the dirty washcloth.

"Wise ass. Here is my list: I want to know more about what you would be doing. I don't want to be left alone all-night long. I understand once in a while, but not all the time. How dangerous is it? How many days a week would you work? Shouldn't you be writing this down?"

"I got it all committed to memory." I smile. She takes Patrick and heads out of the room. "Hey where are you off to?"

"I'm going to give him a bath while you find out more information. Oh, and for the record, there's a pool going around about you putting in your papers."

"Really? Is it too late for me to get in on it?" I ask. She's already gone.

I decide to do a group text.

Me: Hey, guys, I'm interested but I need some more information. Can we get together?

Lucas: Sure, when and where?

Sal: Let's meet tomorrow at the diner by the precinct at ten. That will still give you enough time to turn in your papers.

Me: Are you in the pool, too?

Lucas: We all are, including Hart.

Me: What kind of odds am I getting?

Sal: You don't want to know. See you then.

I get to the diner to find them already waiting for me. Manny comes by with my usual coffee. "No food today." He leaves and now we can get down to business.

"Okay, are you really that busy that you need investigation services?"

"Yeah, I've already got a case lined up for you."

Now I'm intrigued. "What's it about?"

"I can fill you in on it later. Right now, we need to hammer out the details for this partnership."

"How is this going to work?"

"You work your own hours. If it gets slow on the investigative side, you can come over and do some security work."

"Nights? Weekends?"

"Like I said, you set your hours. As far as pay, you get paid per job. So, if you brought in a fifty-thousand-dollar job, you keep thirty and the rest goes back into the company."

I finish my coffee, push the cup away, and pull my papers from my jacket. “Well, I guess it’s time I turn these in. When do I start?”

“We signed the lease on the place yesterday. Here’s the keys and the address. This is the schedule for the private investigator exam. There’s an opening for the exam tomorrow. Once you have that, you’re good to go.”

Turning in my papers was a lot easier than I thought. Captain Hart won the pool. He said when he saw me with Patrick, he knew. I passed my exam for my PI license and MJ even put it in a nice frame for me. She also framed a picture of her and Patrick together for my desk. The office is on 5th avenue and 78th street, so I could walk to work.

Today is my first day on the job. When I get there, I find two desks. I thought I would be alone. When I get inside, I start setting up my desk. I’m about to bring my empty box in the back room, when I notice a picture on the other desk. It’s Jin Chen. I’ve seen this picture before, it belongs to Hudson. I’m about to call Sal when she comes walking in with two cups of coffee and puts one down on my desk.

“Fitz, are you checking up on me?”

“Me? I work here and, by the looks of things, so do you. What exactly do you do here?”

“You’re the new investigator? Lucas told me the new investigator was starting today, but no one told me it was you. I started yesterday. I do everything from answering the phones to research.”

“Why here?”

“When I was hold up at Hart’s cabin with Sal, he asked me if I was doing forensic accounting because of my dad. I thought about that for a long time. I was doing it for my dad to prove that he was innocent. That was before I knew everything. In the past six months, my entire life has been turned upside down. Now, I need to figure out what I want. What about you? Why are you here?"

"I turned in my papers; I'm officially retired."

"Aren't you too young for retirement?"

"I've been a cop for twenty years. I've seen the lowest of the low. I've also got to meet some of the most remarkable people. However, every time I was assigned a case, I lost a little bit of me along the way. I want to enjoy my life and my family. It's time for a new beginning."

"Well you're starting off with a bang. I put the file on your desk for our first case."

She holds up her coffee and we toast. "To new beginnings."

The End, for now . . .

ACKNOWLEDGEMENTS

This year, I learned how short life can be. There is no greater gift in this world than the unconditional love and support of family and friends. I would like to say a very special thank you to Detective Louis Georgetti (Retired). You are always there to help me, no matter what I ask of you. Thank you, Mrs. Phyllis Georgetti, for sharing him and always supporting me. Do you miss me, yet?!

I'd like to give a special shout out to Brett Young. Your music touched my soul. You can follow him at: brettyoungmusic.com

I'd like to extend a special thank you to Colleen Noyes and all the girls at Itsy Bitsy Book Bits.

To all my fantastic Beta readers: Felicia Griffith, Sandra Timmins, Loraine Oliver, Janett Gomez, Michelle Roberson, and Shell Williams. Knowing that I can always count on everyone to help me polish my manuscript is priceless.

A very special thank you to Stacey Ryan Blake of Champagne Book Design. You make my books come to life.

Jacquelyn Ayres, you are the Louise to my Thelma. No matter what, we always know that—together—we can.

Finally, thank you to all the readers who have fallen in love with this close-knit, crazy family. Hang on, because they are just getting started. #TeamFitz

For more information on how you can help fight Human Trafficking, contact The Ricky Martin Foundation at rickymartinfoundation.org

For more information on American Sign Language and the Deaf, contact The National Association of the Deaf at www.nad.org/resources/american-sign-language

For more information on the Hear The Music Project, contact them at www.nashcountrydaily.com/2016/08/04/rascal-flatts-gary-levox-draws-inspiration-from-deaf-niece-and-hearthemusic-project

Other Books

The Unraveled Trilogy

The Unraveling of Raven

Darkness Into Dawn

Shattered Lies

Uniquely Mine

The Letter: Dear Michael

The Bench

www.ingramcontent.com/pod-product-compliance
Lightning Source LLC
Chambersburg PA
CBHW070850260626
47170CB00007B/2574
9780997669268